Starlit Summer

by

KATE FROST

LEMON TREE PRESS

Paperback Edition 2021

ISBN 978-1-914544-00-2

Copyright © Kate Frost 2021

Cover design by Jessica Bell.

A

Starlit Summer

by

KATE FROST

LEMON
TREE
PRESS

Praise for *A Starlit Summer*

"I absolutely loved this story. Set in Cornwall, the descriptions take you away from the chaotic, humdrum city life and transport you to sandy beaches, picturesque ports, and the perfectly named Bramble Cottage... A beautifully written, heart-warming story that evokes memories of endless summer days and true love." Helen Pryke, author of *The Healer's Secret*.

"This was yet another great story by Kate Frost. As always she drew me into her tale with her skilful setting of the scene. She always writes so beautifully and this was no exception... It's partly a story about finding yourself and what your values are, but it's also a bit of real escapism into sunny Cornwall with sexy boy next door builders and impossibly gorgeous film stars... There weren't any black or white characters, just real flawed people. The romance was great too and there was plenty of angst!" Elaine Jeremiah, author of *Love Without Time*.

"I absolutely loved this story! The author's acting knowledge is evident in the detailed descriptions of life on set, her characters are endearing, and her descriptions of Cornwall swept me away. I'm missing the ability to travel in 2020, but reading one of Kate Frost's books is the best remedy." Kim Rigby, author.

For Tom and Teresa

Chapter One

'You're a dreamer, that's your problem.'

Jenna resisted huffing like a teenager. 'Why exactly is it a problem?'

'Because it's never allowed you to concentrate on a career. You're always flitting from one thing to another. It used to be singing, then you wanted to be a potter, an interior designer, then you did modelling, voice-over work, now it's acting.'

'It's always been acting, that's never changed, it's just I'm fully focused on it now.'

Her mum didn't say anything. She didn't have to; Jenna knew what she was thinking, that she didn't have a serious career. Bit parts in film and TV wasn't a regular income or a job her parents could show off to their friends. They had her older brother for that, a lawyer in a multinational company.

Jenna downed her tea and stood up. At least she wasn't living at home any longer; they couldn't complain that she wasn't supporting herself.

'I get that you're acting now, but tomorrow you might want to do something else, I don't know, open up your own cafe. Anything.'

'It actually pays quite well, the acting.' She rinsed her mug out in the sink and stacked it in the dishwasher.

'Maybe it does,' her mum said, 'but it's not exactly constant work… It's unpredictable, that's all I'm saying. It worries me.'

Jenna sat back down opposite her mum at the kitchen table and tapped her finger on the photo of the cottage. 'I only said I'd love to do the cottage up, not that I'm *going* to do it. I mean look at it. Can you imagine what it'll be like when it's renovated?'

'I can. I remember spending summer holidays down there when I was a kid, before Aunt Vi was unable to look after it.'

'Yeah, but still, it must have been pretty old-fashioned even back then.'

'Thanks, Jenna, I'm fully aware of how old I am.'

'Sorry, I didn't mean it like that. It's just it needs modernising, but in a tasteful way.'

'It had a country cottage charm about it, that's for sure. It was always a little rough around the edges but then Auntie Vi was on her own, no husband or children to help.'

'You could argue that gave her more time to look after the place.'

'Not after she had trouble with her hip, and she wasn't keen on company in her later years despite our best efforts to visit and help out. She was even more stubborn than my mum and that's saying something.'

'Is that why we've not been there since me and Jack were little?'

'Sad isn't it.'

Jenna's dad strode into the kitchen, a frown on his face and a tape measure in his hand. 'What you two gassing about?'

'Aunt Vi's cottage.'

'You could do it up, Dad.'

'I'd love to, just haven't got the time. Your mum's keeping me far too busy here.'

'He's measuring in our bedroom to build fitted wardrobes.' She turned to her husband. 'We're going to have to get someone else to do the cottage, aren't we, love? It'll cost too much to keep it on without renting it out, and it can't be rented in the state it's in at the moment.'

'Prime location though. Shouldn't be a problem filling it with holidaymakers once it is done up.' He switched on the kettle and leant against the worktop.

'If you're so interested in the place,' Jenna's mum said, gathering together the photos on the table and glancing at her, 'then come down with us next weekend and help sort through Aunt Vi's stuff.'

Jenna couldn't stop thinking about the cottage all the way home from Guildford to her flat in a supposedly 'up and coming' area of west London. She felt guilty for thinking it, but her mum was so lucky being left it in the will. She knew her mum was focused on the responsibility and cost rather than the many possibilities. Jenna had to admit there was a lot to do, but…

She gingerly backed her car into her space in the underground car park. She grimaced as she squeezed herself through the gap between her car and her neighbour's. They continuously parked on the edge of their space leaving Jenna having to do weird yoga-type poses just to get out. She slammed the door shut and made a mental note to talk to them again.

The modern building she lived in had a secure car park but it was crammed with soulless one and two bedroom flats. The letting agent details had described her flat as cosy and charming. The cosiness was because it was tiny, and she assumed the charm was down to the incredibly distant view of a park on a hill above a sea of rooftops. But it was a view of sorts and it was a place of her own with a living, dining and kitchen area, a small bathroom, and a bedroom with enough space to fit a bed and a wardrobe. Most importantly it was *her* space.

Jenna dumped her bag on the floor and flopped on the sofa. With no job lined up for tomorrow, she texted Carla about going out. She didn't have anything scheduled for the rest of the week either, which usually worried her, but she had spent Monday and Tuesday filming a sunglasses advert. Not only had it been a lot more fun than expected, it was decent money, so she wasn't freaking out about the rest of the week being quiet.

They met at a Middle Eastern restaurant almost exactly between where they lived. The large window below the deep blue sign, Baba Ganoush, was steamed up from the heat and people inside. Carla was already there, easy to spot with her short pink hair, sitting on the bench that lined the far side of the restaurant, clashing with the mustard-coloured wall behind her.

'Hey, Jenna!' Carla stood and enveloped her in a hug, her nose-ring cold against Jenna's neck.

Jenna sat on the chair opposite. 'I thought I'd be the one waiting for you.'

'Unbelievably we wrapped early.'

'You were that good were you?' Jenna smiled and poured herself a glass of water.

'I was the only dancer in the end; they wanted a one-on-one scene.'

'I'd love to be in a music video.'

Carla reached across and touched Jenna's long blonde hair. 'Trust me, with your looks, you absolutely will be one day. But hey, getting gigs in film and TV is pretty awesome.' She picked up the menu. 'Do you know what you want? I'm starving.'

'Didn't they feed you well on set?'

Carla scanned the menu. 'Yeah, too good as always, but totally stodgy stuff that I avoided considering I was in little more than a boob tube and leggings.'

Jenna smiled, knowing full well Carla had little to worry about and she'd make up for the lack of food this evening. 'I'm going to have my usual. Kofta, pilaf, grilled Turkish pepper and baba ganoush'

'Nice. I might have the chicken sheesh with those creamy leeks.'

They dunked strips of flatbread into beetroot and tahini dip while they waited for their main course. Jenna sipped her large glass of wine, something she never did if she was working the next day, as it always made her head groggy and sent her into a panic about sleeping through her alarm. But tonight she could relax.

'Have you heard from Heidi?' Carla picked up her wine, sat back against the cushioned bench and looked across the table.

Jenna shook her head.

'Not since you moved out? Not at all?'

'Nope.' Jenna dabbed the side of her mouth with a napkin.

'Wow, you really are pissed with each other.'

'Are you surprised? I'm fuming. Why the hell does she get to be pissed at me? I did nothing wrong and yet it feels like I've taken the blame.'

Carla held her hands up. A tattoo of a snake wriggled from her wrist down the length of her arm. 'I know, I know, you don't have to tell me. It's just you were always inseparable, practically since the first day of drama school. My two favourite blondes.'

Jenna swirled her wine around the glass. 'Doesn't that make you wonder why the hell she'd treat me the way she did?'

'It was underhand…'

'That's an understatement!' Jenna leant forward and rested her elbows on the table. She kept her voice low, despite the anger churning in her stomach. 'She stole a role from right under my nose; it was more than underhand; it was utterly deceitful.'

'I totally get why you moved out, but don't you want to try and have some sort of friendship with her? At the very least have a conversation about it.'

'Honestly, I don't care if it feels like I'm being childish or holding a grudge or whatever else anyone thinks; she needs to make the first move. She needs to grovel. An apology would be nice. Ignoring the situation isn't going to make me come running back with open arms.' Jenna placed her glass on the table. 'Have you spoken to her?'

The waiter appeared next to them. 'The kofta?' He placed the plate in front of Jenna. 'And the sheesh kebab. Enjoy.'

Carla picked up a knife and fork and smoothed a napkin on to her lap. 'I saw her the other day at a casting for an ad. We were there for different roles… This is the thing though, isn't it, you two were always going to end up competing with each other for parts. You're too bloody similar – looks-wise at least, if not personality.'

'What, cos I have integrity and she doesn't? However much I want a role, I'd *never* do what she did. Never. Us being competition for each other doesn't excuse what she did.'

Carla skewered a piece of grilled chicken with her fork and pointed it at Jenna. 'I agree, it doesn't. It really doesn't. I just want my two best friends to kiss and make up. Selfish reasons on my part. We were an awesome team.'

Jenna reached across the table and took Carla's hand. 'I know how tough this is on you. I don't want you to feel like you have to choose sides or not talk to her...'

'I don't feel like that, Jen, honestly I don't. You're too good a friend to make me feel like that. And Heidi, well, thanks to her deceitfulness, she's too bloody busy most of the time filming with Bond himself, the whole 'effing reason why we're in this mess to begin with.'

Jenna left Carla with a hug and they went home to their own flats. Jenna loved Carla's independence and how uncomplicated their friendship was, unlike her and Heidi's. Carla had always rented a room in a shared house but never with a fellow actor. Smart really, Jenna thought as she cycled home, to ensure life outside work was free of drama queens and the complicated egos of actors.

It had only been at the end of last year when Jenna had moved out of the flat she'd shared with Heidi. Although she liked having her own space and was free from the tension that had been created after what *she* did, it still felt strange not having a flatmate to come home to, to chat, laugh and watch Netflix with or to eat cheese toasties with in the kitchen at midnight.

Since living on her own, Jenna had got into the habit of checking her voicemail and email the moment she got in. She kicked off her boots and sat on the sofa with her laptop. Nothing interesting in her messages, so she emailed her agent to update her availability. Unless there was something happening on the weekend like a wedding or someone's birthday, she liked to keep herself free in case she got a last minute job. But instead, she emailed Beth to say she was unavailable for the upcoming weekend. She was going to go to Cornwall with her parents to help them sort through Aunt Vi's things. Most of all she wanted to see the cottage for herself.

Chapter Two

It was a hellishly long drive to Cornwall. They left before rush hour on the Friday as Jenna's dad Tony decided it was the best way to avoid the worst of the traffic, while her mum Kath was keen to give themselves as much time as they could to sort through the cottage. It was years ago that Jenna had been on a long journey with her parents. The drive reminded her of family holidays when she was a kid, squabbling in the back with her brother, heading to a caravan park on the Norfolk Broads or down to Dorset or Cornwall camping.

The landscape changed from the suburbs, to the fields and countryside of middle England, to the winding narrow roads boxed in by hedges and trees as they got closer to Aunt Vi's cottage. After more than four hours in the car she was feeling sleepy, but she perked up when her dad said they were about ten minutes away. She'd already looked on Google maps to see where the cottage was, and had become even more excited when she discovered it had a perfect location; on its own surrounded by countryside, just a short drive to the nearest beach, and a little further to the coastal town of Falmouth. It had everything going for it. Jenna got butterflies as she glimpsed a smudge of deep blue sea on the horizon. Tony turned off on to a narrow road and they were once again swamped by leafy trees lining each side, forming a tunnel of luminous green above them.

'It shouldn't be far now,' Tony said, leaning forward in the driver's seat. 'So keep an eye out.'

There was nothing but green hedgerows and trees. The

lane even had grass and weeds growing along the middle.

'Dad, I think you missed it,' Jenna said as they whizzed past a wooden gate half-hidden by foliage.

'Damn.'

They had to keep driving for another mile before they found a gateway to turn around in. Tony took it easy on the way back, slowing down in time to pull into the space in front of the worn wooden gate with a faded sign saying 'Bramble Cottage'. Jenna jumped out of the car and struggled to push the rickety gate open over the stones. Branches slapped the sides of the car as her dad drove into the driveway. Jenna closed the gate and followed her parents' car as it slowly rocked its way down the stony uneven drive. Overgrown shrubs and grasses lined each side, encroaching on the already narrow lane. Her dad stopped the car in a space just big enough to park two cars.

Her parents got out and slammed the car doors shut. Birds shot out of a beech tree and flapped into the air.

'Well,' Kath said. 'It doesn't look like anyone's touched this place in a long time. You can barely even see the cottage.'

The cottage was right in front of them. At least the side of it was – an outbuilding with a partly collapsed roof was built against the end wall of the cottage. A rose clambered up the side, obscuring most of the faded white wall, and entwined itself into the broken slate tiles of a roof that was in desperate need of repair. It was early spring and the recent rain, followed by sunshine, had left the garden overgrown. Trees loomed on all sides so Jenna couldn't even tell where the garden started. Leafy greens and pink and white blossom swamped the place, making the cottage feel enclosed.

Jenna followed her parents along a weed-covered path around to the front of the cottage. Her immediate negativity about the place and how much needed to be done vanished as the whitewashed cob and stone building was revealed, along with the front garden, a wilderness with steps leading up to an overgrown lawn bordered by shrubs. A breeze rustled the branches of trees, wafting the scent of hyacinths in their direction. Apart from the crunch of their feet on the gravel path, the only sound was the breeze and birds twittering.

They reached the front door and Kath fumbled in her bag for the keys. Jenna wandered up the stone steps to the lawn; long grass swiped at her skinny jeans as she turned to get a proper look at the cottage. It was a tired dirty grey instead of the gleaming white it must have once been. The wooden sash windows looked original, but the paintwork was peeling. Jenna was certain the wood beneath would need some major TLC.

Kath pushed open the front door. 'Oh my.'

Jenna followed her mum inside. It took a moment for her eyes to adjust to the gloom. Although the three windows in the kitchen and dining area were a decent size for a cottage, they were engrained with dirt and hardly let in any light. Kitchen units ran along the back and side wall, but they were worn and dated. In the middle of the room was a small wooden table and two chairs that looked a little lost in the large and empty space. Jenna guessed with only her Great Aunt Vi living here for decades, there was no need for a bigger table or updating anything at all.

'This is going to be a money pit.' Tony remained in the doorway with his arms folded. He looked at Kath. 'Are you sure you don't want to sell it, love?'

'I'm positive. It's been in my family for decades. It was my grandma and grandad's before it was Aunt Vi's. I have such lovely memories of being here as a child. I want us to be able to enjoy it; I want other people to enjoy it too, so all the more reason to get it done up and in a fit state to start renting out.'

Jenna poked her head into the living room. It smelt stale like the windows hadn't been opened in years. 'It is the most amazing location for a holiday let, Dad.'

'Jenna's right. We'll have no trouble renting it out.'

'Once the bloody place is done up.'

'Stop moaning; you're going to love planning how we're going to transform this place.'

'Yeah, from blinking two hundred odd miles away.'

The living room was sparse with a velvet armchair and a flowery two-seater sofa. The fireplace had a large stone surround with a small gas fire in front of it; Jenna hoped the original fireplace was hidden behind. Two windows looked out over the gardens at the front and the back, a sea of green framing them, overgrown shrubs blocking out both the light and most of the view.

'That'll be a lovely room once it's done up.' Jenna returned to the kitchen to find her dad still frowning, and her mum delving into cupboards. 'It's got the original slate floor too, that's something positive, Dad.' She tapped her foot against a dark grey slate tile.

Tony grunted.

She smiled. 'I'm going to look upstairs.'

Tony nodded and headed for the living room. Kath wiped her dusty hands down her jeans, and wrinkled her nose as she leant over the Belfast sink and fought to open the window. Jenna went up the creaky stairs that started by the kitchen and curved round, ending on a large landing with windows to the front and back of the house. Upstairs felt more spacious than downstairs. The landing, which was actually the size of a small double bedroom, was cluttered with old newspapers, an ironing board, stacks of boxes, and a large butterfly palm in a pot, its drooping leaves edged with brown. But it was lighter too as the windows were clear of foliage and not as dirty as the ones downstairs. There were two decent-sized bedrooms and a bathroom with a roll-top bath, white sink and loo, all reasonably tasteful apart from the mismatched pink and olive green swirly tiles that decorated half of the wall.

Jenna went back on to the landing. 'Mum!' she called down the stairs. 'I've found what needs sorting.'

Kath took the stairs two at a time. Her face dropped at the sight of the clutter. 'We should have hired a skip.'

'That's all right, love,' Tony said, joining them on the landing. 'I'm quite happy to take stuff to the tip while you two sort.'

Fully aware of what limited time they had, they got stuck in. Kath started upstairs, going through the boxes on the landing before tackling her aunt's bedroom. It was the best kept room in the place with a dressing table still filled with powders, lipsticks, perfume and her jewellery box. Jenna started downstairs in the kitchen, rifling through the dusty, cobwebbed cupboards. She pulled everything out and placed them in piles of things to go to the tip, things to sell, and things her mum might want to keep. The third pile remained pretty small, while the one for the tip grew as most of Aunt Vi's kitchen equipment was either ancient or broken. There were a few gems among the rubbish, a couple of enamelled dishes and blue-rimmed cups that Jenna put to one side. As they got on with the jobs, the cottage filled with their chatter, a stark contrast, Jenna thought, to the way Aunt Vi must have lived with only herself for company.

They carried on sorting until they were hot, tired and it became too dark to see in the dim landing light. Tony managed one trip to the tip before it closed, but he went out again later to get fish and chips, and the three of them sat in the living room, eating straight out of the paper.

'It's sad, isn't it, thinking of Aunt Vi living here on her own.' Kath crumpled her empty fish and chip paper. 'We really should have made the effort to visit her.'

'It's not like she gave you the choice though, did she? She was adamant she didn't like visitors; not a lot you can do when someone feels so strongly.' Tony collected the used wrappings and took them out to the kitchen.

'But she only had us, no one else,' she called after him.

'Well,' he said, returning to the living room, 'she couldn't have minded too much about us not forcing ourselves upon her. After all, she left this place to you.'

'Well yes, but only because she didn't have anyone else to leave it to.'

Whatever Aunt Vi's reasoning for being on her own, and for leaving her cottage to her niece, Jenna was pleased that she had. Despite the grubby corners, the cobwebs, the out-datedness, there was a charm about the place. It was also blissfully peaceful. Back at her London flat there was constant noise whatever time of day: cars whooshing past, the drone of a radio or TV filtering through open windows; drunken shouts late at night.

Kath had brought bedding, so they stripped the beds, hoovered the mattresses and made them up with fresh, clean sheets, pillows and duvets. Jenna had thought her mum had been over the top packing the car with so many extra things, but lying in the clean bed, the smell of freshly laundered sheets enveloping her, she was beyond glad. Even though she kept her flat reasonably clean, it wasn't the same as being here with the sash window wedged open, fresh country air and the scent of blossom and damp soil drifting in. The window of her bedroom back home looked out over the main road – car fumes, greasy chips from the Chinese, and her neighbour smoking pot were the less pleasant smells. Living close to London was essential for acting work, but the pull of the countryside was never far away.

Chapter Three

It was the peacefulness that woke Jenna the next morning. She hadn't felt the need to draw the curtains, and had left the window open allowing cool fresh air in. No one overlooked the cottage; she didn't know where the nearest neighbour was, but if there was another house close by it was hidden by trees.

She'd slept in the spare bedroom, sparse apart from the bed, a chest of drawers and peeling flowery wallpaper stained from the damp. A stack of letters was piled on the wooden window seat and, warmed by the morning sun streaming in, Jenna sat and looked through them. The same spidery handwriting appeared in every one. The ink was faded and the cream paper yellowed at the edges. They were in date order though, starting from April 1940 with the last letter dated September 1941. All were addressed to '*My dearest Vivian*' and signed off with '*All my love, Henry*'. Tucked in among them was a black and white moth-eaten photograph of a man in a soldiers' uniform who she assumed was Henry.

Jenna put the letters back exactly as she'd found them, unsure if she really wanted to pry into the private life of her spinster great aunt or to find out the presumably sad story of why she ended up alone.

Breakfast was a quick bowl of cereal while they leant against the kitchen counter, and then Jenna and Kath continued to sort through Aunt Vi's belongings. Paperwork, photograph albums or anything of particular interest, they put straight into the boot of the car to be sorted out at home. The aim of the weekend was to empty the house of everything that wasn't to be kept, in preparation for the builders to start work. It felt weird for Jenna to go through the personal items of a woman she'd only met a couple of times. Over the day she pieced together more about her great aunt, a woman who loved crosswords and knitting, kept piles of old *Radio Times*, had china dogs on the shelves but didn't have any family photos on show apart from one of her parents. Jenna bundled up the letters from the window seat and put them in the box of things for her mum to take home. It upset her to think that any chance of happiness with the Henry who wrote the letters had been short-lived.

Tony had been proactive in contacting builders before they'd come down to Cornwall and one builder came by to give a quote in the morning. Another was scheduled for the afternoon. Jenna liked the way her parents were cracking on with the place. She guessed it was a less emotional job when it was a distant relative. She understood their worry about it being financially draining, but like her mum, she was pleased the place wasn't going to be sold. She imagined coming down here for a holiday with friends once it was finished.

It was typical March weather; a cluster of dark clouds filled the sky early in the day and short sharp showers dumped heavy rainfall, yet by the afternoon the grey clouds had dispersed and high white clouds with pockets of blue allowed sunshine through. Hot and dusty, Jenna escaped to explore the garden. The drive was to one side of the cottage and the garden surrounded the other three sides. There was a smaller area to the front, with the raised lawn surrounded by borders that she'd briefly seen when they'd arrived. A weed-filled path meandered from the front lawn around the side of the house to a much larger area of overgrown lawn at the back. It was hard to see where the garden ended. The edges were shaded by trees, enough to warrant calling it a wood. Where the garden did eventually end, it was edged by a weathered wooden fence with a view across fields to patches of woodland. Was that the sea in the distance? Jenna tried to make out if the blue was sea or sky, thinking how amazing it would be if it really was a sea view, however far away. A cottage in Cornwall with a partial sea view. How lucky had Great Aunt Vi been to live here. Jenna turned back and looked at the wild garden through the trees. Had her great aunt ever really appreciated the place or spent any time out in the garden? It was evident that she hadn't recently. It was sad to think she'd been on her own for so long. There was a battered picnic table on the overgrown lawn at the front, but she didn't imagine a ninety-two-year-old lady struggling up the steps and through the long grass to sit out there even on a beautifully sunny summer's day.

Jenna wandered back through the wooded depths of the garden. Once the grass was cut and the foliage among the trees was thinned out, it would not only open up the garden and make it spacious, but it would draw the eye to the woodland. It was a fairy-tale setting. Jenna imagined summer parties outside, bunting strung through the trees, the lawn filled with people, and barbecue smoke drifting into the air.

Tyres crunched on the drive and Jenna caught sight of 'Harrison & Son Builders' in grey and red on the side of a van. She headed back round to the front of the cottage to find her mum and continue sorting through the kitchen cupboards.

Jenna caught snippets of the conversation as her dad gave the builder a tour of the cottage, starting upstairs.

'If you want work to start over the summer, it will mostly be my son working on it as I'll be busy on another job,' the builder said. 'But a place like this we can squeeze you in…'

'What if it's a two-man job like the kitchen?'

Their footsteps clumped downstairs and Jenna looked up from the kitchen cupboard she was emptying at a tall, broad, tanned man with greying hair emerging into the room with her dad.

'I'll be available for bigger jobs when more than one person is needed, like the roof for starters. We have an electrician we work with and we can do everything from the windows, gutting the kitchen, plastering the walls, fitting a new kitchen… whatever needs doing.'

'That sounds great; we want this place up and running as soon as possible.'

'Money pit otherwise, isn't it?' The builder shook Tony's hand. 'I'll get you a comprehensive quote by tomorrow, then we can take it from there.'

Tony walked him out of the cottage and Jenna watched them go past the front window. A car door slammed, an engine started and then silence returned as the van drove away.

'I like the sound of them,' Tony said, re-joining Jenna in the kitchen. 'How are you and your mum getting on?'

'Okay. I just had a little break. Have you seen the garden? It's loads bigger than I thought. It'll be amazing once it's been tamed.'

Kath joined them in the kitchen with flushed cheeks and a duster in her hand. 'I think we might have to come up another weekend and finish sorting a few things out. But we're getting there.'

The cottage played on Jenna's mind long after she got back home. Everything about it felt special: the location, its setting, the promise of what it would be like given enough love and attention – and money of course. Although the cottage was never a place she'd spent any time at as a child, unlike her mum, it was somewhere she wanted to return to.

But the call of London and work drew her back into city life. Jobs trickled in, confirming for Jenna what she loved about being an actor, the variety of things she got to do. One day she found herself as part of a select group of walk-on actors on a period film in a private mansion just off the M25; the next day she was off to central London for a casting in an indie film; the following week she was on a train to Cardiff to stay overnight with a friend before a two-day shoot on *Casualty* playing a young woman who'd been beaten up by her boyfriend. Despite the early call times, the long days, and often a lot of waiting around, Jenna could hardly call her job boring; she rarely knew what she'd be doing from one week to the next, something she thrived on. She knew her parents didn't understand how she could be comfortable with the unpredictability of work, along with often not knowing the location of the shoot until the evening before, but Jenna craved the excitement and flexibility. She'd never had an office job in her life and she was going to keep it that way.

The dreary wet days of March gave way to spring and sunshine, fresh days with patchy blue sky, more blossom on the trees, and the distant promise of summer. Jenna worked as much as possible, always saying yes to jobs passed to her by her agent and putting herself forward for castings as often as she could. The one thing that frustrated her about the bit-parts she was getting was the thought that she could have had a steady job on a major movie, if it wasn't for Heidi. At least Heidi being tied up with filming meant that Jenna avoided having to see her.

Jenna gritted her teeth as she waited for the Tube doors to slide open, praying it wouldn't be packed and she'd have to stand jammed against someone's smelly armpit. She breathed a sigh of relief as she found an empty seat opposite a woman reading *House & Home*. It had been a long day with a 5am call time, an hour in costume and make-up to be turned into a character who looked the worse for wear after a night out in central London. She'd spent the day filming in a grubby back alley behind restaurants in Soho. She'd endured take after take of being chased along the lane and slammed against a bin by an actor called Harry who was lovely and polite in real life, but was playing a thug called Jay in the scene. Her shoulders ached from being grabbed and Harry had apologised profusely after each take. Despite that, it was one of those days that was immensely enjoyable because she got to actually act and be a part of a pivotal scene and story, plus Harry, with his chiselled jaw, bright blue eyes and muscles, was easy on the eye. But it was physically exhausting and not at all glamorous, and made Jenna fume at the thought of Heidi and what an amazing time she would most certainly be having.

Jenna yawned, rubbed her eyes and hugged her bag. The make-up artists had done their best to remove the dirt and fake blood that had been smeared down the side of her face, but she was longing for a shower to fully remove it. She definitely still had some in her hair. A hot shower and something to eat before falling into bed, alone but with thoughts of Harry playing over and over, was what she craved.

The image on the front cover of *House & Home* was of a country cottage kitchen, all cream units and a central island with a wooden work surface, purple rhododendrons in a vase and dried herbs hanging from a mint-green rack beneath a wall unit. It took Jenna back to Aunt Vi's cottage and what the kitchen could look like once its old-fashioned units were transformed into a smart new cream kitchen to offset the delicious dark grey of the original slate floor.

The Tube pulled into the station. More commuters piled on; a smart-suited shiny-shoed man with a briefcase sat down with a thump next to her. Maybe Jenna would buy a copy of *House & Home* on her way home; it could be her bedtime reading, imagining what the cottage could become. The builders had already been booked, her dad had been quite happy with the father and son team he'd spoken to when they'd been in Cornwall, but there was no harm in Jenna coming up with some ideas. After all, once the place was done up she hoped she'd at least be able to spend a bit of time down there, perhaps with someone special. A blue-eyed, tanned and toned actor like Harry would do rather nicely.

Jenna got off the Tube and emerged from the Underground into dusk. She wrapped her chunky knit cardigan tighter and set off down the road. Her phone beeped. Two missed calls, all while she'd been on the Underground and from her agent too. She listened to her voicemail.

'Jenna, call me back as soon as you can. Thanks, hun.'

Jenna quickened her pace. It was late and she'd be lucky if she made it home before it got dark. She'd had an insanely long day, and the last thing she wanted to think about was more work. Part of her was too nervous to phone Beth back in case she had a last minute job lined up for tomorrow. She shouldn't have that attitude, she knew, but she was dog-tired and the thought of another early start and a long day of shooting made her feel even too tired to tackle the ten-minute walk home.

At a crossing she phoned her agent back.

'Jenna, hun. Sorry to phone you late, I know you've been working all day. I hear it went well, they were super impressed with you.'

The lights changed to green and Jenna started across the road. 'Yeah, it was good, totally shattered now though. Although there are worse ways to spend a day than getting chased by a fit bloke for hours on end.'

'I bet.' Beth laughed, a throaty chuckle that always made Jenna smile. 'Well, the reason I'm phoning out of hours is I've just heard back about the casting for the period feature film you went to.'

'*The Affair*?'

'That's the one and they want you.'

'Oh my God, Beth, that's amazing. When's the call-back?'

'There isn't one. They loved you, said you've got exactly the look they want. The job's yours. A part like this is incredible, you never know what it might lead to. So, what do you think?'

'It sounds too good to be true – what's the catch?'

'There's no catch – honest! It's an eight-week shoot and I need you to let me know ASAP. The only issue I can foresee is that it's not in London. You'll have to relocate for two months; it might not be something you'd want to do.'

'Relocate where?'

'Cornwall.'

Chapter Four

Jenna's heart was racing by the time she reached her apartment building. Instead of going into her flat she made her way to the underground car park, got into her car and joined the tail-end of rush hour traffic heading out of London. The moment Beth had said the location was Cornwall, an idea began to formulate. She could have just gone into her flat and phoned her parents, but she was too excited. She needed to see them in person in case they needed persuading that her idea would work. If her mum would agree to it, more like. Her dad was pretty laid back about things, but her mum, an eternal worrier, would find reasons to say no to Jenna's idea. She was already thinking about the cottage as a headache rather than an opportunity; the last thing Jenna wanted to do was make her stress about it even more.

She pulled into her parents' road and slowed down. It was half eight and not quite dark yet. How amazing would it be if Jenna got to spend the whole summer in Cornwall, by the sea, a world away from the choked-up streets of suburban London. Both work and her summer sorted. The combination could not be any better. If this worked out… The bubbling in the pit of her stomach was something she'd felt countless times before at auditions or call-backs for roles she really wanted. She was so disappointed when she didn't get chosen. She knew she had to contain her excitement, and that her parents might not agree to her idea.

She backed into the drive behind her parents' car and got out. The lamp in the living room was on, the TV flashing, but she couldn't see her parents. She rang the doorbell. Her palms felt sweaty, a completely irrational reaction. All she was going to do was ask her parents a simple question.

Her mum opened the door. 'Hiya, love. This is unexpected. Everything okay?'

'Sorry, yes, I was on my way home but my agent phoned and she kinda got me thinking… I thought I'd come and ask you something.'

'Okay,' Kath said slowly. 'Come on in. It's just lovely to see you.'

The sound of the TV filtered into the hallway as Jenna followed her mum through to the kitchen. Her dad was sitting at the kitchen table tucking into a half-eaten plate of spaghetti bolognese.

'Hello. Well this is a nice surprise. Didn't expect to see you.' He shovelled a forkful of pasta into his mouth.

'Have you eaten?' Not waiting for a reply, Kath grabbed a plate from the cupboard.

'I did, at lunchtime.'

Kath dolloped a large spoonful of pasta on to the plate, topped it with meat sauce and placed it on the table. She sat down and patted the empty seat next to her. Jenna joined them.

Kath picked up her fork, went to dip it into her pasta and looked again at Jenna. 'Is that blood in your hair?' She lifted Jenna's fringe from out of her eyes.

'Yes, fake blood, Mum.'

'What on earth were you doing today?'

'Getting beaten up by a six-foot bloke in front of a dumpster.'

'Of course you were, why do I even ask!' She laughed. 'I'll never get used to the strange days you have. And you call it work.' She shook her head and sprinkled a handful of parmesan over her bolognese. 'Will it be on TV at some point?'

'Uh huh, not sure it's the kind of programme you'll fancy watching though.'

'Lots of sex and violence is there?' Tony asked.

'Yeah, just a bit. Past the watershed type of programme.'

'Just your dad's cup of tea, then.'

Tony wound spaghetti on to his fork and looked at his wife. 'Not if my daughter's getting beaten up, it's not.'

'I am playing a character you realise; I'm not actually getting hurt.'

Her dad grinned at her.

'You don't do anything else, do you?' Kath raised her eyebrows. 'You know… S.E.X,' she mouthed.

'No, but it's sort of implied, but not in a nice way if you know what I mean.' Jenna frowned. She'd come over to ask them something and she was getting grilled about what her character had been getting up to. 'I've got another day filming next week when they find my body.'

'Oh right. No, I'm definitely not going to be watching that then.' She touched Jenna's hand. 'You should eat, love, if you've not had anything since lunchtime.'

Jenna sighed but stuck her fork in the spaghetti.

'So, you wanted to ask us something?' Kath reached for her glass of red wine.

'Um yeah, so my agent phoned this evening to say I've been offered a part in a movie filming over the summer. It's a featured character who crops up in various scenes, so it would be lots of work, really good money, and they hand-picked me.' Jenna took a breath and chewed a mouthful of pasta. Her hands were sweating.

'Well, that sounds fabulous, doesn't it, Tony?'

'It does. But why do you need to ask us – surely not permission to say yes to it – guaranteed work sounds bloody good to me.'

'No, not your permission as such, it's just, it's filming down in Cornwall. The base is near the Lizard peninsular. I'd need to relocate there for the summer, and I just thought…'

'You want to stay in the cottage, don't you?' Kath set down her wine.

'It's eight weeks' constant work, Mum, the whole of July and August, with filming five days a week. It's perfect. I've been thinking about it all the way over here. I can stay in the cottage and oversee the building work, film during the day and work on the garden in the evenings and weekends. Once the major stuff's done I can even do the finishing bits like painting. I'd love to stay there and it saves you time and stress worrying about being miles away from the cottage while building work is going on.'

Jenna sat back in her chair and folded her arms. She held her breath and waited. Her dad nodded; her mum frowned.

'It would be easier to not have to project manage from two hundred miles away, love.' Tony smiled at Jenna and looked at Kath.

'But Jenna's never project managed anything in her life, plus she'll be out working most of the time.'

Jenna decided not to give a smart-arse reply – she was confident that she'd be able to organise the work on the cottage by herself and work on set during the day, particularly if she was staying there. After all, she'd have a vested interest in getting the work finished and done on time if she was having to live in the mess. 'You and Dad will be at the end of the phone if there are any issues or if I'm unsure about anything, won't you?'

'That's true,' Kath said slowly.

'And it would be easier having Jenna down there keeping an eye on the place and how things are going – means you won't worry quite so much. Helps her out too.'

'Thanks, Dad.'

'Well.' Kath placed her wine on the table. 'I suppose you two are right. If you think you can do film work and manage the building work, then you're welcome to try, love.'

After more chatting, half-finishing her plate of spaghetti and being force-fed a bowl of strawberries and cream, Jenna made it home. She closed the door behind her, any last bit of energy dispersing the moment she slipped her aching feet out of her shoes. Her one-bed flat was small, but it was her sanctuary.

It was dark and late and she was desperate for sleep. She went into her bedroom and looked in the mirror. Her blonde hair fell in waves around her shoulders, and she could see the red stain in her fringe from the fake blood. Her blue eyes, framed by long lashes, were her best feature, but tiredness showed in her pale face. She took her laptop and sat cross-legged on her bed, propped up by pillows. She had an email from Beth with more details about the role in the 1940s-set Cornish film including dates and filming locations. The role she'd been offered was for a natural blonde, pretty, bubbly twenty-something woman and apparently she was it. Getting parts really was pot luck at times, but luck had been on her side, landing her a role that would make her decent money over the summer and allow her to escape to Cornwall.

Jenna was uncertain if the next few weeks dragged or flew by. They were filled with interspersed days filming mostly in or around London, but she had a night shoot in Brighton where she played a clubber, and spent four long hot sweaty nights dancing with and snogging a twenty-six-year-old called Liam. No wonder her parents thought she had a crazy job. But it paid the bills and was as far from a 9-5 office job as she could get; the complete opposite of her older brother.

The plan was for Jenna to go down to the cottage the Friday before she started filming, so she'd have the weekend to get herself organised. The builders were due to start work that week too. It was all falling into place. She'd been to costume fittings in London, and by the middle of the week before she was due to start filming, she already had her bags packed. She'd given herself two days off before her Cornish adventure, although it felt wrong turning down work. It seemed to be a snowball effect, the more she worked, the more she was offered. It felt good getting her name and face out there.

'I'm going to miss you.' Carla wrapped Jenna in a bear-hug.

The remains of their Indian takeaway littered the coffee table in Jenna's apartment, their plates stained yellow and red from chicken pasanda and a lamb rogan josh.

'I so wish you were working on this film too.'

Carla pointed to her choppy pink hair, twisted into curls.

'Was never going to happen – not a period film looking like this.'

'You have to come and stay with me for a bit.'

'I'll try. You're so effing jammy with this role. What a way to spend the summer. Filming on location in Cornwall, staying in a cute as anything cottage…'

'It will be cute but it's not at the moment.'

'Beats living here and commuting into London.'

'You've got stuff lined up though, haven't you?'

'Yeah, course.' Carla reached for a poppadum and broke a piece off. Crumbs dropped on to her baggy black and white harem pants.

'You sound down.'

Carla shrugged. 'Nah, not really, I'm being flaky. Just a bit fed up of the whole audition cycle, but we came into this knowing it's a shit-hard way to make a living.'

'I thought it'd get easier, the more auditions I went to but it doesn't, does it?'

'Gets fucking harder. More pressure that we should know what we're doing.'

'But you're getting stuff, right? You're always working.'

'Yeah, I'm just being over sensitive. I get work as the kooky, weird friend, the raver, the homeless woman, the drug user, the crazy person going mental in a music video… I'm never going to get the kind of roles you or Heidi get.'

Jenna's fists clenched at the mention of Heidi. Despite everything that had happened, it was weird her not being here with them, saying goodbye, sharing their successes and fears.

Carla sighed. 'I just need my luck to change and get a role like yours, something permanent and secure for a few weeks.'

'You'll find something, you always do.' Jenna reached for her friend's hand. 'I hate seeing you looking down. Remember at drama school you were so positive about getting to play the interesting characters and not the blonde girl-next-door type. I'm never going to get chosen for those quirky parts that you're awesome at. The tutors loved you for that too.'

'Yeah, I know. Like I said I'm being over sensitive. I turn up to an audition and there's a sea of pretty blondes waiting to be called and I know I have no chance.'

'You've dyed your hair pink; you know that's not helping, right?' Jenna laughed.

Carla playfully whacked her arm and ran her fingers through her short choppy hair. 'It was for a role, that quirky lesbian nightclub owner. I quite like it, although it's fading pretty quick; almost back to blonde.'

'There you go then, you'll fit right in with that "sea of pretty blondes" soon enough.'

'Yeah, right. I should get "quirky" tattooed on me.' She reached for the bottles of Cobra and passed Jenna one. 'Anyway, enough of me moaning. Congrats to you on getting a great job and here's to you having an amazing summer in Cornwall.' She knocked her bottle against Jenna's. 'You might find a cute guy down there…' Carla winked. 'I mean, you're going to get to work with Milo Blake. He is so hot right now.'

'He is, but…'

'Yeah yeah, I know, this year's all about you, but never say never…'

Jenna tucked her legs beneath her on the sofa. 'Going out with another actor, well you know, has its challenges…'

'We're all bloody neurotic, that's why.'

'And a "normal" bloke, well, they just don't get what we do, that it's acting. We play act for a living, for God's sake, it doesn't mean anything.'

'Elijah was a prick.' Carla sipped her beer. 'Not every normal bloke will react the same way as he did. He was jealous as fuck with no good reason.'

'He kinda did have a good reason though, didn't he?' Jenna folded her arms. 'I spent a week filming half naked, writhing around with a male model.'

'Yes, but you were *acting*.'

Jenna glanced at the cloudy night tinged yellow from the street light right outside the kitchen window. 'He didn't see it that way.'

'And that was *his* problem. He lost out big time because he lost you, all because he couldn't handle what you do for a living. You've got to do what makes you happy. If acting's it, then you need to find someone who understands that it's a job and you have boundaries.' She pointed her bottle at Jenna. 'You know what, you've just cheered me up. I don't have that problem. I never get to snog a hot man – or hot woman for that matter – seeing as though I always get cast as the quirky sidekick. They never get laid.'

Early the next morning Jenna heaved her bags into the boot of her car. She crawled through traffic and regretted not waiting until after rush hour to get going. Despite the overcast morning, she kept her window open. The heat and humidity mixed with exhaust fumes made her long to leave suburbia behind and feel fresh air on her face. Cars splintered off at each junction, people dropping their kids off at school or heading to work, while Jenna followed her satnav for the M3 and the 260 more miles to Bramble Cottage in the depths of Cornwall.

Although Jenna grew up within commuting distance of London, family holidays had always been in the country or close to the sea. Even when they went abroad, her parents opted for a village setting or somewhere away from built-up touristy areas. Work had kept her parents in Guildford, but their love of the countryside had influenced Jenna from an early age. To be successful as an actor she needed to be close to where auditions and the majority of roles were. Either that or she'd have to be prepared to travel a lot. This opportunity of a long shoot in Cornwall was rare and she couldn't quite believe she was on her way to a summer that promised so much.

The motorway turned into a fast A-road and the clouds began to thin out revealing glimpses of blue sky and sunshine the further south-west she headed. Work commitments had meant she hadn't been able to go with her parents when they'd gone down to the cottage for a second time to finish sorting things out. That had been three months ago in early spring. Now, the countryside was bursting with leafy greenness. The landscape changed dramatically during the nearly five-hour journey, from a cityscape to bright yellow fields of rape, grazing sheep and wooded hilly areas. The roads narrowed the further into Cornwall she drove, making Jenna's heart pound every time she met a car coming the other way.

Jenna slowed when she thought she was close to the turning to Bramble Cottage. The lanes all looked the same, a tunnel of trees casting patchy sunlight through gaps in the branches.

A van pulled out up ahead. She caught the name on the back, 'Harrison & Son Builders' and realised it was the builders who would be working on the cottage. She slowed even more, indicated and turned into the narrow driveway that led to the cottage.

The lane desperately needed clearing; brambles and weeds snagged the side of the car as she drove the short distance to the parking area. It seemed smaller than she remembered, but then after all the spring rain followed by the summer sun everything had grown like crazy. She turned off the engine and stepped from the car and on to a bramble snaking out from the undergrowth. It was easy to see how the cottage got its name.

Silence.

It was such an odd sensation, listening to, well, nothing. There wasn't even a breeze to rustle the leaves. Jenna crunched her way along the path, pulled the keys from her bag, and opened the front door. Her parents had done a good job of emptying the place. Her mum had scrubbed the kitchen too, so although the old-fashioned units remained, it was now at least dust, dirt and cobweb free.

Jenna set her bag on the kitchen table and did a quick tour, opening windows as she went to rid the cottage of the smell of bleach. Her mum had bought a few things for the cottage to replace lots of the old stuff they'd got rid of, so Jenna spent the next hour unloading the car and putting new saucepans, a frying pan, wok, toaster and a kettle away. She made the bed in the main bedroom, put her toothbrush in the bathroom, and slowly turned the place into her home from home.

Chapter Five

The rumble of an engine turning into the driveway set Jenna's heart racing. She jumped out of bed. It was Saturday morning and she'd planned to lie in knowing that sleeping in would be non-existent once filming started. She assumed it was the builder but she'd also assumed he wouldn't be back till Monday.

It was as humid in Cornwall as it had been in London, and so she'd slept in a vest top and knickers with the windows wide open. At least some air drifted in and it was fresher than when she'd gone to bed. Sunshine slanted through the window on to the carpet, promising a brighter day. In a sleep-haze she searched the room for something to wear and pulled on the leggings she'd been wearing the day before.

Footsteps crunched along the path below the bedroom window and someone knocked on the door. She dived across the landing and into the bathroom, splashed cold water on her face and rubbed toothpaste across her teeth with her finger.

'Hello?' a deep voice called from the kitchen.

Jenna grimaced and spat toothpaste into the sink. Of course the builder had keys and could let himself in. How else was he expected to do any work on the place when she'd be out all day?

'Hey there!' she called back. 'Be down in a second!' She swept a damp hand through her bed-hair before deciding to tie it back into a messy bun. She pulled a face in the mirror, wrinkling her lightly tanned nose. There was no getting away from the fact that she'd just got out of bed, but at least she looked reasonably fresh-faced.

Unable to find her slip-on trainers, she padded barefoot downstairs. Slowly steel toe-capped boots and tanned muscly legs in shorts came into view.

She stopped on the bottom step and frowned. She'd expected the fifty-something builder her dad had been talking to, not a twenty-something man with tattooed arms, windswept dark-blonde hair, a beard, and smiling eyes.

'Hey there, I'm Finn. You're Jenna, right? Dad said you're going to be staying here while the work's going on.'

'Your dad… Oh, right. Yes, of course. So you're the um "son" in "Harrison & Son". Sorry, for some reason I was expecting your dad. Actually truthfully, I wasn't expecting anyone today.' She motioned to herself and immediately regretted pointing out how under-dressed she was.

Finn's eyes followed her hands, dropping from her face downwards, then immediately snapping back up to her face. 'Yeah, sorry if I woke you. We're squeezing in this job so I thought I'd get started sooner rather than later. I didn't think you'd be here yet.'

'I came down early to have a bit of time before starting work on Monday.' The more she looked at him and the more he looked at her, the more flustered she felt. 'I was taking the opportunity to have a lie-in while I could…'

'I don't have to work today, totally fine if you want the place to yourself or to go back to bed.'

Jenna waved her hand. 'No, it's fine, I'm up now and have things to do anyway. I don't want to mess your day up if you already have work planned.'

'Okay great.' He was taller than her even though she was standing on the bottom step.

'Coffee. I need coffee.' Jenna slipped past him, her feet slapping on the cold slate floor. 'Would you like one?

'Yeah, love one thanks.' He placed his work gloves and toolbox on the kitchen table. 'So you're down here for the summer?'

Jenna filled the kettle and flicked on the switch. She turned to face him. 'Yeah, for the next few weeks. I've got a part in a film.'

'You're an actress, are you?'

'Uh huh.'

'Oh right, yeah, I know. It's that film where they're taking over the place all summer. Filming around Porthleven.'

'That's the one.'

'Cool.' He sounded upbeat about it but Jenna wondered whether the locals actually enjoyed having a film crew descend on their beautiful part of the world for weeks at a time. Maybe hotel, restaurant, shop and bar owners did, reaping the benefits of lots of extra people on top of the usual tourists, but tradespeople probably found it all a bit inconvenient.

The kettle boiled. Jenna made two mugs of coffee. She didn't even know him and she was making assumptions from the tone of his voice.

'Milk?'

'Just a splash, thanks. No sugar.'

She took the carton of milk from the fridge, added a dash to the mugs and handed one to Finn.

'So, my parents said you're working on the outside of the cottage first, sorting out the roof and damp and stuff?'

'Yeah, that's the plan. Starting outside and working our way in. Dad will be working with me on the roof next week. We can work around you though, one room at a time but that won't be for a couple of weeks yet.'

'I'll be out quite a bit of the time anyway so it shouldn't matter where you work. We just thought – well my parents agreed – that having me down here to oversee everything would be useful. Easier to make decisions.'

'Sounds great.' Finn nodded and sipped his coffee.

They were both standing, leaning against the work surface. Maybe she should suggest they sit down. No, that was a stupid idea. The heat of the coffee was making her even more flustered than she already felt. He was way too good looking to be confronted with first thing in the morning, braless, make-up free and having only just got out of bed.

'Right, well…' Clutching her mug, Jenna pointed to the stairs.

'Yeah course, I need to get on too. It'll be good to get the roof underway while the weather's like this. Supposed to be sunny for the next few days.' With his mug in one hand, he picked up the toolbox with the other. 'Thanks for the coffee.'

'No problem.'

All Jenna could think about as she went upstairs was how much of a distraction Finn Harrison was going to be. She hadn't thought anything about his dad Gary working on the place, but his son…

The scaffolding was right outside the bedroom window. She shut the flowery curtains and started unpacking her suitcase. Apart from the old-fashioned decor and furniture, Aunt Vi's room was the best kept room in the place. It was strange sleeping in her old room and waking up to the sound of the birds her great aunt would have heard every morning. There was very little of hers left in the room; her mum had cleared the dressing table but had left a perfume bottle that had a subtle musky scent, along with a postcard of Whitby that Jenna's grandparents had sent to Aunt Vi in 1989 before Jenna had even been born. She leant the postcard back against the mirror and finished hanging up her clothes in the empty wardrobe.

There were no curtains at the landing windows. The floorboards creaked beneath her feet as she nipped across to the bathroom. Knocking sounded from the roof. She peered out of the window but couldn't see Finn, only hear the rhythmic thudding. She pulled the curtains closed and ran the shower until it was warm. After living on her own for the last few months she'd underestimated how odd it would be to share the space with someone else – even if that someone was a builder rather than a housemate. She was very aware of him being around and it didn't help that he was young, good looking and had so far left her completely and utterly flustered.

By the time Jenna had showered, dressed and put on her make-up it was mid-morning. The heat hit her the moment she stepped out of the cool cottage. She ate her toast sitting on the steps that led up to the grassy area with the battered picnic table. The steps were bathed in sunshine and the humidity from the day before had been replaced by a drier heat. She could happily sit here forever, soaking up the sun and listening to the birds singing. The scaffolding was at the back of the cottage and every so often there'd be knocking and the sound of something dropping to the ground.

A garden was the one thing Jenna missed since she moved from the garden flat she'd shared with Heidi. There was so much potential both inside and out at Bramble Cottage, and until work inside had been finished, there wasn't a lot Jenna could do, but outside…

Jenna grabbed the gardening tools she'd brought with her and decided to start tackling the front garden, away from where Finn was working at the back. She searched through the lean-to at the side of the cottage, but apart from being thick with cobwebs, there wasn't much except a few rotting logs, an open bag of coal, rusty shears and a dozen or so chipped flower pots. Nothing she could really use and no lawn mower. Jenna emerged back into the sunshine, brushing off dirt from her arms and stray cobwebs from her hair. Taming the grass would have to wait till she'd had the chance to buy a lawnmower – pretty essential considering the size of the garden. No wonder it was in this state if Aunt Vi had no way of keeping it under control.

Dressed for the heat of the early July day in shorts and a sleeveless top, Jenna started ripping and digging out dandelions, creeping buttercups and nettles that crowded the borders. She worked slowly and systematically along the largest border, making a mental note of the plants and bushes she found among the weeds. Her brain was already in overdrive thinking how best to tame them without losing the natural country garden look that she loved.

A thud from over the other side of the cottage made Jenna stop and look up. She swept her hair from her eyes and stood upright, stretching her aching back. There were more thuds followed by the squeak of wheels. Jenna shaded her eyes. A wheelbarrow appeared around the side of the cottage first, pushed by Finn. He stopped by the side of the lean-to and peeled off his T-shirt, stuffing it into the back pocket of his shorts, leaving half of it hanging out. He was tanned from working outside and toned from all the physical work. His muscles flexed as he lifted the handles of the wheelbarrow and pushed it along the narrow path and up the wooden ramp. Jenna's eyes followed him, her face feeling hotter and hotter as she took in the tattoos that crept across his broad shoulders and down his arms. He dumped the contents in the skip and manoeuvred the wheelbarrow back down, then turned and caught her eye. Flustered, she smiled, waved and dropped her gaze from his six-pack as she crouched down again. She yanked out the weed in front of her and decided she needed to cool down inside and concentrate on something else for a while. In fact, sod that, she needed to go and do some shopping. She was too hot and bothered, plus getting out of here and away from Finn and his muscles would be a good idea.

It was a few miles to the nearest town, and although she had a car, Jenna reminded herself that she needed to be organised here and make sure she always had the basics in like bread, milk and fruit. At least she'd be fed well on set. It was usually late and she'd be past eating by the time she got home after a day filming and she was certain it would be the same here. Also, the location for filming next week was a good twelve miles away, and it was unlikely that the shoot would stay there for the whole eight weeks. She was prepared for early starts, lots of travelling, and getting back to the cottage late. Life as an actress had made her flexible. It also made her anxious. She gripped the steering wheel, her palms sweaty despite the cool air rushing in through the open window. She always had the same fear when starting a new job, all the unknown elements of getting to know a new cast, crew and location. With one- or two-day shoots, she often wouldn't know her call time or the exact location until the last minute, then she'd have a mad rush to work out her journey, prepare for the next day, plus get enough sleep while worrying about sleeping through her alarm. And yet despite all of that, she enjoyed the excitement and variety of her life, and the interesting people she got to meet. There were extra perks too like meeting famous people, having the opportunity to film in unusual places, or getting a bonus payment because her role was changed to a speaking one on the day, even if she only uttered a simple 'excuse me' or 'hello' and it was removed and left on the cutting room floor.

Jenna had the cottage to herself on the Sunday and she spent the morning pottering, before heading out in the car to explore the surrounding area. It was another blistering hot day with an endless blue sky and only wisps of clouds that looked like they'd been painted on with the gentlest brush stroke. Jenna wondered how long the good weather would last. Schools hadn't broken up yet, but it was still busy particularly on the coast with holidaymakers, mostly couples and a few families with younger children.

Having grown up in Guildford and lived in London ever since, she relished being far away from motorways, from the traffic choking the road in front of her flat, and the constant noise of the city. After the events of the past few months, getting away from it all was exactly what she needed, even if work started tomorrow. A change of scene and pace though, that was priceless. And what an opportunity to be able to stay in a place like this for the whole summer. She was going to make the most of it, knowing that the eight weeks would probably whizz by.

Two-hundred and fifty miles away from home and the landscape couldn't be more different: coastal villages with pastel-painted cottages, harbours packed with white boats bobbing together, and sparkling turquoise sea. It almost felt like she should be abroad. She didn't like the thought of tucking into a roast dinner in a pub on her own, so she bought fish and chips, and ate them sitting on a bench by the harbour, a salty sea breeze taking the edge off the heat, the soothing sound of water slapping the harbour walls mixed with the screech of gulls.

Even though staying in the middle of nowhere on her

own could have left her feeling a little on edge, that was furthest from her thoughts as she drove back to the cottage along narrow lanes at dusk. Despite looking forlorn and in desperate need of some TLC, the cottage was surprisingly inviting, particularly once the front door was closed and the lamps in the living room were switched on.

Jenna drew the flowery curtains on the darkness descending over the garden and settled in the armchair with a book. She'd craved this absolute peace for such a long time. Relationships had become too hard over the past year, and it wasn't just the romantic ones. Even though men weren't the main issue, she was quite happy being single. It was complicated friendships and being let down by the one person – besides her immediate family – who was closest to her. It was a situation she needed to face at some point, but being on location in Cornwall for the summer was the perfect way to avoid a huge amount of awkwardness and tension.

Chapter Six

The signs pinned to trees and telegraph poles gave away the fact a movie was being made. Even though Jenna had the postcode plumbed into her satnav, she followed the 'BASE' signs, rather than risking the satnav leading her down a scarily narrow lane. She was used to city driving and some of the roads in this part of Cornwall seemed impossible for two cars to pass each other and she didn't fancy trying. It was early in the morning on a Monday and it wasn't like rush hour back home, when the road outside her flat was choked with cars, buses and lorries for at least two hours. Here, in the middle of nowhere, she seemed to be the only person around.

She always got a nervous buzz rocking up to set on the first day of filming, particularly to a film set. Although her mum accused her of flitting between jobs and careers, acting had always been at the top of her list and that excitement never diminished. Even though her job wasn't as glamorous as her non-actor friends and family assumed – long hours, often lots of waiting around, shooting in all weathers – she still felt the thrill of working in the industry and being a part of a group of like-minded people.

The 'BASE' signs led her off a lane and into a farmer's field. A parking area had been cordoned off and trailers had been set up with signs like 'Hair', 'Make-up', 'Production Office', along with a couple more set back for the lead actors. There was also a huge marquee where Jenna assumed most downtime would be spent and where meals would be served. A handful of the crew were already gathered around the catering van, with steaming cups of coffee in one hand and bacon sarnies in the other. It was the lifestyle she loved; the excitement of working on different projects, getting to meet new people all the time, seeing old friends, making new friends, and not feeling tied down by a traditional job. Exams hadn't been Jenna's strong point, but anything creative had been: drama, art, music, woodwork, gardening – she enjoyed anything practical and was good at it. Drama school had been hugely competitive to get into, and yet she never felt her parents regarded it as quite the same achievement as her brother studying law at Cambridge.

The make-up truck had enough space for four actors at a time, and even early in the morning with the door wedged open and a fan whizzing around what little air there was, it was warm inside. Jenna sat in the first empty chair and looked in the mirror at her make-up free face.

One of the make-up ladies, a pretty round-faced woman with a dark-brown bob, smiled at Jenna through the mirror. 'Well, don't you look lovely and fresh-faced this morning.'

'It's all the fresh Cornwall air and a good night's sleep.'

A slender woman around the same age as Jenna came in and sat in the chair next to her. The other make-up artist swept the woman's auburn hair off her freckled face and into a band.

'I'm Lily,' the redhead said and smiled at Jenna. 'I think we'll be working together a lot. I'm one of the three friends.'

'Yeah, me too. I'm Jenna.' She looked at Lily through the mirror and then at herself. The make-up lady did the same with Jenna, twisting her hair back into a band.

'That's a lovely face to work with.' The make-up lady smiled at her and dabbed a sponge into a creamy foundation. Jenna always felt like it was a treat having her hair and make-up done. Even if it was part of her job, it felt like she was being pampered, with the added bonus of getting paid.

'This is the first major film I've worked on. How about you?' Lily asked.

'I've worked on films before – all bit parts. This will be

the longest shoot I've ever done.'

'The whole summer in Cornwall. Pretty exciting. I've not seen you at the hotel?'

Jenna closed her eyes as the make-up lady dabbed the sponge on her cheeks and forehead and swept it across her face. 'I'm not staying there. My parents have a cottage down here, left to them by my mum's aunt, so I'm staying there.'

'Oh nice.'

'What's the hotel like?'

'A-maz-ing. Right on a clifftop with sea views. It's lush. You'll have to come and see it.'

Jenna was comfortable with the routine of a day of shooting, even if it differed slightly from project to project. Hair, make-up and costume kicked the day off with filming in-between a lot of downtime. People new to the film or TV industry were always surprised by how much waiting around there was: waiting for scenes to be set, lighting and sound checks, and walk-throughs. Jenna was also relieved that her first day of shooting didn't involve having to learn any lines, although she'd done her homework and was prepared. She only had a light splattering of lines over the whole film, but her character was featured a lot. Day one was an easy scene with the three girls played by her and Lily, and Amanda who she'd met in the costume tent. They giggled together as they walked along the harbourside in front of fishermen's cottages.

As a first day went, it was a good one. It was also Jenna's first experience of being a part of the named cast on a major film and on a period one too. There was something even more special about going through hair, make-up and getting into costume when you got to peel away modern day clothes and step into the life of someone from long ago. Or on this film, the 1940s. The World War II backdrop made her think of Aunt Vi and the soldier she'd been in love with. The women Jenna, Lily and Amanda were playing were glamorous with beautifully curled hair, red lipstick, and costumes that were much more comfortable than when she'd been squeezed and pulled into a corset for an eighteenth century period drama. Two months ago she'd been in a skin-tight top and a mini skirt filming a scene in a south London nightclub, now she was in the depths of Cornwall, the unspoilt surroundings perfect to depict summer in the 1940s. She had to pinch herself that this was really happening and that she was in a film on location for two months. Life couldn't get much better than this.

Jenna settled into a routine of early starts and long filming days. The weather was warm and sunny, the ideal conditions for both the shoot and the work on the cottage. Leaving early in the morning, Jenna hardly saw Finn, but mid-week she had a later call time and Finn and his dad arrived before she'd left. She made them coffee, talked through what they'd been doing and said goodbye. Each day when she arrived back an improvement had been made with the slate roof tiles slowly being removed and replaced.

It was four days into filming when Jenna had her first scene with Milo Blake, the lead actor. She'd worked with big-name actors before but had never shared a one-on-one scene with them or had played the love interest like she would with Milo. There was a buzz at the base the morning when Milo Blake was first on set. Jenna could sense it with extra security on the gate to the base, supporting artists whispering together as they waited to be bussed to location. Milo's trailer was a focal point for everyone's attention.

'He arrived at the hotel yesterday,' Lily said as the three girls walked together from the costume trailer to hair and make-up. 'Bet you regret staying at that cottage now.'

'Not really, I think it would do my head in everyone going dippy over a film star.'

'He is hot though.'

'Only the second sexiest man alive though according to *Hot Now Magazine*.' Amanda hooked her arm in Lily's and Jenna's.

Jenna laughed. 'Only number two, eh?'

'They're obsessed by him.'

'Who?'

'The magazine. And women in general.'

Milo Blake was hot, in a movie-star kind of way. He had luscious dark hair with brooding full lips and large deep brown eyes. He was clean shaven, tanned and wasn't averse to getting his top off at every opportunity. Jenna imagined he'd look just as good in a soldier's uniform from the Second World War as he did in jeans and a T-shirt. She was also certain of the distraction he'd be at the hotel where he was staying with the rest of the main cast. She was pleased she would escape the craziness, yet she was also anxious that she was the only one who had yet to meet the infamous Milo Blake.

'Lily, Jenna, Amanda. You're all on the minibus that's about to leave.' The First AD scanned the paper on the clipboard he was holding. 'Head over to the car park and you're in the first minibus.'

Freshly out of hair and make-up with their long hair pinned neatly back in 1940s style waves, the three of them walked arm in arm across the base.

'Timothy's nice too,' Amanda said as they reached the car park. 'He arrived a couple of days ago and I think him and Milo already know each other.'

'Yeah,' Lily said. 'He said they worked together before.'

'Aah, here she is.' A deep brooding voice took her by surprise. 'Jenna Wilson, last but not least of a very lovely trio of ladies.'

He'd spotted her before she'd clocked eyes on him. Lily nudged her and Jenna looked to her left and came face to face with Milo Blake.

He held out his hand. 'Milo.'

She shook it. 'Hey there, it's good to finally meet you.' She stopped herself in time from spilling the beans that *everyone* had been discussing him all morning. But she guessed he knew that already.

'I hear you're not staying with us at the hotel. Holed up somewhere by yourself.'

'Yeah, I wasn't sure what the arrangement was going to be

when I said yes to the job. If I'd known everyone was going to be put up in a fancy hotel...'

'I'm sure it's not too late to change your mind and come join us.' He slid open the minibus door and let her on first.

'Ah, well I'm overseeing the building work on the cottage for my parents, it's how I negotiated staying there for the summer. I kinda like it there too.'

'The hotel has a hot tub and a swimming pool.' Milo winked and sat next to her, while Lily and Amanda slid on to the seat behind them. Lily caught Jenna's eye and raised an eyebrow.

'That is tempting...'

It was a short journey to that day's filming location, just enough time for Milo to tell her a bit about the last film he worked on. She didn't mind sitting back and letting him talk. The whole minibus could hear him; it was evident he liked being the centre of attention and thrived on it. Jenna imagined he had plenty of stories to tell from working and partying with Hollywood's elite. He moved in completely different circles to her. She knew actors who'd performed at the RSC and worked on TV series for the BBC, even someone who'd got a part in a Netflix film, but no one who'd made it in Hollywood like Milo Blake had. Here she was, literally rubbing shoulders with him, as they bumped along a potholed lane to a secluded Cornish farmhouse with far-reaching views of the ocean.

Jenna had worked as a film extra before and during drama school and her one worry had been getting snubbed by the actors. As with everything in life, some people were lovely, some were arseholes, and actors were no different. Jenna vowed that however successful she got, she'd always make time for everyone – cast, crew and extras alike. A handful of bad experiences when she was younger made Jenna notice how actors treated people. The more famous they were, the more she noticed. Milo commanded attention, but he also made time for everyone, chatting with the crew, flirting with the make-up ladies, teasing one of the supporting artists, and that made him all right in Jenna's mind. She came to that conclusion during the first two days of filming with him. He was good looking and fit as anything, but that didn't always go hand in hand with being decent.

She mostly had scenes with Lily and Amanda, but there were plenty with Milo too, and Timothy, plus a few of the older character actors who she hadn't met yet. There'd be plenty of time to get to know everyone better, and she was already firm friends with Lily and Amanda who were a similar age and at a similar point in their career. And although Milo was hugely successful and much further along in his career than she was, he sought her out, chatting to her between takes, inviting her to sit with him at lunch and waving her over whenever he saw her. It was noticeable because he didn't do that with Lily and Amanda, unless they were all together.

The heat increased as the week went by and continued over the weekend and into the second week of the shoot. A heat wave from Spain caused chaos in the UK which was unused to those kinds of temperatures and not set up for working in such conditions. The location where Jenna was filming also changed from the cool but cramped farmhouse and yard shaded by a sweet chestnut tree, to the suntrap of a sandy beach backed by cliffs. By the afternoon on the hottest day, everyone was flagging with the sun relentlessly beating down and a shimmery heat haze over the golden sand. Jenna envied the holidaymakers who got to spend lazy days on a beach beneath the shade of an umbrella, swimming in the sea and splashing about in rock pools. Filming on a beach wasn't quite the same when downtime was beneath the shade of a roasting-hot marquee wearing a 1940s swimming costume. And no sunbathing was allowed. No one wanted to risk the cast getting sunburn. There were times she had to remind herself how lucky she was to work on a big-budget film on location in a beautiful part of the world.

Chapter Seven

'That's a wrap!' The First AD's announcement was met with a collective sigh of relief from everyone. 'Let's get out of here before we all get heat stroke.'

It was nearly two in the afternoon and the temperature wouldn't have been out of place in the Mediterranean. The beach had little shade, the marquee for use between takes was as hot as an oven. Even umbrellas held over the actors plus copious amounts of cold bottled water did little to help. Everyone was hot, sticky, sweaty and miserable. No wonder countries like Greece and Spain had siestas. All Jenna could think about was lying down somewhere cool.

In the minibus on the way back to the base everyone was talking about cooling off in the pool at the hotel before heading to the nearest pub for a beer. It sounded rather appealing to Jenna, but at least the cottage with its thick stone walls kept the heat out. It was unbearably hot in the costume tent, and no one stayed longer than they needed. With relief, they slipped back into more comfortable summer clothes.

'Come back to the hotel with us,' Lily said as they escaped the stickiness of the tent for the equally humid air outside.

'Maybe later.'

'I'll message you.'

They split off; Lily to the minibus that was taking some of the cast back to the hotel, while Jenna got into her baking hot car. Sweat immediately beaded her forehead. She started the engine and wound down the windows, cursing that her car didn't have air-conditioning. Her top stuck to her back as she bumped out of the field and turned into the lane. Warm air rushed in as she picked up speed. She squinted in the brightness even with her sunglasses on. As she went over a hill, the countryside spread out in front of her, a mirage of greens with splashes of colour breaking up the view: the gleaming white of a cottage; the mustard-yellow of a field of rape; the red, pink and blue of wild flowers in the hedgerows; the deep blue cloud free sky.

She'd only been in Cornwall for little more than a week but driving back to the cottage felt like she was going home. Even more than her flat in London did – it was where she slept, showered and cooked food, but she had no affinity to the place. Yes, she liked having her own space but she didn't feel as relaxed as she did here. It was also an oasis, away from the heat on the coast, with the garden surrounded and shaded by tall trees.

Jenna turned into the drive and parked alongside Finn's van. The slam of the car door was loud in the quiet of the garden. Startled wood pigeons flapped into the air from the trees. As she headed to the front door she heard scraping and assumed Finn was working round the back of the cottage.

Compared to outside, the kitchen with its flagstone floor, thick stone walls and small windows was cool. She dumped her bag, went over to the sink and peered out of the window. She could just make out a bucket and the side of Finn's tattooed arm as he worked on the cottage wall.

Jenna opened the fridge's freezer compartment, pulled out two ice creams and went outside. She made her way round to the back of the cottage and on to the lawn. As soon as she'd got the lawn mower at the weekend, she'd cut the grass and it had transformed the garden. It looked even bigger with some of the wildness tamed. The sun pounded down, and out of the shade it was even hotter than by the sea. The trees surrounding the cottage garden were completely still, the only movement the occasional bird swooping between branches.

'Just you today?' Jenna shaded her eyes and watched Finn repairing the stone next to the kitchen window. 'Fancy a break?'

'Hell, yeah.' Finn turned and dropped the trowel into the bucket.

Jenna smiled and chucked him a mini Magnum.

'I didn't know if your dad was here.'

'No, just me today.'

Jenna waggled the remaining Magnum. 'I'll have this one then.'

Finn wiped his arm across his forehead and stepped out from the shadow of the cottage. 'You're a lifesaver.'

Sweat glistened on his face and chest, and with no T-shirt tucked into his back pocket, it looked like he hadn't even bothered to wear one at all.

'Bit hot isn't it?' Jenna sat on the dry grass and peeled the wrapper off. The chocolate beneath was already beginning to melt. 'The heat even shut down filming today, which hardly ever happens.'

'So you've got the afternoon off?' He joined her on the grass and sat next to her. He leant back on one hand with his Magnum in the other.

'Yeah, back in early tomorrow though.' Jenna cast her eyes away from him to the cottage. 'You seem to be getting on well. The roof looks great.'

'Yeah, Dad's on another job for the rest of the week now the roof's done. I've started on the wall; there's a really damaged bit which probably accounts for the damp you've got in the kitchen beneath the stairs.'

The reclaimed slate tiles Finn and his dad had used blended in with the original tiles, but now the roof was crack-free and water tight, a hint at how the whole cottage would look once Finn had finished with it. Jenna couldn't do anything to the inside of the cottage besides clean it, until the work putting in new sockets, unblocking fireplaces, repairing the windows, ripping out the kitchen and re-skimming the walls with plaster had been done. Until then she was happy to tackle the garden.

'This,' he said, waving the ice cream, 'is the next best thing to a cold pint in a pub garden.'

'Oh God, I couldn't think of anything better.'

'But I'm working, so this is perfect.'

'There must be some good pubs around here though. Where do you go?'

'Not to the really touristy ones, although lots of those have the best beer gardens or are close to the sea. We usually just go to the one in the village.'

'Where do you live?'

'In Mullion.'

'Oh really? That's near to where most of the cast are staying. Bet it's a bit different living down here rather than being on holiday for a couple of weeks though.'

'Yeah, part of me wants to get away from here; live somewhere more exciting.'

'Seriously? I'd love to live down here.'

'You are.' He motioned to the cottage in front of them.

'Only for eight weeks.' Jenna bit into the ice cream. The coldness made her cheeks clench and a piece of chocolate dropped on to her bare leg. She whipped it off her skin and popped it into her mouth. 'I'd love to live somewhere like this. I'm fed up of city living. It's not all it's cut out to be.'

'Neither is living in the country or by the sea.'

'Shame we can't swap.'

'I guess you need to live near London for work? I mean I know you're working down here but I presume it's a one-off?'

Jenna nodded. 'Most jobs are in or around London.'

Finn finished the last bite of his ice cream and rested back on both elbows. The sun beat down and even with Factor 30 on, she could feel her skin sizzling in the heat. Finn looked like he was used to working outdoors, his chest golden, no tan lines on his arms. His skin gleamed, the tattoos edging the top of his chest and down his arms, black and bold in the sunshine.

Jenna realised she was staring. 'When did you get your first tattoo?'

'At eighteen.' He pointed to the tribal band at the top of his arm. 'Kinda got hooked. Saved up to get one each year ever since – or at least expand on the ones I've already got.'

'Nice.'

'Have you got any?'

Jenna smiled. 'I may have.'

'You going to show me?' He met her eyes and grinned.

'They're not exactly in an obvious place – it's easier in this job not to have tattoos on show, really. I've done quite a few period dramas. Easier getting cast without them.'

'Do you get typecast?'

'What, the girl next door parts?'

'I didn't mean it quite like that, but yeah I guess. I mean you're pretty. Like really pretty.' He dropped his gaze from her and looked at the cottage instead.

Jenna brushed a stray hair from her face; she was already hot but her cheeks flushed even more. She didn't want the silence to grow and it to suddenly be awkward between them.

'It's funny, I was having a similar conversation with my friend back in London. She's got this epic, like totally unique look which sets her aside from other people and bags her some great roles, but she was saying her looks rule her out of so many other opportunities, like the love interest. The sort of stuff I get to audition for.'

'Is that who you're playing on this film?'

'Sort of. There's a group of three friends and I'm the one who catches the attention of the lead character. It's a supporting role though, mostly scenes when we're in the background or in a big group scene. But I do have some lines.'

'Sounds like a big deal to me.'

'Let's just say I had the right look.' She wiggled her toes in the grass, her red toenails glinting through the green blades. She blew hot air over her face. 'We so should have sat in the shade.' She couldn't help glancing at his chest again, glistening in the sun, probably from the sunscreen he rubbed on himself earlier…

Finn sat up, his stomach muscles tensing as he did.

'I've got a bit more to finish off, then I'm going to call it a day and stop early. It's too hot to work round the front in this heat.'

'Absolutely, finish early and go have that pint in a beer garden.'

'Thanks for the ice cream and company.'

He leant his hand on the grass as if to push himself up but instead moved closer and kissed her cheek. His beard tickled her skin, sending a shiver through her. He lingered for a second too long and instead of pulling away, his lips brushed against hers.

'Sorry.' Within a heartbeat it was over. 'I um, didn't mean to… that was inappropriate.'

He stood up, shoving his hands in the pockets of his paint-splattered shorts.

Jenna didn't know what to say; her senses were in overdrive. He tasted of chocolate mixed with a delicious smell of aftershave, sunscreen and hot skin.

She picked up the ice cream wrappers and scrambled to her feet. 'Don't worry about it; sun's obviously gone to our heads.'

They set off across the grass together, Finn heading to the shade of the wall, and Jenna escaping around the side of the cottage.

The kitchen was dark and cool, a welcome respite from the mid-afternoon heat. Jenna dropped the wrappers in the bin, leant on the edge of the sink and gazed out of the window at the spot where they'd been sitting. With the kitchen window open, she could hear scraping. Finn was continuing to repair the cottage wall where the mortar had come away. All she could think about was that kiss, the lightest brush of his lips against hers, and yet it was so sensual. So unexpected. It seemed to take him by surprise too.

It was too hot to do any work in the garden, and she was too flustered to concentrate on anything else, mainly because her thoughts kept flitting back to Finn and his muscles flexing as he re-grouted the cottage wall. She planned on waiting until he finished for the day and then she'd take up Lily's invitation of joining them at the hotel. She bit her lip; she could suggest to Finn that they go for a pint in a pub garden together, but somehow that seemed even more forward than that briefest of kisses. Anyway, she was certain he was planning on going with his mates. Feeling even more hot and flustered, Jenna decided to have that siesta she'd dreamt about earlier.

Lying on her bed, she listened to the scrape scrape scrape of Finn working on the wall. The image of his full lips, bearded chin, blue eyes and sandy hair made sleep impossible.

Chapter Eight

Jenna did eventually drift off. She woke to silence, the room darker than it had been when she'd come upstairs. She went over to the window and peered out. The sun had moved around the cottage leaving most of the grass now shaded. The scaffolding was in the way so she couldn't make out if Finn was still there or not, but the rhythmic scraping had stopped. She walked across the landing in bare feet to the spare room. One of the windows overlooked the side of the house and drive, but only her car remained. She wondered if he'd tried to find her to tell her he was finishing for the day. Maybe he thought she'd been hiding away so there wasn't any awkwardness over that kiss.

Oh God, thought Jenna, *let it not make things awkward.* All she'd been able to think about since she'd got back from work was Finn. She needed a distraction. The hotel, a pool and the rest of the cast was the simple answer to that. She'd been invited over nearly every day and it was about time she showed up.

The cast staying together at the hotel reminded Jenna of being a student at drama school, and even though she relished being on her own at Bramble Cottage, there was a certain appeal to that kind of camaraderie. After the ups and downs of the last few months, Cornwall and the cottage had been her escape, but as she drove into the grounds of the hotel she felt a pang of envy at the rest of the cast being in a place like this.

Jenna didn't mind that Bramble Cottage wasn't right on the coast; it was surrounded by trees and countryside, quiet and unspoilt. It was close enough to easily reach the sea but far enough away from the summertime crowds. She parked in the car park at the front of the hotel and walked around the side of the building, immediately understanding why Lily and Amanda, and even Milo, thought she was mad staying at the cottage. The hotel was breathtaking. Perched on a cliff top, its white walls gleamed in the sunshine and the large windows made the most of the far-reaching views, the blue sea, craggy cliffs, and lush tropical gardens studded with colour.

Jenna felt jealous of the beauty and openness of the location compared to the overgrown tangle in the garden at Bramble Cottage. She didn't need to go into the hotel to ask anyone where any of the cast were, she could hear their laughter and screeches from the car park. She paused for a moment on the edge of the patio. There were guests sitting out with cocktails and wine, making the most of the sunshine. The lawn swept down to the edge of the cliff, part of it lined by bushes, the rest of it dropping away to reveal a sandy cove studded with dark grey rocks.

She took the path along the edge of the lawn towards the noise. The outdoor pool was set away from the hotel, surrounded by a sandstone terrace with sunloungers. There was nothing but the green of the surrounding grounds and the blue of sea and sky.

'Jenna, you made it!' Amanda jumped up from her sunlounger and ran across to her in bare feet.

'This is the life you're leading outside of filming?'

Amanda grinned. 'Not bad is it. A taste of a Hollywood A-lister lifestyle.'

Jenna clocked Milo and Timothy along with a couple of the older actors laughing together around the other side of the pool. Both Lily and Amanda were in bikinis with floaty beach kaftans thrown on over the top. Jenna felt overdressed in shorts and a T-shirt. The intense mid-afternoon heat may have dissipated, yet it was still sweltering and the pool was a suntrap exposed on top of the cliff. Jenna longed to dive into the cool clear water of the pool.

'You've got a bikini with you, right?' Amanda asked.

Jenna nodded.

'Come up to my room and get changed.' Amanda took Jenna's hand and led her back along the path to the hotel.

'Wait for me,' Lily said, catching them up.

The inside of the hotel was as swish as Jenna had imagined with a light airiness that continued into the rooms. Amanda's bedroom was huge, the walls white, with splashes of colour from seaside pictures and the silver and blue bedspread.

Lily wandered over to the window. 'Your sea view's even better than mine.'

'Wishing you were staying here now?' Amanda flopped down on the bed.

'Actually, I'm happy staying in my great aunt's cottage. It's got heaps of character.'

Lily turned back to face them. 'That's what you call something that needs a hell of a lot of work doing to it.'

'Well, that's true, it does. But it does have loads of character – beamed ceilings, gorgeous stone walls. You should come over and see it sometime.' Jenna headed to the bathroom.

'He fancies you, you know,' Amanda said.

Jenna turned back. 'Who does?'

'Milo. He definitely fancies you.'

Jenna shook her head and closed herself in the en suite.

'You don't have a boyfriend, Jenna?'

Jenna sighed. Amanda had been fixated on her and Milo since the moment he turned up on set. Jenna rested her bag next to the sink, unzipped it and hunted for her bikini.

'Nope. Been single for just over a year,' she called back.

'Who finished with who?'

'I did with him.'

'Was he an actor?'

'Nope.' Jenna wriggled out of her shorts and T-shirt and pulled on the bikini bottoms and top. She stuffed her clothes in her bag. There wasn't a full length mirror in the bathroom so she couldn't scrutinise herself, which was probably just as well. She tied her hair into a messy bun, threw on her beach cover-up, slipped her feet into flip-flops and went back into the room.

Amanda whistled. 'He's going to fancy you even more now.'

Jenna playfully whacked Amanda's arm. 'Stop it. We're working together, that's all. And he's a flirt, he's like it with everyone.'

Lily raised an eyebrow. 'Not everyone. Although if I didn't have a boyfriend, I'd be all over him.'

'You're the only single one of us, Jenna, you gotta have some fun.'

It seemed like they were having more fun trying to set her up with Milo than she was having. She might be an actor and good at playing the part of confidence but in real life she still felt out of her depth at times, particularly when she was around someone like Milo who was as easy to talk to as he was easy on the eye.

'Come on, let's get back out there and soak up the last bit of sun.' Amanda scrambled off the bed, pulled down her sunglasses and led the way out of her room.

'At last, you join us!' Milo patted the empty sunlounger next to him and Jenna slid on to it, dropping her bag on the ground.

She was used to being around actors and had worked with a few famous names, but Milo left her feeling star-struck. It wasn't like she was a huge fan or anything. She liked him, she'd seen a few things that he'd been in, but he had an air of confidence about him, of someone who knew just how popular, good looking and successful he was. A confidence that often eluded Jenna, even though countless people told her she was talented, that she was pretty...

'You don't have the whole place to yourselves, do you? Looked like there were some couples out on the terrace when I walked past.' Her attempt at small talk was lame but the best she could do under Milo's gaze.

'There are a couple of regulars — presumably the hotel manager didn't want to cancel and piss them off. Think they're quite excited about being surrounded by a load of luvvies.'

'At least you're all out most of the day.'

Even beneath the shade of the umbrella it was still hot, and being flustered was making the situation worse. Lily and Amanda had settled themselves back on their sunloungers at the one shady spot of the terrace and Adrian, who she'd met on set earlier that day, and another couple of actors were sitting together chatting by the wall.

Jenna wedged her sunglasses in her hair and stood up. 'I'm going to cool off in the pool.'

'I think I'll join you.'

Jenna sensed Milo's eyes on her as she peeled off her beach top and left it crumpled on the lounger. Her bikini was a sunny yellow and looked good against her light tan. She slipped her feet out of her flip-flops.

Milo brushed past her and dived straight into the pool.

Water splashed on to the terrace and Lily screeched as it reached her. Timothy was already in the pool doing laps and he ducked his head under, shot back out and wiped beads of water off his face and through his hair as Milo swam past.

Jenna entered the pool via the steps, relishing the cool water connecting with her skin, first her feet, legs and body, until she was submerged. After sweltering on set in the morning, it was blissful to float, relax, and stare up at the cloudless blue sky.

Water splashed in her face. She turned to look but there was no one there, only a shadowy figure beneath the water coming at her like a rocket. Jenna shrieked as Milo's hands slid around her waist. As he emerged from beneath the water he pulled her upright so they were floating together, his grinning face inches from hers, dripping with water and sexy as hell.

'He'll never let anyone be,' Timothy said, swimming past and looking between them with raised eyebrows. 'Always fun and games with Milo. Get used to it.'

Jenna wasn't drinking, but everyone else was. As the sun retreated, the laughter got louder, the drunken antics rowdier.

After her dip in the pool, Jenna had dried off and settled herself beneath the shade of an umbrella with a book. It wasn't often that she was the one in the position to be looking after everyone else. She was driving though and so didn't have a choice. This year had been a tough one in many ways. Lily and Amanda's comments about her being single and available and that she should be trying it on with Milo Blake had hit a nerve. She'd been fine being single this past year, focusing on herself and her career, even though that had been sabotaged by her so-called friend. Men or lack of them weren't the issue, she was surrounded by good looking blokes on a day-to-day basis. It was the nature of her job. It was the same story dating another actor, roles and ego always got in the way. Not that the boyfriend was always to blame; she knew she was too. Maybe she was too self-absorbed, too focused on chasing a dream.

Fingers clicked in front of her. She looked up and came face to face with Milo's crotch in burnt orange board shorts. Her head snapped up to meet his eyes.

'You're in a daydream.'

He reached down, took her hand and pulled her to her feet. The last remnants of the sun were bleeding across the horizon, a deep red and a vivid pink merging with black night. Outdoor lights had come on, lighting up the pool, with lamps edging the paths. Timothy and Amanda were in the pool, the others chatting on the side. Lily had been keeping Jenna company before disappearing up to her room, Jenna couldn't remember what for. Tiredness was sweeping over her; Milo's hand was warm and firm in hers and she realised he was leading her away from the others.

He stopped before the end of the terrace, just where the stone paving was edged by a border packed with bushes. He kept hold of her hand. Even in the night air she could smell the sweetness of honeysuckle.

'You should be staying here, you know.' His fingers stroked her hand.

She was conscious of her heart beating. What if he invited her up to his room, what would she say? She liked him, but she didn't know him, and what little she did know had been gleaned from magazines. But then she was single, what harm would a bit of fun do? Even with a movie star…

'You're beautiful.' He was slurring his words, his eyes were glazed, not quite focusing on her. He caught hold of her waist, almost as if he was swaying so much he needed something to hold on to, to steady himself. The last person she'd been this close to had been Finn, earlier that day sitting in the sunshine. No alcohol involved then, just a bit too much summer sun. And what? The kiss had happened so quickly she'd barely had time to process it, and yet she was thinking about it now when a semi-naked Milo Blake had his arm around her waist.

'You're drunk.'

He tugged her closer, so their bodies were pressed together, hot damp skin connecting. She expected him to kiss her, but instead he leant closer, his stubble brushing the side of her face, one hand tightening around her waist, the other hand dipping down and resting on her bum.

'You're sexy as hell, you know that right?' he whispered.

Light pooled around them, making him look more tanned than usual, his hair darker, his cheekbones even more defined. His lips brushed her cheek and then he pulled away. He smiled, and sauntered back towards the splashing in the pool, leaving damp footprints on the pale stone.

Jenna shivered. She looked around, sensing someone watching her. And there was, although they were trying to be subtle about it. Amanda was looking in her direction as Timothy tapped a blow up ball towards her. She needn't have worried about what her answer would be if he asked her up to his room, yet her emotions were now even more conflicted.

Chapter Nine

The second week merged into the third and Jenna found herself spending more and more time with Milo. After the evening at the hotel's pool, he sought her out, inviting her to sit next to him if they had a lunch break together. It didn't go unnoticed. She saw the looks and witnessed the hushed discussions between the supporting artists. He was interested in her; asking questions about her family, friends, the jobs she'd worked on – and the jobs she'd lost out on.

Jenna had the attitude that she'd sit wherever there was space or next to whoever looked like an interesting person to talk to, whether they were cast, crew or an extra. Having worked as a supporting artist in the past, she loathed the cliqueiness of some principal actors who stuck together and ignored everyone else. She strived to not be like that and yet found herself in the difficult position of bonding with the main cast, who she was working with on a daily basis, but still trying to get to know the extras.

It was the middle of the third week of shooting when Milo waved her over. She'd been heading to a table filled with crew but it felt ruder to ignore him than it did to go and sit with him, so she headed over and Amanda joined them. Timothy was already there, sitting next to Milo, and Jenna could see Lily in the lunch queue, jumping ahead of the extras. It was a normal part of filming, the principal actors and crew getting special treatment. She understood the reasoning that they had to be back on set and working, but she knew what it felt like to work in the background. It was very different from being in the limelight, something she'd not yet got used to, unlike Milo who seemed one hundred per cent comfortable with his Hollywood star status.

'I've missed seeing you this week, Jenna. Only had Timothy for company. Although we've got a scene together this afternoon, haven't we?'

Did he actually wink at her? It wasn't like the scene was anything major. All it involved was Jenna brushing past him and Milo giving her 'a look'. Their actual kissing scene would come later in the shoot. They'd been slated to wrap early today – how hard would it be to muck up a scene with absolutely no dialogue?

'Learnt your lines?' He definitely winked at her that time.

'Ha ha.' Jenna stabbed her fork into the pasta salad.

'They're my favourite scenes.'

'What? The ones where you don't have to learn any lines?' Amanda grinned across the table at him.

'I should be an extra.'

'Rather than a bona fide Hollywood star?' Timothy raised an eyebrow. 'I'd stick to learning lines, mate.'

Jenna chewed a mouthful of pasta. Their casual put-down made her squirm.

Milo finished his food, pushed his plate away and leant back in his chair. His dark eyes focused on her. 'So, when are we going to get to see where you're staying, Jenna? You're this mysterious woman, disappearing off every evening on your own. I want to see where you hang out away from the rest of us.'

'Why don't you all come back this evening?'

'A party.' Amanda clapped her hands.

'Well, I mean, sort of. A few drinks, some food…'

'Sounds good to me.' Milo met her eyes and held her gaze. She squirmed again, but less from annoyance this time and more from his ability to make her feel flustered.

It was strange doing the familiar drive back to Bramble Cottage with Milo. His tanned arm rested on the open window and sunglasses shaded his eyes. Jenna relished the breeze buffering her face as they bombed along narrow lanes. She'd got to know where the passing places were and her confidence in country driving had increased.

Jenna pulled into the driveway and stopped on the gravel parking area. Apart from the cottage still being clad in scaffolding it exuded peacefulness the moment she switched off the engine.

Milo got out of the car, took off his sunglasses and looked around. 'This place is actually yours?'

'My parents. Left to my mum by her aunt.'

'It's fucking ace.' Milo took the box of wine and beer from off the back seat and walked to the front door.

Jenna followed him, her eyes fixed on his broad shoulders and his flexed arm muscles as he carried the box of booze. It was more than just his fame that made him noticeable; he was confident and sure of himself. Fame probably helped with that, but Jenna got the feeling he'd always been like this. He'd probably been an infuriatingly cocky kid. They'd gone to the same drama school but he'd graduated four years before her and even back then, everyone had heard of Milo Blake. Everything about him screamed film star: his lusciously thick dark hair, tanned skin, handsome face with defined cheekbones, full lips and dark brooding eyes.

He reached the door and Jenna squeezed past him. His aftershave mixed with the scent of the garden. She fumbled for the key in her bag. He was only a little bit taller than her but lean and muscular in all the right places as far as she could tell. Who was she kidding? She'd seen the shirtless photos in magazines – the top 100 sexiest men. He always made it on to those lists, rubbing shoulders with the likes of Chris Hemsworth, Tom Hardy and Benedict Cumberbatch.

She sensed him behind her, so close she imagined him sliding his arms around her. She hurriedly pushed open the door and they went inside.

Jenna switched on the light and dumped her bag on the kitchen table. 'It needs work doing to it, mostly cosmetic though.'

'It's awesome.' Milo put the box next to her bag and

wandered across the kitchen. He peered up the stairs and then poked his head into the living room. 'Bet there's a fireplace hidden behind that monstrosity.'

'Yeah, knocking that out is on the list for the builder to do once he's finished working on the outside. There's damp upstairs which is hopefully sorted now the roof's fixed.'

'I'd love to have an old house like this but the upkeep must be a nightmare.'

'It's okay if you've got the time and money to spend on it – or get someone in to fix it.'

Silhouetted in the living room doorway, Milo turned and grinned. 'I like my modern-as-hell apartment in central London, but a bolthole like this would be cool. Maybe in the South of France though.' He winked and sauntered over, reached past her and pulled a bottle of beer from the box. 'Got something to open this with?'

Jenna searched through the drawer next to the cooker and pulled out a bottle opener. She opened two bottles and Milo clunked his against hers.

'Cheers.' He took a swig. 'When are the others getting here?'

'I think they were nearly done when we left. They should have wrapped by now.' She took a sip of her beer, suddenly feeling star-struck at the sight of Milo Blake in the cottage kitchen. 'Let's go outside.'

Clutching her beer bottle, she escaped into the warm but fresher evening. It wouldn't get dark until much later, but the sun had dipped and its heat was filtered out by the trees surrounding the garden. She'd spent time with Milo over the past couple of weeks but she didn't feel like she really knew him. She was flattered by his attention, though, and the chance to hang out with him. His interest in her was welcome but surprising. She knew Carla would scold her for not thinking she was worthy or pretty enough for his attention.

They rounded the corner of the cottage and went past the scaffolding.

Milo stopped. 'Okay, this is awesome too.'

The sun cast a glow across the garden – it was so still and

quiet, almost otherworldly. They walked over to the worn wooden table and chairs that Jenna had rescued from the fallen-down outhouse.

They sat down next to each other, both facing the cottage. Jenna glanced at Milo. 'Do you like it, the fame?'

'I like aspects of it. The intrusion sucks but I can't be choosy, it comes with the territory. Who knows how long it'll last – I plan on milking it for as long as I can. There's always the threat of a new up and coming actor. It's got easier over the years as I've become well known, but I still have to audition and chase roles...'

'Join the club.'

He swigged his beer and looked at her intently. 'You got this job easily enough though, didn't you?'

Jenna put her bottle down and frowned. 'I was expecting a call-back but my agent said they liked my look. How did you know?'

'*I* liked your look.'

Jenna's frown deepened. 'Wait. What? You got a say in choosing me?'

'I got to choose a couple of roles, yours included.'

'Who were the others?'

He tapped the side of his nose. 'Now that would be telling, wouldn't it?'

'Why did I get the part?'

'Why do you think? I mean, look at you.' His eyes travelled from her face downwards.

Jenna's heart sank as his eyes lingered. If he was expecting her to put out just because he'd got her the job, then he didn't know her very well.

'So, I really was picked for the role because of the way I look.'

'Get used to it, Jenna. The entertainment industry is ruled by the way people look. You're beautiful, blonde and slim. You'll go far. If you play the game.'

Jenna's eyes narrowed behind her sunglasses. Did he really mean what she thought he meant? Was he actually suggesting that being with him would advance her career?

'I'm not sure that's really what I…'

A taxi turning into the drive ended their conversation. Timothy, Lily and Amanda piled out, slamming doors and shouting 'hellos'. The taxi reversed down the drive and out on to the lane. The silence returned as it sped away.

'I'm glad we didn't have to drive and find this place.' Timothy plonked a four-pack of cans and a bottle of gin on the table. 'It's in the middle of bloody nowhere, Jenna.'

'I know. Perfect isn't it?'

'I miss the city.' Timothy flopped on to one of the chairs.

'I love it.' Lily hugged Jenna. 'I'm not surprised you're staying here. I mean, the hotel's great, but this place is stunning.'

'Even with the scaffolding and mess.'

Amanda held up a bag that was straining with the amount of things in it. 'I have food and stuff that needs to go in the fridge.'

Jenna stood, avoiding Milo's gaze. He'd made her worried that she could actually mess up her career by saying the wrong thing. She motioned Amanda to follow. They headed back round to the front of the cottage and went inside.

Jenna opened the fridge. 'It's pretty empty.'

She stood back while Amanda stacked tubs of snacks and dips on the shelves.

Amanda closed the fridge and stood up. 'So, anything happen before we got here?' She raised her eyebrows, giving Jenna a knowing look.

'No, nothing. Sorry to disappoint.'

'He so likes you though.' Amanda gestured in the direction of the garden.

She shrugged. 'He likes everyone. He's a total flirt.'

'Rumour has it he likes beautiful blondes too.' Amanda nudged Jenna's arm.

There were worse things to be, but Finn's comment the other day in the garden about her being typecast was spot on. Would she ever have a diverse career like Carla, or even Lily and Amanda? Both were undeniably attractive but there seemed to be more scope to the roles they could go for.

Maybe she should dye her hair, mix things up a little, but then she'd worry about not getting jobs. She wanted work on the strength of her acting ability not because of the way she looked, although she guessed that worked both ways. Carla got work on the strength of her looks too, it's just Jenna was competing against every other pretty blonde twenty-something actress.

'You're in a daydream, Jenna.' Amanda clicked her fingers in front of her face. 'Come on, let's join them.'

They left the dim kitchen for the light evening. At least with everyone here now, the tension she'd felt at Milo's suggestion had eased. Not that being with everyone else would stop him from pursuing her.

Drinks flowed, the sun set, the laughter and chatter got louder and more raucous disturbing the birds in the trees. Maybe Jenna was overthinking things. Maybe she should go with the flow and welcome Milo's advances? After all he was rich, famous, good looking, fit as anything, and they had plenty in common, both British, both actors, striving for the same thing, recognition, longevity, success. And despite her reservations, she was flattered by his attention and the idea of Milo and her… Jenna's laughter was as loud as everyone else's, her smile as big, her appetite for a good time equally matching Lily and Amanda's thirst for a big night, and yet, in the pit of her stomach there was an uneasiness that just wouldn't budge.

Chapter Ten

It was gone midnight before they started to head inside. Lily and Amanda had gone first complaining it was too chilly in their summer clothes with bare legs and arms pinpricked with goosebumps. Timothy lit a cigarette and remained sitting at the table puffing smoke into the clear night. Milo had wandered off to explore the garden, not that he could see much.

Jenna cleared away the last of the glasses, smiling at Timothy before heading inside. She dumped the glasses next to the sink, finding the tiniest bit of space among the mess. They'd pretty much used every glass, mug and plate in the place. Lily and Amanda were chatting in the living room, the only sound disturbing the peaceful night. She was about to join them when she realised she'd left her mobile outside.

It was much cooler now. The sky was black and twinkled with the silver of tiny stars. It was so different to the washed out sky back in London, polluted by the glow of the city. Earlier in the evening she'd strung outdoor lights around the picnic umbrella, but what little light they gave off only pooled around the edges of the table. The moon cast a silvery glow over the cottage but the trees surrounding the edges of the garden were shrouded in darkness.

Timothy was no longer sitting at the table and her mobile wasn't on it either. She searched around and found it on the grass. She began to head back around to the front of the cottage to join Lily and Amanda when she glimpsed movement. She paused, straining to look through the night, expecting to see a fox or possibly a deer. The moonlight gave just enough light to make out Milo and Timothy half-hidden among the trees with their arms wrapped around each other, kissing.

She couldn't look away, needing to make sure she'd seen right. Her heart thudded and her palms were sweaty. Milo had been flirting with her on set and the other evening at the hotel, plus after what he'd said in the garden before the others arrived... She was staring at them, with her mouth open. Gripping her mobile, she backed away and crept across the lawn.

Laughter filtered into the night air from inside, amplifying the stillness and silence of the garden. A screech from the living room startled something in the undergrowth. Jenna shuddered at the rustling and exchanged the fresh night air for the warm kitchen. She closed the door behind her.

'Hey Jenna,' Lily called. 'Where you been?'

Jenna walked across the slate floor to the living room. 'Just clearing up.'

Amanda's legs were curled up on the armchair and her usually pristine chestnut hair was now wild. 'Where are Milo and Timothy?'

Jenna flopped down on the sofa next to Lily giving herself time to reply and not really sure what to make of what she'd seen. 'Still outside; I think Milo's having a smoke.'

'How are you still looking so with it?' Lily sighed.

'I don't feel it. I'm going to regret how much I've drunk in the morning.'

'Good genes, that's what it is.' Amanda pointed across the room at her. 'You always look amazing even first thing in the morning before the make-up girls have had a go at us.'

'Hey, I'm not the only one.' Jenna threw a cushion at her. 'You two have the loveliest clearest skin...'

'Freckles,' Lily said. 'I have freckles.'

The front door creaked open and footsteps pounded across the slate floor. Milo appeared in the living room doorway.

'We okay to crash here tonight?' He looked at Jenna. 'I'm

dog-tired.'

'Of course. Wherever there's space; there's a spare room upstairs, this sofa.'

'Thank God I've not got an early call time tomorrow,' he said.

Jenna pulled a face. 'Unlike me. I've got to be there by seven.'

'Me too.' Timothy sidled in, squeezing past Milo. He caught Milo's eye and sat down in the empty armchair opposite Amanda.

Jenna looked between Milo and Timothy. She was certain they hadn't seen her outside. They were behaving completely normally. Milo squeezed into the space on the sofa between her and Lily, his thigh touching hers. She was utterly confused. She'd been flattered by his attention. After all, he was the lead on the film, a big-name actor, a proper Hollywood star, and although his suggestive comments earlier had taken her by surprise, the more she thought about it as the night went on, the more the idea of being with Milo Blake appealed to her. Famous and influential with his model looks, dark hair and those deep brown eyes that made Jenna believe she was the only person in the world when he looked at her. And yet, she knew what she'd seen outside.

'I'm bagging the spare room,' Milo said with a grin.

'Of course you would, Hollywood star and all,' Lily said. She looked past him to Jenna. 'I've already called a taxi for me and Amanda. We're going to head back to the hotel in a bit. You can join us if you want, Tim?'

Timothy yawned. 'Not sure I can be bothered. Might crash on the sofa if that's okay with you, Jenna?'

'Of course it is.'

Was that another look between Milo and Timothy or was she imagining things?

Lily and Amanda left half an hour later. The bright headlights of the taxi punctured the darkness as it backed out of the drive and disappeared along the lane. Jenna closed the front door and locked it.

She poked her head around the living room door. Timothy was lying on the sofa, a blanket over him, his hands tucked behind his head.

He looked up at her. 'See you bright and early in the morning.'

Jenna nodded. 'Night.'

She took the stairs two at a time. Light spilt from beneath the spare room door. She walked across the landing to her room and a door creaked open behind her. She turned. Milo was just in his pants, a shadowy figure silhouetted by the light behind him. He ran a hand through his thick dark hair and stepped across the landing.

'Thanks for a great night.' His warm hands slid down her bare arms. He leant in, his lips gently brushing her cheek before he pulled her into a hug. Conflicting and confusing thoughts flooded her head as their hug continued a bit too long, his firm hot body pressing tight against hers. Was this what he'd been insinuating earlier, his meaning behind 'playing the game'? Was he expecting her to make the next move? How easy would it be to take his hand and lead him into her room? But the image of him and Timothy together made her falter. What the hell was she thinking? She knew what she'd seen out in the garden, and yet here he was, suggesting he wanted more than friendship. Maybe he liked men and women... But before she could make a decision, he released her.

'Night, Jenna.'

'Night, Milo.'

She watched him retreat across the landing and close the door behind him without a backward glance. Jenna sighed and went into her room. This was the second time he'd teased her, and then nothing. What was he playing at? Maybe he was confused. She opened the windows as far as they'd go and breathed in the cool air. It was stuffy in her room so she left the curtains open in the hope of a bit of breeze finding its way through. She changed into her pyjama shorts and a vest and climbed into bed. She closed her eyes but her head immediately filled with thoughts of Milo in his underwear.

That hug out on the landing, the blatant flirting on set. She'd be kidding herself if it hadn't crossed her mind that she'd end up in bed with him tonight.

She flung the sheet off. She'd been single for far too long. The only action she'd got in the last few months was kissing that hot model on a pop video she'd filmed a couple of months ago, and that didn't count. Even though it was hardly an ordeal snogging a fit bloke all day long, they had been acting. And he of course had a girlfriend – it was the first thing he'd mentioned, setting clear boundaries.

She swung her legs out of bed and sat on the edge. She was tempted to stride across the landing, push open the door and slide into bed with Milo. That would be one way of finding out if his attention towards her meant something or not. But then, the other day in the garden when Finn had kissed her, that lightest of touches had sent shock waves through her… Anyway, she'd sworn herself off relationships with fellow actors; in her experience they always ended in tears. Milo would be no different. In fact, it would be a lot worse to get involved with someone so famous. The pressures of the job mixed with the price of fame – there must be so much expectation on him at all times. Lily had said there were quite often paparazzi outside the hotel. Every part of his life was written and talked about.

Jenna made her decision and got back into bed, pulling the sheet over her bare legs. She'd had too much to drink and wasn't thinking straight. They'd all had fun tonight, but she had to be up in less than five hours for work, and here she was considering seducing the lead actor on the film. If he'd wanted something to happen, he had every opportunity out there on the landing…

Despite both windows being open and only a sheet covering her, Jenna slept fitfully, unable to get comfortable. Too much drink had made her head woozy.

Footsteps creeping up the stairs pulled her out of an uneasy sleep. She glanced at her watch; 02.27am. She had to be up at six and she desperately needed sleep. A door opened and closed, the flush sounded loud in the quiet of night-time, a tap briefly running. The footsteps paused on the landing, but instead of going back downstairs, another door opened, the now familiar creak of the spare room door closing really slowly like someone didn't want to make any noise.

Silence.

Jenna rolled on to her side and tucked her hand beneath her pillow. In the middle of the Cornish countryside with no neighbours and no passing cars, it was painfully quiet, making it impossible to ignore the moans from across the hallway. Jenna closed her eyes tight, burying her head in her pillow, willing sleep to erase the sound of Milo and Timothy moving together on the spare room bed.

Chapter Eleven

Beep-beep-beep.

Jenna shoved her hand out, felt for her mobile on the bedside table and swiped it to snooze. Her head thumped with tiredness and she desperately wanted to go back to sleep but she had thirty minutes to get up, dressed and leave the house.

She groaned as she forced herself out of bed. She crept on to the landing and stood there for a moment, listening. She couldn't hear anything from the spare room. She bit her lip; Timothy had the same call time as her. The last thing she wanted to do was go knocking on the door waking him and Milo up. She was not ready for that kind of awkwardness at such an ungodly time in the morning with a thumping hangover.

Coffee. She needed to get her priorities right. She went downstairs instead, filled the kettle and switched it on.

'Morning.'

The voice behind her made her jump.

She swung round. 'Bloody hell, Timothy, you scared the shit out of me.'

'Sorry.' He ran a hand through his messy hair. He was bare-chested but had at least put on the shorts he'd been wearing the day before. 'You forgot I'd crashed in the living room?' He met her eyes and held her gaze.

'Something like that.' She turned away and grabbed two mugs. 'Coffee?'

'Please, you're a lifesaver. Drunk far too much last night.'

Not slept enough either, Jenna thought. She knew what she'd heard. Had he crept downstairs so she wouldn't realise he'd been with Milo? He was acting like nothing had happened so maybe he thought she didn't have a clue.

'It was a good night, last night. Just maybe next time we should do it on a weekend rather than mid-week.'

Jenna made the coffee and handed him a steaming mug. 'My bad; it was all a little spur of the moment.'

'Good though. I really enjoyed myself.'

Jenna murmured 'uh-huh'; she'd heard exactly how much he enjoyed himself. 'So, I'm going to get a quick shower, then you can have the bathroom.'

'Great, thanks Jenna.'

The lukewarm water left Jenna feeling a little more alive. Timothy showered while she went to her room, towel-dried her hair and threw on a skirt and top. At least she didn't have to bother doing her make-up as that would be done once they got to the base. And they'd be able to have breakfast before being taken to location. Her stomach rumbled. She could actually face a cooked breakfast this morning to counteract all the alcohol.

Jenna grabbed her bag and closed her bedroom door. Timothy had finished in the bathroom. The door to the spare room was still closed. She stood in the middle of the landing and listened – she could just make out gentle snores, so Milo was still asleep. It wasn't her responsibility to wake him. He had a later call time than her and Timothy and would have to sort himself out. He was the star of the film so a car would pick him up and drive him to set as long as he let them know where he was. *Oh God*, Jenna thought, *what would that seem like to everyone, Milo being picked up from the cottage?* That would fuel the rumours he'd already ignited with his flirting. Nothing she could do about it now.

Timothy was dressed and smoking on the steps outside the front door. Jenna tore a blank page from a notebook and scribbled a message for Milo, leaving the keys for the cottage next to it. Hopefully he'd have the sense to lock up and bring the keys with him. She grabbed her bag and joined Timothy outside, closing the door behind her.

'Milo's still asleep; didn't want to wake him.'

'Uh huh.' Timothy stubbed his cigarette out on the step.

'Figured he'll realise we've already left. Come on, let's go. We've got twenty minutes to get there.'

An early start and a short easy scene to shoot meant an early finish. She'd spent the day running along the beach and laughing with Lily and Amanda, who were both as hung-over as she was. Spending the day outdoors, splashing in the shallows and laughing together was a great tonic. In-between shooting, the three girls retreated to the shade beneath the umbrellas on the edge of the beach while they waited for the scene to be reset.

'So, what happened with you and Milo after we left last night?' Amanda nudged Jenna's arm.

She'd been waiting for this question all morning. 'Nothing.'

'Yeah, right, he was all over you last night.'

Jenna smoothed the creases in her chocolate-brown 1940s skirt, leant her elbows on her knees and gripped her water bottle in her hands. The sea curled on to the sandy shore, a rhythm that soothed her aching head.

'He's a flirt, that's all. I told you this last night.' She looked at them both over her sunglasses. 'Everyone knows he's a flirt.'

'You're his type though. I mean, it's rather shallow of him if he can't see past someone's looks, but he does love blondes.' She motioned between herself and Lily. 'Never going to be interested in us.'

Jenna knew her looks had helped her to get the role, Milo had told her as much. Amanda with her chestnut hair and pale skin and redheaded Lily with her freckles were both pretty – it was a requisite of the film – but Milo had taken a shine to her over the others.

Timothy was fair-haired. Maybe Milo really did have a thing for blondes.

'We should have made Timothy get the taxi back with us, given you and Milo some alone time.' Lily nudged her arm.

Jenna stood, stretching her aching back and turning her face to the sun. 'Seriously you two, nothing happened. There's no gossip. I'm sorry to disappoint you.'

'Imagine what hooking up with Milo Blake could do for your career…'

Jenna turned to them. 'Seriously? You're seriously suggesting I sleep with him to further my career?' She felt angrier at Lily suggesting it than she'd done when Milo himself had hinted at the idea last night.

'Everyone else does it given half a chance.'

'Yeah, well, I don't want to be the type of person who will do anything to get a role.' The First AD was walking towards them. Jenna wedged her bottle in the sand. 'Come on, they need us back on set.'

Lily's comments left her feeling annoyed for the rest of the morning. After a handful of takes on the beach they were wrapped by 1pm and bussed back to the main base where they headed straight to wardrobe to change out of their costumes. It was a relief to ease into a comfortable and cool skirt and sleeveless linen top. The weather did not go with spring-time 1940s costumes. Whether she wanted to or not, she had to find Milo to get the keys off him before she could head back to the cottage.

He was easy enough to find. The first crew member she asked knew where he was, and when she reached the marquee his popularity and dark smouldering looks worked like a beacon. Jenna breathed deeply and strode over, weaving her way past the tables filled with extras and crew having lunch.

Milo spotted her and grinned as she reached him.

'Thanks for letting me sleep in this morning.' He didn't say it quietly and the two older female actors sitting opposite him glanced at each other.

Milo pulled Jenna down on to the chair next to him and leant close, his hand on the small of her back. He smelt delicious, fresh and spicy, and for the briefest of moments she imagined him back at the cottage, getting a shower and the possibility of what could have happened…

'It was a good night last night; we should do it again.' He smiled and winked, but she knew it was for show. No doubt it was Timothy he was thinking about. She could feel eyes on her though; the actresses opposite were definitely watching them. 'You're finished for the day?'

'Yeah, but I need the keys for the cottage.'

'They're in my trailer. Can you wait a minute?'

'Of course.'

He stabbed the last piece of salmon on his plate with his fork, popped it in his mouth and washed it down with a swig of Coke Zero.

'Let's go.'

Jenna followed him. She knew how this looked. She knew they were being gossiped about. She felt Timothy's eyes on her where he was queuing for lunch as they left the marquee. Was Milo playing a game? Putting on a show to give an impression of someone he wasn't? He was a bloody good actor; that was evident on camera and off.

The grass had been worn away by so many feet walking between the trailers and the marquee. The earth was hard and cracked, baked by the never-ending sunshine.

Jenna matched his stride and wondered if she should say anything about last night. Did he even have a clue that she knew about him and Timothy? She knew his flirting with her was for show, she was certain he didn't really like her in that way, and yet it was messing with her head regardless.

'I shouldn't have drunk so much,' Milo said as they reached his trailer. 'Alcohol and acting doesn't mix, not when I have a goddam serious scene to shoot today. Next time, we party on the weekend.'

'That's what Timothy said this morning.'

'Uh huh.' Milo unlocked the door of his trailer and pushed it open. 'Well, he's right.' He turned to her. 'Don't be shy; come on in.'

Jenna stepped into the trailer but left the door open. It was the stuff of dreams to have a private trailer, somewhere to escape to on set, but right this minute she wanted to get off base and back to Bramble Cottage.

'Your keys.' He dangled them in front of her. She opened her palm and he dropped them into it. 'You should join us at the hotel for drinks later.'

'I will sometime. Not tonight though. Like you, I drank way too much last night, school night and all. I'm planning a quiet evening.'

'You don't get lonely on your own at the cottage?'

Jenna shook her head and clasped the keys firmly in her hand. 'Nope.'

'I guess you have that builder for company.'

Jenna frowned.

'Think I surprised him this morning.'

Finn. Shit. She hadn't even thought to let him know that there'd be someone at the cottage when he started work this morning. She'd left a note for Milo, but hung-over and thinking about getting to set on time she'd completely forgotten that Finn would rock up for work not thinking anyone was there.

The tightness in her chest as she said goodbye to Milo and left his trailer took Jenna by surprise. Anger coursed through her. The events of the last twenty-four hours had surprised and annoyed her in equal measure. Working so closely with people always led to gossip, intrigue and complicated relationships, but she never liked being a part of that.

She managed to avoid bumping into anyone else on the way from Milo's trailer to her car. She drove the now familiar route inland to the cottage. She parked the car next to Finn's van and walked round to the back.

Finn briefly turned at the sound of her footsteps crunching over gravel but quickly went back to focusing on the window surround he was working on. He had an open tin of paint next to him and he was wearing a T-shirt with the sleeves rolled right up to his shoulders.

'You're back early.'

'Yeah, short day.' Jenna shaded her eyes with her hand. 'It's looking really good out here.'

Finn glanced at her. 'Been at it all day. Finished the top windows on this side.' He cleared his throat. 'Speaking of which, you might want to warn your boyfriend that I'm working on the windows at the moment.'

'My boyfriend?'

Finn dropped his gaze from Jenna's face. 'Yeah, your boyfriend, the actor. He came out of the bathroom stark bollock naked this morning. I, um, got quite an eyeful from outside the landing window.'

'Oh. Right. Blimey. Yeah.' Jenna's cheeks flushed. 'Milo said he'd surprised you, I didn't realise...' Jenna shook her head, imagining the scene playing out, Finn minding his own business on the scaffolding outside the landing window, and Milo emerging from the bathroom naked.

Finn stirred the paint, and Jenna watched as the white liquid swirled thickly around the tin.

'By the way, he's not my boyfriend.'

He picked up the paintbrush. 'Just thought I'd better mention it. In case he's planning on making a habit of it.'

Now it made sense Milo saying he'd surprised Finn this morning. Walking around the cottage naked would certainly do that. Jenna faltered, unsure if she should say something else or leave it. He'd got completely the wrong idea about her and Milo, yet she knew the more she protested that Milo wasn't her boyfriend and actually they weren't together in that way at all, the less he'd believe her.

The wood around the ground floor windows had been repaired and sanded. Finn dipped the brush in the large tub of exterior woodwork paint and neatly ran the brush down the wood, turning it from pale brown to gloss white.

Jenna turned away; saying nothing else was best. She stalked through the long grass at the back of the cottage and out into the sunshine. The wilderness at the front had been pared back, weeds removed, bushes tamed, showcasing the garden. She felt foolish about a naked man being in the house and Finn getting the wrong idea. What must he think about her? But why did she care? Milo was a colleague, as were all the others who came over the night before. She could have a party if she wanted to. Then why did she feel guilty? She knew why; that kiss in the garden with Finn, that they'd brushed off at the time and hadn't spoken about since. And the unspoken tension between them that she had thought was sexual; now it just felt tense.

She went inside. The brightness of the sunny morning turned to shadows in the dimly-lit kitchen. She glimpsed the devastation in the living room with wine and beer bottles cluttering the coffee table. Her early call time had at least resulted in her having an early wrap, but she was suffering for the late night and too much alcohol now, plus she had a lot of clearing up to do. She was also utterly confused about her feelings. Annoyed at Milo toying with her emotions. And now Finn had got completely the wrong idea.

Chapter Twelve

'Hey, how's it going?' Carla's cheerful voice filled the room. Keeping her on speakerphone, Jenna stirred the chilli con carne bubbling away on the stove. It was late and it had been a long day, but she felt like cooking and eating something homemade, something other than the food they got on set. And occasionally, when she was in the right mood, cooking relaxed her.

'Nearly three weeks done. Lovely crew, great cast. I totally love being down here.'

'I'm still beyond jealous.'

'I know, sorry. You need to come down here for a few days. Whichever weekend you have free, just let me know.'

'I promise, I will. I've got a bit of good news too.'

'Oh yeah?' Jenna lifted the lid off the rice before the water boiled over.

'I didn't tell you because I didn't want to jinx it, but I got an audition for a new BBC mini-series, for a tattooed cool-as-fuck secondary school teacher. Got the call-back earlier this week…'

'And?'

'And I got the part. Starts shooting in October.'

'Aah, that's amazing, Carla. I'm so pleased for you. See, and after everything you were telling me before I left.'

'Yeah yeah, I know. I'm never going to get a leading role, but this is a good part, something I can really get my teeth into. So, that's my news and you're obviously loving being down in sunny Cornwall. How's it been living in the cottage while work's being done?'

Jenna sprinkled a pinch of salt over the chilli and stirred it in. 'Yeah, it's fine. The builders have finished the roof and now that's done it's just been one of them working on the outside of the cottage, plus I've not really been around much during the week.'

'You're not getting lonely on your own in the evenings?'

'It's no different to being home.'

'Apart from you have lots of friends back home. Have you hung out with the cast or crew much?'

'Yeah, a couple of times this week. Everyone's pretty shattered though, you know what it's like, long days. I guess the only disadvantage to staying at the cottage is not being at the same place as most of the cast. I think they hang out in the hotel bar lots. They were over here last night though.' Jenna bit her lip, unsure if she should say anything about Milo and Timothy.

'You don't feel like you're missing out?'

'Not really; I mean it's been fun spending time with them, it's just nice to have the space and place to myself.'

'Apart from the builders.'

'Yes, apart from the builders.' Jenna added a dash more passata to the chilli and stirred it in. It wasn't like she minded having Finn around on the few occasions she saw him before or after work. Being greeted by his smile and a sneaky peak of his six-pack had fast become the highlight of her day, until him assuming Milo was her boyfriend had put paid to that. Now there was an awkwardness and they'd hardly said more than a couple of words to each other since. The thought of his toned chest and smiling eyes, she realised, was also stopping her from listening to Carla. 'Sorry, what did you say?'

'I said, talking about the cast, I kinda have some bad news... Well, not bad exactly, it's just you might not be too pleased about it... Although actually it might be a good thing...'

'Carla, seriously, just tell me.'

'I thought I'd better warn you so it doesn't come as a shock...'

'Shock about what?'

'Heidi. She's got a part on the film.'

'What film?'

'What film do you think? Yours, silly.'

Jenna dropped the wooden spoon into the pan. 'I don't understand? They cast the film ages ago, how is she working on it?'

'She got cast ages ago too, it's just I didn't know because I've not seen her because she was working on... well you know what she was working on. She wrapped on Bond a few weeks ago.'

Jenna bit her lip. 'When does she start filming on this?'

'Monday.'

'Seriously?'

'Seriously. I saw her this afternoon. Said she was getting the train down tomorrow so she can settle in over the weekend.'

'Right.' Jenna tipped in the drained red kidney beans, mixed them in and put a lid on the pan.

'You're pissed off, aren't you? Sorry, I shouldn't have told you and ruined your evening.'

'No, it's fine. Better you telling me now than me turning up on Monday and seeing her.'

'You're still pissed about it though. I can tell. It'll be fine, Jenna, I promise. It'll be good seeing each other again, on neutral ground so to speak. You'll see. Maybe it'll be a way of working things out between you.'

They said goodbye, and Jenna was left with worry gnawing at her stomach and a dull ache spreading across her forehead. Apart from today with the Milo and Finn situation, she'd been so relaxed and carefree since she got here. She put this down to the combination of a change of scene and the slower pace of life away from London. The countryside and sea were a tonic, the role on a big budget film exciting, and with guaranteed work the pressure was off for a few weeks at least. And now she was going to have to confront the one person who she really didn't want to see, particularly down in Cornwall, a place that until this moment had felt like a real escape. It was always the way though, just as everything seemed to be going so well, something happened to stir things up. Heidi Turner-Williams had done enough meddling in her life; she was the last person Jenna wanted to see, work with and have to spend time with. Even if, as Carla had suggested, being forced to confront their issues might be a good thing in the long run. No longer hungry, she switched off the gas and put a lid on the chilli. She went and stood on the step outside, breathing in the night air in an attempt to calm the rage creeping from the pit of her stomach and up to her chest.

Jenna was out of sorts from the moment she woke. She was on edge throwing her clothes on, locking the front door and starting her car. The feeling only worsened the closer she got to the base.

Even though she knew Heidi wouldn't be on set until Monday, she couldn't undo the knot of tension in her stomach as she headed to wardrobe or when she was sitting in the make-up trailer. The usual relaxed banter between the make-up artists and the cast continued as usual, yet Jenna knew she was quieter than normal. The thought of seeing Heidi was as uncomfortable as the anticipation of bumping into an ex boyfriend. Heidi had hurt and betrayed her far worse than an ex ever had. She was probably worrying for nothing; if Heidi was travelling today, the chances were she'd go straight to the hotel and wouldn't even be at the base until after the weekend. Now more than ever Jenna was glad she was staying well away from the hotel and everyone else.

She spent Saturday on her own in the garden, ripping out weeds, hacking back bushes and cutting the grass. Her hard work was beginning to pay off. The garden looked twice as big as the overgrown and tangled mess it had been when she'd first arrived. She didn't even have Finn's company. She'd expected him to turn up but neither him nor his dad had. Although to be fair, Finn had finished the windows and most of the damaged stonework had been repaired. Apart from still being clad in scaffolding, the cottage had transformed from looking tired and grey to rejuvenated and appealing. She knew they were fitting in the cottage between jobs and probably Finn was helping his dad on another job this weekend, but she missed seeing him. Next week, her fourth since arriving in Cornwall, Finn would be starting on the inside of the cottage on Monday, and her ex-best friend would be working on the same film as her. After the initial feeling of space and freedom, life was beginning to feel increasingly claustrophobic.

She needed to do something. She needed to get away from her own company and her muddled thoughts. She messaged Lily and Amanda to see if they fancied going out somewhere other than the hotel. A proper night out with food and drinking, to a pub with a beer garden, that's what she fancied. That thought took her right back to thinking about Finn again.

'Aaaghhrr!' She threw her mobile on to the sofa, stalked into the kitchen and downed a glass of water.

While she was waiting for them to reply she went upstairs and got ready. After spending most of the day working in the garden she needed a shower. She'd moved around as the sun did, catching the shade rather than the rays, but it had still been hot, even beneath the trees. She washed away the sweat, sunscreen and dirt and by the time she was towelling herself dry in her room, Lily and Amanda had replied. Jenna arranged to meet them in Mullion, walkable for them and an easy-enough drive for her.

The pub was old and thatched. It was set further into Mullion and away from the sea, and its beer garden was the perfect place for a Saturday night drink, spacious and tree-lined with plenty of large wooden picnic tables. It was good to get away from the cottage for the evening and also to be somewhere other than the hotel with the cast and crew.

It was stuffy inside the pub, so they escaped outside with their drinks, finding a free table on the far side of the garden. The evening was fresh but it was still warm enough to be sitting outside in short sleeves. Who needed to go abroad when there was this weather and surroundings right on the doorstep – well, a few hours' drive away for Jenna.

'Are you missing home?' Amanda asked, as if reading her thoughts.

Jenna cupped her hands around her cool pint of lemonade. 'Nope, not a bit. I've swapped a tiny flat in a soulless block for a cottage and garden full of character. Are you?'

'I miss my boyfriend but not the everyday stuff, you know. I haven't had to cook since I got down here. Don't have to think about cleaning or when my next job's going to be. I'm fed up of spending days on the Tube heading across London from one casting to another.'

'It can be soul destroying, can't it.' Jenna sipped her lemonade. 'It's good to have the security of a steady job for a few weeks at least.'

'I am beginning to think what to do come September though,' Lily said. 'I don't have anything lined up, do you?'

'Shush.' Jenna put her finger to her lips and grinned. 'Not tonight, let's not stress about it, there'll be plenty of time for that. This evening is about enjoying ourselves.'

A group walked into the beer garden, their laughter and voices arriving before they did. They looked like surfers, in board shorts and Ripcurl hoodies. There was one woman with them, her arm around the waist of one of the blokes, his arm resting across her shoulder.

It was the tallest bloke who caught Jenna's attention with his windswept hair, beard, and tattoos snaking down one arm. As they reached an empty table the familiarity of his features became clear.

Chapter Thirteen

Finn was the tallest of his friends and also the best looking. Although he was unassuming when you talked to him, from afar it was his looks that caught people's attention. Jenna clocked a few other women looking in his direction. Almost as if he was a film star. Finn clambered over the bench at the table on the other side of the garden, sat down and caught Jenna's eye. He smiled and waved.

'Who's that?' Amanda asked.

'The builder.'

'*He's* your builder?'

'Well, not my builder. Him and his dad are the builders working on the cottage.'

'Why are you going red?' Lily clasped her fingers around the stem of her wine glass and leant closer. 'Oh. My. Goodness. You like him, don't you?'

'I can see why. Easy on the eye is an understatement.' Amanda whistled and folded her arms.

'I bet he's a joy to watch working on the cottage, all hot and sweaty.'

Jenna shook her head. 'What are you two like.'

'Living out the excitement of being single through you. I mean with him and Milo, you are one lucky lucky lady. Milo's all over you at work.' Amanda nodded in Finn's direction. 'Bet it's the same back at the cottage with him.'

Lily looked at Amanda. 'Oh, to have so many men falling at my feet.'

Jenna swung her legs over the picnic bench and stood up.

'I don't have men falling at my feet. You have no clue. That "thing" with Milo isn't what everybody thinks. And Finn,' Jenna lowered her voice and avoided looking in the direction of Finn and his friends, 'is a lovely normal bloke and is pretty bloody sensible steering clear of us neurotic actors.'

She walked away weaving between tables across the spongy grass, going the longer way round to avoid Finn. Inside, the pub was traditional and cosy with beamed ceilings and thick stone walls that probably held the heat out like Bramble Cottage, but packed with people and on a still and hot evening, it was roasting inside.

'A Budweiser, please.' She'd been good and stuck to lemonade but one bottle of beer would be fine for her to drive back.

She had no idea why Amanda's comment had got under her skin so much. Well, she did. The thing with Milo had annoyed the hell out of her and she hated that Finn had got the wrong idea.

Amanda appeared next to her at the bar and slid her arm around her waist. 'I'm sorry. I didn't mean to take the piss. I wasn't thinking. And yes, us actors can be neurotic and hard to live with. My boyfriend is a saint putting up with me.'

'He's not an actor?'

'A financial advisor. Go figure.'

The barman passed Jenna her bottle of lager and she handed him the money.

Amanda hooked her arm in Jenna's as they made their way back across the pub. 'I love my boyfriend to bits but I always think how exciting it would be to be single and have the opportunity to have a fling with an actor. I think I'm living my fantasies about Milo Blake through you. Sorry if I've been a bit full on.'

They emerged back into the beer garden. The air was warm but fresher outside.

'You don't have to apologise; I overreacted. I don't know why I'm feeling so uptight about everything. Milo's messing with my head…' They joined Lily back at the table and Jenna placed a hand on her shoulder. 'Sorry for getting upset.'

Amanda took Jenna's hand. 'How's he messing with it? Your head?'

Jenna bit her lip. She was conflicted about telling them the truth and exposing Milo when it was obviously a secret. Yet, without explaining it, it simply looked like she was making a huge fuss over one of the hottest actors on the planet giving her attention and no one understood that.

'When you said before that I like Finn, it's true. But I *really* like him.'

Lily raised her eyebrows and looked in Finn's direction. 'The builder?'

'Yeah, the builder. Which is why I don't want to get involved with Milo.' It was partly the truth and hopefully it would stop them from pushing the point further and avoid her spilling the beans about Milo and Timothy. The possible consequences about the truth being revealed and her being the one to reveal it unnerved her.

'I can see the appeal,' Amanda said. 'I mean they're both hot as hell but in different ways. They're like chalk and cheese. Blonde-haired, bearded surfer type guy, compared to dark-haired brooding Hollywood actor. What a choice.'

Lily picked up her wine. 'Why don't you go over and talk to him.'

'He's with his mates.'

'So?'

Jenna sipped her Budweiser. 'We kinda had a thing.'

'You've slept with him?' Lily nearly spat out a mouthful of wine.

'No, nothing like that. We had, like, the briefest of kisses on that really hot day last week. You know the day we wrapped filming early because of the heat. We were sitting out on the grass at the cottage and he just kissed me. And then I didn't see him for the rest of the day and then we sort of haven't spoken about it since.'

'So it's weird?'

Jenna shrugged. 'Kind of. It was spur of the moment and amazing.'

'You have got to talk to him.' Amanda swung her legs

over the bench and grabbed her drink. 'Come on.'

'Amanda, no,' Jenna hissed.

But Amanda was off across the daisy-speckled grass making a beeline for Finn.

Lily picked up her glass. 'Do you really want to let her talk to him on her own?'

'Not really, no.'

Jenna grabbed her bottle and followed Lily. She reached their table and met Finn's eyes just as Amanda was introducing herself.

'Hey,' he said.

'Can we join you?' Amanda asked.

'Of course.' Finn shuffled along the bench to make room and Jenna found herself sitting down next to him.

Amanda sat opposite, Lily squeezing on the end of the bench next to her. 'This is Lily, and you obviously already know Jenna.' She gave Finn the biggest grin and Jenna felt the blood rush to her cheeks again.

'This is Tom.' Finn motioned to the brown-haired guy next to him and then across the table. 'And that's Jake and his girlfriend Stef.'

'So you're all actresses?' Tom asked.

Amanda nodded. 'For our sins, yes.'

'And you're working on the film that's been shot around here?' Tom continued.

'That's the one,' Jenna said.

'Isn't that the one with Milo Blake in it?'

Jake nudged his girlfriend. 'Stef's got a thing for Milo Blake.'

Stef ignored him. 'Do you three know him?'

'As much as you can really "know" an actor as famous as him,' Lily said. 'But yes, we're all working with him although Jenna has more scenes with him, don't you?'

And so the conversation turned to Milo Blake. Jenna felt increasingly uncomfortable as she was forced to talk about him, while sensing the tension ebbing off Finn.

It was nearly midnight before Lily and Amanda decided to call it a night. The conversation had eventually moved on from Milo, films and acting, to surfing, Cornwall and the jobs Finn and his friends did.

Amanda moved around the table and perched on the end of the bench next to Jenna. 'We're going to walk back to the hotel before we get too wasted.' Her usually bright eyes were nearly half-closed.

'I can drive you back, if you like.'

Amanda placed her hand on Jenna's arm. 'It won't take long to walk and it'll sober me up. Don't rush your drink.' She did a comical one eyebrow raise, while Lily grinned from across the table. Amanda kissed Jenna on the cheek and with a wave she linked arms with Lily and they walked away across the beer garden.

'They're not subtle, are they?' Finn said.

Jenna laughed. 'No, they're not. They're actors, bloody drama queens, what do you expect.'

'You didn't want to go back with them?'

'Nah, I fancied staying a bit longer.' They were sitting together at one end of the picnic table, Jake and Stef were whispering together at the other end, and Tom had wandered off to talk to another friend.

A prickle of excitement crept across the back of Jenna's neck at the thought of being alone again with Finn. His hands were clasped around his pint. It was the first time she'd noticed the small tattoo on his middle finger. Tattoos crawled down his arm, poking out beneath the right-hand sleeve of his T-shirt. He was watching her intently, his usually blue eyes dark in the dusky light of the pub garden.

'We talked about this the other day, while sweltering in your garden, wishing we were having a pint in a pub somewhere.'

'Did you make it to the pub that night?'

'Yeah, I was going to see if you wanted to join me but you weren't around when I left.'

'Yeah sorry, I, um…'

'It was nice what happened in the garden… I didn't mean to come on to you like that – if I'd known you were with someone… I know what it's like to be the one cheated on; I'd never intentionally do that to someone else.'

'Honestly, Milo's not my boyfriend. He's a total flirt. He's a movie star, so bloody confident about himself. He stayed over in the spare room, that's all. So did a couple of the others. I mean, who walks around someone else's house naked?'

'He's got confidence; I'll give him that.'

'I also hadn't warned him about you being over early in the morning or given you the head's up that there'd be someone in the cottage.'

'Well, I'm sorry, for assuming too much and not believing you when you said you weren't together. I like you, that's all.' His hand found hers beneath the table. Jenna had a momentary flashback to them sitting in the garden at Bramble Cottage, that unexpected kiss that had surprised her and then left her wanting more, whereas being alone with Milo had left her stressed and worried that she'd say yes to him when really she meant no.

'Where have you gone?' Finn leaned closer, waggling a hand in front of her face.

'Sorry, I was thinking.'

'About what?'

'That I like you too.' It hardly took anything for Jenna to close the gap and kiss him. He didn't pull away like the first time as if it had been the wrong thing to do. And this time it felt *so* right. They shuffled closer on the picnic bench, Jenna not caring if anyone was watching. Their hands slid around each other's waists. She'd admired him plenty of times when he was topless in the garden and his chest was pleasingly firm beneath his T-shirt. His kiss was tender, un-rushed, and Jenna savoured it until the chatter and clatter of glasses flooded back and the people around them came back into focus.

Finn was grinning at her. 'I don't think we have the excuse this time of the sun having gone to our heads.'

'I can't even claim it's because I've had too much to drink.'

His hand was warm where he held hers in his lap. 'Maybe

we don't need an excuse.'

'Maybe you're right.' She ran her fingers up his chest, reaching his beard and cupping his face. She kissed him again and lingered, playing out in her mind if she should be brave – or reckless – and ask him back to the cottage. She imagined him in her bed and walking naked to the bathroom in the morning.

She pulled away and let go of his face. 'Do you fancy a walk?'

It was a balmy summer's night, away from the noise and busyness of the pub. Lined by houses and bungalows, the road was quiet with only a few cars passing and it was even quieter once they headed along the narrow lane that led to the hotel the cast were staying in. They turned off before the hotel car park on to a track that joined the coastal path with a view over a deserted Polurrian Beach. The night was starlit, the sea an endless black, the only colour the white surf catching the moonlight as it foamed on to the beach. They were close to civilisation with the hotel on the hilltop behind them and the village only a short walk away, and yet Jenna felt truly disconnected from the world.

Finn's hand was warm in hers as they walked. Just before they reached the steep path that led down to the sandy beach they stopped. Finn kept hold of her hand as they gazed out over the dark expanse of sand below. 'Is acting what you've always wanted to do?'

'One of the things. My mum always complains I've flitted from one thing to another, although I guess acting's always been my constant. How about you?'

'It was kinda expected that I'd go into the family business.'

'Did you want to?'

He paused. 'Yes.'

'You don't sound sure.'

'I wanted to be a builder like my dad. I mean, it's all I know; I've been helping Dad since I was twelve, probably even younger. I'm good at it and it's a successful family business. I'd have been foolish not to go into it.'

It wasn't hard to hear the justification in his voice. 'I guess that's great if there was really nothing else you wanted to do…'

His thumb rubbed along the side of hers in time to the waves breaking on the shore. 'I wanted to surf, that's all I did as a teenager and still do, every chance I get. What about you? What do you do when you're not working?'

'At the moment downtime is either on my own at the cottage or meeting up with the cast and crew in the evening – like Lily and Amanda tonight.'

'But back home?'

'You know, the usual, going out, meeting friends. Go to the theatre, cinema, gigs. I have a gym membership…'

'That you actually use?'

Jenna playfully slapped his shoulder. 'I do. I play netball as well and years ago I used to love working on my parents' garden – not very cool, I know, and a bit odd a teenager being into gardening. I've been on a waiting list to get an allotment for the last two years. Never surfed, though.'

'Never?'

Jenna shook her head.

'We'll have to do something about that.'

'Yeah, you can teach me some time.' She grinned and he held her hand tighter.

'So, is that why I always see you in the garden at Bramble Cottage?'

'Yeah, I love it. Taming it but holding on to its wild beauty at the same time. I find it therapeutic. Maybe it's because it's the complete opposite of my job – the nature of being an actor is social, constantly meeting new people, going to auditions. Working on set you're always surrounded by people – hair, make-up, costume, ADs, lighting, sound, other actors. It's pretty full on. So gardening is an escape from all that.'

'I like Jenna the Gardener – it's the only side I've really seen of you.'

'The acting stuff is a whole other world. It's weird.

Sometimes I feel completely comfortable and a part of the acting world, and other times totally disconnected from it.'

'Maybe it's not what you really want to do deep down? Maybe your passion lies somewhere else. Like being outdoors doing what you love?'

His words hung in the night air, toying with her. Jenna knew that right this moment being out here, looking at the ocean was what she loved – the peacefulness, the beauty of the starlit night with the moon reflecting on the glass-like sea.

It also helped that Finn was with her, his hand firm in hers, their shoulders touching sending tingles through her. They remained standing side by side looking out over the beach.

'This has been a good night,' she said.

He turned to her and the moonlight caught one side of his face, defining his cheekbone. 'I'm very glad we bumped into each other.'

'For that cold beer.'

'Exactly.' He leant closer and kissed her. The tingling in the pit of her stomach intensified. Her hand dropped from his and circled his waist which was hard and toned from all the building work and surfing. His hands ran up her sides, finding her face as they kissed each other deeply, the only sound the continual breaking of the waves.

Chapter Fourteen

Jenna drove him home. It wasn't far, only on the edge of Mullion, walkable but it was late and his friends had already left the pub. Jenna didn't want the evening to end.

She pulled up outside a large and modern semi-detached house in a leafy cul-de-sac. He turned in the passenger seat to face her. 'I'd invite you in but my parents are home. Not that they'd care, it's just… well, it's not particularly cool living with my folks.'

Was he waiting for her to invite him back to the cottage? Maybe she should… But then again it was probably a bad idea. He was the builder working on her parents' cottage and she was supposed to be overseeing the work, not actually seeing the builder.

'No worries, it's late anyway and I still need to drive back.'

He undid his seat belt and slid his hand on to her thigh. 'Are you going to be okay?'

'I'll be fine.' Jenna strained against her seat belt as she moved closer to kiss him. 'And maybe we should do this again sometime.'

'How about tomorrow, if you're not working?'

'No work on the weekend. I'm free. I'm always free.'

'How about I take you to my favourite beach.'

'Sounds amazing.'

'I'll pick you up at nine.'

'Perfect.'

His lips brushed hers again, his beard tickling as he pulled away. He opened the car door, letting cool air in. The door slamming shut was loud in the darkness. She watched him walk up the path. The security light switched on, bathing him in light, accentuating his broad shoulders beneath his pale T-shirt, and his muscly legs in jeans that hugged him in all the right places. He turned, waved and closed the door behind him. The security light switched off, returning the cul-de-sac to darkness. Jenna sighed and did a three-point turn, her headlights cutting through the night as she drove away.

She wished he'd asked her in; it didn't bother her that his parents were there. Was it so strange that at twenty-eight, only a year older than her, Finn was still living with his parents? He worked for the family business after all, and buying your own home must be crazy expensive in this part of Cornwall. It was probably the easier and most sensible option. She'd only moved out from her parents' because of work, to be closer to London and jobs, otherwise wouldn't she still be there? And maybe she should have gone back when she'd moved out of the apartment with Heidi – she was spending a fortune on rent for a tiny place with no outside space.

Her head hurt from concentrating on the dark narrow roads, difficult to navigate even with full beams on. She was relieved when she pulled into the drive and switched off the engine. She got out of the car and shivered – it was so much cooler this late at night. A bat flew between the trees, its dark shape silhouetted against the moonlit sky. She shivered again, but this time more from the eerie stillness of the night rather than the cold.

She power-walked to the door, trying not to think about the beady eyes of an owl watching her from the treetops. It would feel quite different with Finn's strong arm around her waist. Once again she regretted not having the nerve to invite him back.

She closed the cottage door firmly and locked it. At least she'd see him tomorrow. Deep down she knew that this evening was enough, to know they felt the same way about each other. More could wait; she had enough going on without jumping into bed with him and into a new relationship. That was the last thing she'd expected when coming to Cornwall, but like everything over the last couple of weeks, life had a way of surprising her.

After bumping into Finn, she realised just how much she looked forward to seeing him. It was a good start to the day if he arrived before she headed off to work. She hadn't been able to get him out of her head from the moment they shared that kiss in the garden.

It was late and she was sober but tired. It had been a long week filming mainly outdoors in stifling heat. The cottage was cool, although warmer upstairs and she stripped down to a vest and knickers, leaving the curtains drawn and the windows wedged open as far as they would go. She closed her eyes and fell asleep thinking about Finn.

It was difficult to sleep much past dawn with birdsong and daylight streaming through the windows. Jenna didn't fight it and got up. She had a shower and put on a bikini beneath her denim shorts and T-shirt. The sun shone across the lawn promising another beautiful day; so far it had been a charmed summer and Jenna wondered how long it would last.

She made coffee and toast and ate it outside. A peacock butterfly fluttered around the purple flowers of a hebe. Jenna still hadn't got used to how peaceful it was with no traffic, only the rustle of leaves, the sway of branches in the breeze and the buzz of a lazy bee. There were no man-made sounds, not even the rumble of a lawnmower, which was so reminiscent of summer when Jenna was growing up. She loved being able to potter out in the garden whenever she wanted to.

There was still plenty to do outside and loads of weeds to remove. Bare patches of soil needed replanting, while other areas were overgrown and threaded with brambles. It was the best time of day to work on the one border that always got the sun. Jenna retrieved her gardening gloves and secateurs from the lean-to, and started cutting her way through the brambles making a spiky pile next to her. There were already a few deep red juicy berries and she picked those and ate them. She was still hacking away when she heard an engine and crunch of tyres on the drive.

Jenna dropped the secateurs and gloves on the grass, wiped her brow with the back of her hand and walked across the grass to the driveway.

Finn emerged from his van and grinned. His hair was windswept, his T-shirt sleeves rolled up to his shoulders showing off his muscles and tattoos; he was in board shorts and grey Converse trainers.

'Morning.' He slammed the door closed.

'Morning.' Jenna wondered if it'd be inappropriate to kiss him… daytime felt very different to the end of last night.

His hand found the small of her back as they walked to the cottage together. He didn't attempt to kiss her so she restrained herself too.

'Is it strange being here and not having to work?'

'It's nice not working and even better spending the day with you.'

Warmth flooded through her at his words. 'Fancy a coffee? I've made a pot.'

'Love one.'

They sat outside in the same spot Jenna had sat on her own an hour or so earlier. The sun made Finn's tanned skin look even darker than it had inside.

Finn took her hand. 'I wish I'd invited you in last night.'

Jenna knew her cheeks were flushing. Before falling asleep last night she'd played over and over in her mind what could have happened…

'I should have invited you back here, it's just…'

'I know, a bit forward. We had a nice night. It didn't need to be more, it's just, well you know…'

Jenna laughed. 'Yeah, I know.'

'I love my folks to bits but there are times… Sheesh, it'd be good to have my own place.' He cupped his hands round his mug of coffee. 'I haven't always lived with my parents. I spent a summer in Newquay and then I shared a flat with Jake in Falmouth until he moved in with Stef.'

'You couldn't stay there on your own?'

'Couldn't afford to and no one else was in a position to move in with me. And I didn't fancy sharing with a stranger.'

'I know that feeling.'

'You do?'

'I fell out with my best friend – we'd lived together at drama school then moved in together afterwards. Heidi's parents bought a flat in London, they said as an investment for their retirement, but were happy enough for me and Heidi to live there and pay a fraction of the rent we'd have to pay anywhere else. They're loaded anyway. Then end of last year me and Heidi had a massive argument and I moved out. I had the choice of back with my parents making it harder to get jobs in London, or rent a poxy little flat closer to train and Tube links.'

'So you went for the flat.'

'Yep. It's nothing special, but it's my space and I've kinda liked living by myself these last few months.'

'No boyfriend?' He grinned.

'No boyfriend. And you had no girlfriend to move in with?'

He shook his head. 'I've had relationships but the one serious girlfriend who I hoped to move in with broke my heart. I want to move out of my parents' though. A couple of surfer friends are talking about renting a place along the coast. It won't be cheap though, even for a small place, but it'll be worth it. I work with Dad and we get on great, but I just need space. Not all the questions, you know what I mean?'

'Totally.'

'So what happened between you and your friend?'

'It's a long story and one that's going to wind me up too much.'

He held up his hands. 'Say no more.' He drained his coffee and stood up. 'Let's make the most of today, then.'

Finn drove. It was good for a change to not be the one navigating narrow winding lanes. Apart from going to her parents', she mostly took the bus, train or Tube back home. It was a different lifestyle here. Weekends spent surfing, on the beach, in the outdoors, or for her, pottering about in the garden she loved. There were plenty of leafy green open spaces within driving distance of where she lived or reachable by public transport from central London, but it was very different having so much beauty right on the doorstep. It was a joy to wake up and smell air free of exhaust fumes or stale greasy chips from the local Chinese. Her tiny flat overlooking a main road just didn't compare to the period cottage in the middle of an acre of garden and woodland, with not another building in sight.

They parked in a large and busy car park that overlooked the sandy expanse of Dayton Bay. Finn passed Jenna's rucksack to her from the back of the van and swung his on his back. They didn't head to the beach as Jenna expected, but set off along a sandy path that cut through grass to the headland and away from the village and bay. Although the sun was high in a nearly cloudless blue sky, the breeze coming off the sea was fresh. Where the path narrowed, long grasses tickled their bare legs, while the sun warmed her arms enough to keep goosebumps at bay.

'So,' Jenna said, matching Finn's long stride as he led the way. 'You're taking me to your favourite beach?'

'Yep, one of them. Been coming here for years; well, for as long as I can remember. It's my mum's favourite place too, near where she grew up. I don't think Dad was ever too keen on lugging everything we needed for a day on the beach along this coastal path but Mum always liked the peacefulness away from the worst of the summer crowds.'

With Dayton Bay behind them, their surroundings were just grass and trees on one side and to their left jagged rocks jutting down into the sea. As they rounded the corner, the view opened up with sloping grass leading to white-walled slate-roofed coastal homes. The sandy path cut between the swathes of green grasses and colourful wild flowers swaying in the breeze. They kept going until a sandy rock-studded beach backed by sloping grassy cliffs began to reveal itself.

Finn stopped. 'It's worth the walk.'

Jenna stood next to him, gazing at the pale sand and

sparkling sea. It was worth the walk for the views alone; the coastal path edged by tall grasses and studded with tiny mossy flowers, the view of blue sky and an even deeper blue sea stretching to the horizon and beyond. Endless. Jenna liked that, being on the edge of something, at the start with all the possibilities that promised.

Chapter Fifteen

The beach was practically empty apart from a couple of young families camped in sandy sheltered spots with colourful wind breaks and umbrellas. It was always the same, the effort of getting to a place put people off. Jenna didn't mind one bit.

They made their way down the steep path. The steps cut into the rocky hillside making it slippery underfoot with loose stones. Finn took her hand at the steepest part, guiding her down. Although she was quite capable of looking after herself and navigating the steps, she liked chivalry and that he was looking out for her. She loved the feel of his hand in hers, the way his strong arm supported her until they jumped the last couple of steps, landing in the soft sand. They walked across an almost pristine beach, leaving their footprints in a meandering line behind them as they headed around a rock closer to the sea and then back up the beach a little way to a sheltered rocky outcrop.

They didn't have a windbreak or an umbrella; they'd travelled light with just a rucksack each and a picnic blanket tied on to Finn's. He laid it out on the sand in front of the rocks and kept it down with a couple of stones at the edges. Jenna sat down, resting her back against the hard smooth rock.

'This is the life.'

Finn sat next to her and leant his arms on his knees. 'I try and get to the beach every weekend.'

'I've been on a beach nearly every day since I got to Cornwall, but it's different being on location and filming on a beach rather than just being able to enjoy it.' Jenna stretched her legs out and crossed her ankles, her bare feet already covered in sand. 'It's the weirdest thing. Lots of people would consider the job I have to be the best in the world and yet I find myself moaning about it so much. I should get over myself really. I'm acting in a big movie on location in a beautiful part of the world and I can still find fault with it.'

Finn leant back against the rock, his shoulder brushing hers. 'It's only natural, isn't it, to complain about your job, even if deep down you love it?'

'Do you love what you do?'

'Yes, although I love surfing more, but as a job it's a decent one. I'm not stuck in an office; I get to work in different places on different projects, meet new people all the time. I'm good at what I do. It's pretty sweet really but I complain plenty enough. Some jobs are just boring, they don't challenge me, then I start to wonder what the hell I'm doing. Then others I get to work somewhere interesting or I get to completely renovate a property. It's a good feeling seeing a place transformed from a dump to a beautiful place to live.'

'Okay good, I'm glad I'm not wrong in feeling like that.'

'But getting to work on a big movie… I have friends who'd kill to have that opportunity.' He winked and nudged her shoulder. 'I'm teasing you. But I do know people who'd love to do what you do.'

'This movie is a bit of an exception, but most jobs aren't like this. People see acting as this amazingly glamorous job – and in part it is, getting hair and make-up done, getting to wear some amazing costumes. But most people don't see the reality of every day – the long hours, the boredom of hanging about waiting to be called to set. Unless you're a main actor and are in every scene or have a trailer to escape to, the downtime between scenes can drag. There's all the setting up, the lighting, sound checks, walk-throughs and then numerous takes.'

'I guess I've never thought of it like that.'

'I mean, working on location here, we do get to relax on the beach between takes – although we're in costume and have to sit under a tent, no sunbathing for us. But I've done jobs where I've spent about four hours filming and another six or seven hanging about in a warehouse with nothing to do. There are people to chat to and you can read a book or a magazine but after that length of time it can be soul-destroying. I guess what I'm saying is I've seen and experienced it all, the good and the bad.'

'But this film is good, right?'

'Yeah, this film is great. I've properly lucked out this time. Trouble is, it's given me the taste of the good life now.'

'Something to strive for, right?'

'Right.' She gazed across the unspoilt sand to the sea shimmering in the sunshine. 'But hey, today I don't have to sit beneath a tent out of the sun or wait for someone to call action. We shouldn't talk work.'

'I agree.' Finn sat upright away from the rock and looked at her. 'We should go for a swim.'

'We should?'

'Absolutely. You've got your swim things on, right?' His fingers brushed the bikini strap tied around her neck.

'It'll be freezing.'

'It'll be refreshing.'

'I was kind of imagining lounging about and sunbathing…'

He stood up, kicked off his beach shoes and peeled off his T-shirt.

'Come on.' He gently pulled her off the picnic blanket. 'You'll love it. Refreshing remember…'

She took a deep breath and followed his example, easing off her top and shorts and leaving them in a pile next to his. Her bikini was new, one she'd bought especially for this summer, but she'd only worn it once so far at the hotel pool the other evening.

She felt Finn's eyes on her and she realised although she'd seen him shirtless plenty of times before, he'd never seen her in anything as revealing as a bikini. He held his hand out and she took it. They walked down the beach, imprinting their footsteps on the sand as it changed from dry to damp the closer they got to the sea.

The waves were much bigger close up, rhythmically churning on to the beach. Even with just her feet in the water the sensation made her toes curl.

'Seriously, Finn, refreshing? It's freezing!'

Finn pulled her further into the water. She didn't resist; secretly she loved that he wanted to go swimming, that he didn't just want to stay on the beach lying around doing nothing, even if that's what she'd imagined. He wasn't one for posing – he was a grafter, that was evident from watching him work on the cottage.

A wave broke, splashing water on to her chest. She gasped. In the sunshine, she could try to imagine they were in Greece, the warm shallows of the Mediterranean caressing their skin, but the Atlantic Ocean was still cold and the constant waves brought fresher, cooler water on to the shore. It was revitalising though. Finn dunked himself beneath the water, emerging dripping wet, his hair darker than before and plastered to his forehead. Water beads clung to his beard and he grinned as he wiped the water on his face away with his hand.

Jenna was only submerged to just below her waist but goosebumps pinpricked her skin and her teeth were beginning to chatter. The sun on her shoulders wasn't enough to take away the chill of the sea.

'Get it over with and go under – you'll feel much better afterwards.'

Finn started wading towards her, his movement slow in the water. Jenna screamed and just before he reached her she closed her eyes and dived downwards, her whole body engulfed by cold. Below the surface, Finn's laughter was muffled. She pushed herself upright, emerging in a shower of seawater, her blonde hair stuck to her face like Finn's was to his.

'I wouldn't have dunked you under, honest.' He caught her around her waist.

She slid her hands down his arms, firm and cold, goose-bumped just like hers.

'Usually I'm in a wetsuit,' he said.

'Ah, I see, you're just trying to act tough.'

Jenna slipped away from him, submerging herself in the sea again, allowing her skin to adjust to the cold. With the sun shining down from an almost cloudless sky it began to warm her up. Finn swam alongside her flipping between his front and back, the incoming waves rocking them closer together.

There were only a couple of other people crazy enough to be swimming. Two young boys were by the edge of the sea, furiously digging a hole with spades and screeching with delight every time it filled with seawater. Families camped on the sand were pulling picnics out of bags, and the thought of food made Jenna realise just how hungry she was. They'd been in the water for ages. She stopped swimming and tentatively touched the sandy floor with her feet. It was shallow enough for her to stand, the water coming to just above her bikini top. She held up her hands and waggled them at Finn.

'My fingers are wrinkled and my stomach's rumbling.'

Finn swam past her. 'Race you back.'

He powered ahead, his strong arms slicing through the water. Jenna decided to enjoy the view rather than chase after him. He stood up just before the waves broke and waded the rest of the way, white foam splashing on to his back. Jenna swam a little way and followed his example, slowly walking out of the sea, pushed forward by the surf until she was padding after Finn across smooth damp sand.

'That was lush,' Jenna said when she reached him. He threw her a towel and she wrapped it around herself, shivering from the cool water running down her skin. Finn draped his towel across his shoulders and hugged her to him, the heat of his body making her instantly forget how cold she was. He brushed the damp hair stuck to the sides of her face away, tucking it behind her ears.

'You're beautiful.' He leant closer and kissed her more passionately than the night before. Cocooned in the beach towels their damp bodies were pressed against each other. Finn's hands slid beneath their towels and across her cold skin, brushing the sides of her breasts and skimming her hips. She moved her hands to his chest, making his towel drop away on to the picnic blanket, leaving them shivering and laughing together.

After drying off and having their picnic, Jenna pulled on her shorts over her bikini bottoms and they explored the beach together. Even in the middle of the day it was still blissfully peaceful, and they wandered over to a cluster of rocks on the far side. They picked their way across, finding small rock pools hidden in crevices and larger ones too, deep pools undisturbed by the tide, teeming with sea creatures.

Finn stopped by the edge of a large pool. 'Me and my sister always used to bring nets and spend hours seeing what we could find.'

'Shame we haven't got one now.' Jenna followed Finn and sat on the edge of the rock pool, her feet dangling, submerged in the cool water. Fronds of seaweed swayed beneath the surface from the movement of her feet. Tiny fish darted between rocks, disappearing into shadowed crevices. The water was warm where shafts of sunlight between the rocks created a green watery world.

Being here with Finn reminded Jenna of family holidays, the long days on the beach exploring damp caves and rock pools with her brother, screeching together as they ran into the cold sea and straight back out again. They'd often gone to Cornwall, although Jenna only remembered visiting her great aunt a couple of times. Perhaps she'd been too young. Her memories were hijacked by beaches, rock pools and making sandcastles, rather than cups of tea in a garden with an elderly relative she hadn't really known. By the time Jenna was nine and her brother eleven, her mum, fed up of camping and the unpredictability of the UK's weather, insisted they swapped campsites for a hotel in Spain. The excitement of staying in holiday apartments by the beach won Jenna over for a few years, but as she got older, she thought more and more fondly about those early camping holidays and the beaches they explored in Cornwall.

'Look.' Finn pointed to a rock not quite submerged by water and a small crab scuttling over it.

The longer they waited and the quieter they were, the more creatures they saw, hiding amongst the seaweed and zigzagging across the impossibly clear water.

'I keep thinking something's nibbling my toes,' Jenna said.

'A natural version of one of those fish spas.'

'This is much nicer.'

More families and couples arrived on the beach in the afternoon, but nowhere near enough for it to feel crowded. The place was a hidden gem, and special to Finn, which made it special to Jenna. He had so many memories of the beaches along this stretch of the Cornish coast and told Jenna about family days out, beach parties with his friends, attempting to surf for the first time, barbecues on the beach, and an accident when he'd cut his knee open on a rock. He still had the scar, a jagged white line across his kneecap.

The intense heat of the previous week had dissipated, and in a shady sheltered spot it felt fresh, leaving Jenna glad that she'd brought her hooded jumper. A hoodie and shorts – the ideal combo for a British summer when it could be hot one minute and cold the next, blazing sunshine in the morning and torrential rain in the afternoon. It felt almost Mediterranean, and yet days like this reminded her of the unpredictably of the UK.

She didn't want the day to end and was conflicted again about whether to invite Finn in when they got to the cottage, but on the way back in his van, feeling sun-kissed and sandy with salt-spray hair, Finn saved her from her dilemma by inviting her to his parents' for a roast dinner.

'I couldn't think of anything nicer,' Jenna said as he turned off the road that would eventually lead to the cottage and on to the road that led to Mullion. A home-cooked Sunday roast after a day at the beach was the perfect way to end a perfect day. It also spoke volumes that Finn was happy for her to meet his parents and yet at the same time took away the awkwardness of inviting him back to the cottage, for what?

Although she fancied Finn like crazy she liked the idea of getting to know him slowly and not jumping straight into bed with him.

'They really won't mind me turning up unannounced?' she asked as Finn pulled the van into his parents' driveway and parked it behind his dad's larger van.

'I'm pretty sure Mum expected me to invite you back. Anyway, she makes enough to feed about ten people. You joining us won't be a problem.'

Any anxiety Jenna felt at having dinner with Finn's parents was dispersed by the warm welcome.

'You already know my dad,' Finn said. 'And this is my mum, Sally. Mum, Jenna.'

'It's lovely to finally meet you, Jenna. I've been hearing all about the cottage, and you of course.' She did a sideways glance at Finn before ushering them along the hallway to the large open-plan kitchen diner at the back of the house.

The smell of roast chicken was enticing yet gave Jenna a pang of homesickness that she wasn't at her mum and dad's about to tuck into Sunday dinner with them. Although she'd moved out years ago, she'd occasionally go over to theirs on a weekend and have dinner. It wasn't quite the same cooking for herself.

'Drink, Jenna?' Gary placed a bottle of red wine on the kitchen island. 'We have white in the fridge too or a beer, maybe even a gin and tonic.'

'White wine will be lovely, thanks.'

After spending the day on the beach in the fresh air, swimming and exploring, Jenna's stomach rumbled. Their picnic seemed a long time ago now.

'Have a seat.' Sally gestured to the stools on the other side of the kitchen island. 'It'll be another ten minutes or so until we eat.'

Jenna sat and Finn joined her, his thigh touching hers. Gary and Sally reminded her of her own parents, chatty and warm, her mum cooking, her dad getting the drinks ready.

Gary poured Jenna a generous glass of wine and slid it in

front of her. He waggled a bottle of beer at Finn. 'Fancy one, Finn, or is that a stupid question?'

'Just the one, Dad. I've got to drive Jenna home.'

'Well cheers, Jenna.' Gary knocked his beer bottle against her wine glass. 'It's nice to have you over. We always seem to only see you in passing. They're keeping you busy on this film?'

Jenna sipped her wine. 'Just a bit. It's always the same though, early start times and late finishes, so I'm used to it.'

'Have you filmed on location before?' Sally took four plates from a cupboard and put them on the oven's hot plate.

'Yes, plenty of times, but nowhere quite like this. Most filming takes place outdoors, on beaches, harbour sides, and then inside scenes like cafes and characters' houses are actually filmed on location rather than sets being built.'

'Gives it authenticity that way, I guess,' Gary said.

'There are plenty of period properties round this way that I'd imagine are ideal for filming – this film's not modern-day is it?' Sally asked as she started to stir the gravy.

'No, 1940s.'

'See.' Gary pointed his beer bottle in his wife's direction. 'We'd never get chosen to be in something like that, too modern our house. Worked on some pretty special places over the years though, haven't we, Finn?'

'Dad likes houses with lots of character because they're not straightforward to renovate.'

'I like a bit of a challenge.'

'Otherwise known as a complete headache.' Sally gave Gary a look and turned to Jenna. 'He says he loves working on those sorts of places, listed buildings and all that, but you should hear the amount of complaining and swearing that goes with it when he's in the middle of one of those jobs.'

Gary waved his hand. 'Don't listen to her, Jenna. They're interesting. Doesn't mean they're easy mind.'

'Bramble Cottage must be a breeze for you then? I hope you won't get bored.'

'Actually, your cottage is the perfect job – a place full of character that's not been touched for decades. It's retained its charm, just needs life breathing back into it. I'm enjoying working on it and Finn is too, although probably for different reasons.'

'*Dad.*'

Gary laughed and winked at Jenna.

She smiled and turned to Sally. 'Do you have a roast every Sunday?'

'Yes, pretty much, whatever the weather. It's tradition. The way I was brought up.' Sally pulled on the oven gloves and took a bronzed roast chicken out of the oven and placed it on top of the cooker. 'Although Gary has persuaded me a couple of times this summer to have a pub roast. Much nicer someone else cooking in the heat we've had and eating it in a shady pub garden. Right, if you all want to take your drinks to the table, I'll start dishing out.'

The large polished wooden table looked out over the garden. Bi-fold doors led to raised decking, a neat lawn, and the border in front of a wooden fence decorated with colourful hydrangeas and phlox. There wasn't a sea view, but in a quiet cul-de-sac with no other houses backing on to them, the view was of open fields.

Sally placed the roast chicken at the centre of the table next to the roast potatoes and vegetables and encouraged them to help themselves. She dished up sage and onion stuffing and bread sauce, and soon Jenna's plate was piled high with roast potatoes, parsnips, cabbage and mashed swede and carrots. Gary carved the chicken and placed two large slices on her plate. Gravy cascaded down her roast potatoes and Jenna tucked in, so incredibly hungry. This was the best meal she'd had in a very long time, even with the catering on set being exceptionally good.

'So,' Sally said, after they'd all had a chance to start eating. 'Have you always wanted to be an actress?'

'I think so, yes. I mean I loved performing from an early age and was always into drama and dance at school, then got lucky enough to be accepted into drama school. I've dabbled in other things though, mainly to pay my way through drama school and then while going to auditions.'

'Waiting tables and that kind of thing?' Sally wedged a piece of chicken and roast potato on her fork.

'Not so much waiting tables, although I've done my fair share, but I've had other things on the side to make money like a bit of modelling and writing. I wanted to be a potter at one point. My mum despairs of me.'

'I think it's a fascinating job,' Sally said. 'Must be lots of competition though, going to auditions and not knowing when you'll be working next?'

'Yeah, it's been hard work. You have to have thick skin because the rejection can suck.' Jenna glanced at Finn. 'We were talking about the reality of an acting life today. It's not an easy career. I think I've given my parents plenty of stress about where my next pay cheque's going to come from, while my older, more sensible brother's been building a steady and lucrative career as a lawyer. We couldn't be more different, really.'

'Well, I'm immensely impressed that you're an actress on a big movie.'

'Mum will be telling all her friends about you coming over.'

'And why not, it's exciting, one of the most exciting things that's happened around here, having a Hollywood movie being filmed.'

'It's actually a British film, Mum.'

'Is it? It's got Hollywood actors in it, like that Milo Blake. Do you know him, Jenna?'

Jenna took a sip of wine. 'Only since working on the film.'

'Ooh, tell me more. What's he like? Is he as handsome in real life?'

'Mum, what's with all the questions?'

'I'm just interested that's all.' She turned back to Jenna, her wine glass clutched in her hand. 'So, what is he like?'

Jenna hadn't expected to be talking about Milo, and with Gary and Sally's eyes on her, she squirmed in her seat. 'He's kinda like you'd expect – full of confidence, smooth-talking, the centre of attention.'

'They're all staying at that lovely big hotel on the cliff, aren't they?'

Jenna nodded.

'All the cast are there, are they?'

'Yep, apart from a couple who live in Bristol and Cardiff. They're commuting down for a couple of days when they have filming and going back home in between.'

'But you're at the cottage. Don't you wish you were with the rest of the cast?'

'Trust me, it's a relief to escape – it can be quite claustrophobic on set at times; friendships are formed fast and the nature of the work means you end up spending a lot of time with people you don't know very well. Having a place to escape to is good.'

With her stomach full of roast dinner and still feeling windswept and salt sprayed, Jenna relaxed as Finn drove her back to the cottage. She'd enjoyed the warmth and homeliness of Gary and Sally's, and Finn's company of course.

Finn pulled his van into the drive behind Jenna's car and left the engine running. Should she should invite him in or not? It had been such a perfect day maybe they should leave it with a kiss and nothing more complicated than that. Sod that. Why was she being so good?

'I, uh…'

Finn smiled. 'I need to get home. I promised a mate I'd meet him at the pub tonight; can't let him down, his girlfriend broke up with him recently and he's a bit of a mess.'

Jenna put her hand on his thigh. 'That's fine. What I was going to say is thank you for such a lovely day.'

'You really enjoyed it?'

'I haven't had such a fun and happy day in a very long time.' She leant closer, sliding her hand up his thigh as she kissed him.

Finn shuffled in his seat, moving his hand on to her hip and kissing her back. He pulled away, with a grin. 'Right, I'd better get going before I change my mind.'

Chapter Sixteen

Jenna's first thought when she woke was Finn, but despite having a later call time, she was up and out of the cottage before he arrived. She vaguely remembered Gary saying something about needing to get plumbing parts before they started work.

She sensed something was up the moment she arrived at the base. As she walked from her car people looked her way and started whispering together. Her heart was racing by the time she checked in with the First AD. She passed a group of crew clustered around the catering van, and made it to the make-up trailer.

'Here she is.' August, who'd been doing Jenna's make-up since the first day, smiled as she entered. She tapped the empty chair in front of her. 'The woman of the moment.'

Lily and Amanda were already there, their faces make-up free and about to be transformed into 1940s women.

Jenna sat down in the chair. 'What's going on?'

'You and Milo are the talk of the town,' Lily said. 'Well, talk of absolutely everywhere.'

August slapped a magazine down on the shelf in front of her. 'You've not seen this?'

It took a moment for Jenna to register what she was looking at. The front cover of *Hot Now Magazine* featured Milo Blake in orange board shorts, his tanned and toned chest pressed against Jenna's. It wasn't the clearest of photos, like it had been taken from a distance, but standing in a pool of light with Milo's lips millimetres from hers and his hand resting firmly on her yellow bikini bottoms, it was undeniably them.

No one said anything.

Jenna looked up and caught sight of her frowning face in the mirror. August was standing behind her, make-up sponge at the ready. Jenna looked over at Lily and Amanda.

'I don't understand?'

Lily pulled a sympathetic face. 'There was obviously a pap stalking the hotel…'

'I get that, but there's nothing going on between me and Milo.'

'There's a whole article inside about the two of you.'

'I think "hot sex" is how they described it…' Amanda dropped her gaze from Jenna and stared down at her knees.

'Oh for God's sake. You two were there, nothing happened.'

'It kinda looks like something to me,' August said with a raised eyebrow.

A bubble of panic rose in her stomach. All Jenna could think about was Finn. What if he saw this? He'd know it wasn't true, wouldn't he? Maybe she should tell him, pre-warn him, but it was bullshit. Telling him because she was worried he was going to believe it felt like she was trying to defend herself. She had nothing to defend. But the rising panic after their blissful day yesterday made her sick to her stomach.

'I went home that night remember?' Jenna frowned. 'You believe me, right?'

'I know.' Amanda shrugged. 'It's just, I don't get why you're so upset about it, even if it's not true. It's Milo Blake and everyone's talking about you.'

'That's exactly the problem, everyone talking. Trust me, if I was actually getting to have "hot sex" with him, I'd be perfectly happy for everyone to know about it. But I'm not.'

'If I was you I'd roll with it, make the most of the column inches,' August said, dabbing the sponge into foundation. 'Use it to your advantage.'

It wasn't until she'd had her hair and make-up done and was heading out of the costume tent in her 1940s skirt with her blouse neatly tucked in that she realised the commotion of the last hour had completely made her forget about Heidi starting. Jenna wasn't slated to film with her this week, but that didn't mean she wouldn't see her at some point today. She wouldn't see Milo though as he was off filming at a second location somewhere on the north coast. She couldn't even talk to him about the magazine article or find out what he thought about it. It wasn't like it was the first time he'd been on the front cover of a gossip magazine.

What concerned her the most was Finn. She couldn't care less about Heidi or Milo bloody Blake. She found a quiet sheltered spot well away from everyone, took a deep breath and called Finn's mobile. He'd definitely be at the cottage by now. He always had his mobile on him, tucked into the back pocket of his shorts; there was no way he wouldn't hear it or see who was calling him. But there was no answer. She tried once more before giving up. Her worry intensified at the thought of him ignoring her call.

The morning went by in daze. She was unusually quiet and lost in her thoughts on the minibus to that day's filming location; she noticed the worried glance between Lily and another actor. They spilled out of the minibus and were taken to a harbourside cafe that had been turned into a quaint 1940s tea room. Unable to focus on anything other than the suggestive photo of her and Milo, she was relieved to have no lines.

'You're in a world of your own, Jenna,' Lily whispered on a break between camera changes.

It was an easy day where Lily and Jenna got to sip tea, eat cake and pretend to talk in the background. There were supporting artists there too, as well as an older actress playing the role of the tea shop owner. Ade, the character actor who'd been at the pool party the other evening, played the role of Milo's character's dad.

'I'm just worried about who's seen that article.'

'What, like Finn?'

'Exactly like Finn.'

'First positions!' the assistant director called and

supporting artists shuffled about in their seats. Ade went back outside ready to make his entrance.

Lily leant closer to Jenna. 'Don't worry, it's today's gossip, everyone will be talking about something else by tomorrow.'

Jenna wasn't convinced but she appreciated the support and Lily's attempt at making her feel better about the situation. She sighed and picked up her newly filled cup of tea.

'And action!'

Every time she checked her phone during breaks, there were more and more messages from friends about her and Milo, along with a handful of missed calls from her parents, from their landline, her mum's mobile and even her dad's mobile. She could only imagine that friends of theirs had made them aware of the magazine article and then they'd gone and read about their daughter having sex with a movie star, evidenced by a photo of them semi-naked together. There was no return call or message from Finn. Jenna switched off her phone, stuffed it in her bag and vowed not to look at it again until she finished work.

They were bussed back to the base at lunchtime and Jenna queued to get food. Not that she was hungry; she was too annoyed by everything, her stomach in knots. She sat with Lily and picked at her plate of salad and quiche.

'You're a fast mover.'

The familiarity of the voice made Jenna's heart drop. She looked up and came face to face with Heidi.

Heidi dumped her plate of food on the table and sat down opposite. 'I wouldn't have had him as your type; you like blonde-haired, blue-eyed kinda guys. But I guess Milo Blake is rather rich and famous.'

'Seriously. You're going to do this, are you?' Jenna gritted her teeth and tried to keep her voice low and controlled. She leant forward, aware of Lily listening next to her. 'I promise you, I would never stoop so low just to further my career. Why don't you take a long hard look at yourself before accusing me of messing about?'

There was no hello, no how are you. It had been months

since they'd last seen or spoken to each other and all she could do was accuse her of sleeping with Milo to get ahead in her career.

Jenna dropped her knife and fork on to her plate and stood up. She turned to Lily. 'I'm going for a walk before we're needed back.'

'Are you okay?' She looked at Heidi and back to Jenna.

'Yeah, I'm fine. Just need some air.' She should do the decent thing and introduce Lily and Heidi to each other but the rage burning in her chest told her to get the hell out of the place, away from prying eyes and ears, away from any further conflict. She dumped most of her lunch in the bin and stacked her plate with the other dirty ones. It was stifling in the tent and noisy with chatter and she was relieved to escape. There was nowhere to go apart from across the field. On the far side was a cluster of trees, so she headed for that, walking the long way around the edge.

There had always been a healthy competition between Jenna and Heidi. They were the same age and looked similar with long blonde hair and blue eyes. Jenna was tall and slender, Heidi curvier, but both got lots of attention. They were often up for the same roles and offered the same opportunities. Jenna had honestly believed that they'd learnt to live with that, the healthy competition between them driving them both on to bigger and better things. Until Heidi had abused their situation and destroyed any trust.

The long grass was dry and scratched at her legs. The costume department would kill her if she snagged her stockings. She had thirty minutes until she was needed back and she didn't want to be near anyone, least of all Heidi. The sensible brown shoes she was wearing were nice and sturdy for walking across the hard dry earth; the long-sleeved blouse and fitted skirt were less practical. She slowed down, aware that she'd be a hot mess by the time she got back if she kept up the pace.

The wood was cool and dark and she sheltered from the sun beneath an oak. She leant against the trunk and gazed out. The incline of the field was gradual and she hadn't realised quite how hilly it was. Now she could see all the way down to the base with its white tents and silver trailers, a mini city in a farmer's field in the heart of Cornwall. She could just about make out the sea too, a smudge of dark blue against the pale blue sky.

She couldn't hide away up here. She couldn't hide from the gossip either. She needed to confront Milo, explain herself to friends, family, and her agent. No doubt Beth would have left a message or ten by now. And Heidi. She had to deal with her. They had to talk and clear the air. It didn't mean they had to be friends again but they had to confront each other because Jenna couldn't continue to carry around this kind of anger any longer. More than anything, she needed to talk to Finn.

The afternoon dragged; it was the first time since they'd started filming that she wanted the day to be over. It was back to filming the same scene after lunch, sipping tea and pretending to chat with Lily. When she finally got back to the cottage in the evening, Finn and his dad had already left and there was no message from Finn either. Despite having eaten very little all day she still wasn't hungry. A knot of tension made her shoulders ache and she felt talked about and abused. It was a strange feeling to be a part of such gossip. The only reason she answered her mobile when it rang was because it was Carla.

'Hey you,' Jenna said, her voice sounding as weary as she felt.

'You kept bloody quiet about that.'

'Oh Carla, not you as well. All anyone's talked about today is that flipping picture.'

'So it's not true?'

'Of course it's not true!'

'Woah, okay, I've hit a nerve there.'

Jenna rubbed her forehead. 'Sorry, I didn't mean to snap at you.'

'I get why you're upset being gossiped about if it's not true, but why the hell isn't it true? I mean you're all over each other. You're hot, he's hot; you're single, he's single. Why the hell are you two not banging each other? They're saying you're having "hot sex", so why the hell not have some?'

Jenna wandered from the kitchen into the living room, slumped on the sofa and put her head in her hand. 'It's complicated.'

'You don't want to talk about it?'

'Not particularly. Not right this moment. I've had enough of this shit today and bloody Heidi weighing in on stuff that really isn't any of her business. We aren't friends, so she has no say in my life any more.'

'Oh boy, you're hellishly pissed off.'

'Can you blame me?' Jenna said. 'I could so do with a friendly face. It's feeling a little claustrophobic on set at the moment. Everyone's gossiping. Everyone thinks I'm shagging Milo and the more I deny it the more everyone thinks it's true. I can't win. I wouldn't care if I was actually getting laid, but I'm not.'

'How's Milo reacted?'

'No idea. Haven't seen him. Probably lapping up the attention. And with Heidi down here…'

'You don't have to talk to her though do you?'

'I guess not. I think we'll only have a couple of scenes together and I don't think they're being filmed this week. But she sought me out today and took me down. After what she did how the hell does she have the nerve to talk to me like that? Seriously, Carla, if you have any time, even just a couple of days, please visit.'

'I might be able to this weekend; I'll see what I can do.'

Jenna forced herself to eat a chicken salad outside on the picnic table. She'd ignored text messages from friends who'd seen the magazine, deciding to not even attempt to comment on it, knowing that protesting would be futile and simply encourage more talk. She avoided going on Facebook and Instagram after making the mistake of looking at Twitter and getting a huge shock about how she was being talked about by strangers. She couldn't ignore the voicemail messages though.

At dusk she retreated inside, dumped her plate in the sink, took the cordless phone and went and sat in the living room.

Her parents would have eaten by now and be sitting down in front of the TV. It was ridiculous to feel this nervous about talking to her parents, particularly her mum who she usually confided in about everything.

By the second ring her mum had answered the phone.

'Jenna, love. I tried calling you earlier and couldn't get hold of you. Or this afternoon.'

'I was working, Mum. Had my mobile switched off.'

'Denise... you know Denise from next door, she came round this morning with the magazine. I mean, you're on the front cover kissing Milo Blake.'

'We're not kissing.'

'His hand is on your bottom.' She lowered her voice at the word bottom.

'Yeah, well, it was because he planted it there, same as I'm pretty bloody certain he tipped off the paparazzi to be there and take the shot. It was set up, Mum.'

'Why would he do that?'

'It's complicated.' How many times was she going to give that as an answer?

'You're a grown adult, I don't really care what you get up – it's your life, you can choose who you go out with, and it's not like I disapprove or anything like that. It was just a bit of a shock to have it all paraded about in front of us. Denise was full of it, telling us all the juicy details from the article. Your dad had to leave the room at the mention of the "hot sex".' Once again her mum lowered her voice.

Jenna's cheeks burned at the thought of her dad listening to nosy Denise relaying the details about her and Milo. She tucked her feet beneath her on the sofa. 'It's all made up, Mum. Every bit of it. Apart from the photo and that was staged by Milo. We've flirted and chatted but that's all. I've been back to the cottage on my own every night.'

'Well, how can they write such blatant lies?'

'They always do though, don't they? Gossip and scandal and making out that something's more than it really is sells magazines.'

'I guess that's true. I mean Trump's full of it, "fake news" and all that. It's not so strange that entertainment magazines bend the truth too.'

'Or they're sold lies in the first place.'

Her mum huffed, unconvinced. 'By the way, your agent phoned this evening, wondering if we'd heard from you.'

'Yeah, she's left messages. I'm going to phone her now.'

'Are you sure you're all right, love? You sound down.'

Jenna stared across the sparse living room at the gas fire in front of the blocked up fireplace. She felt like taking a lump hammer to it and smashing it to pieces. 'I'm fine, Mum, really. It's just been a strange day. This kind of attention is normal for Milo; I've never experienced anything like it. Loads of people are telling me it'll do wonders for my career.'

'And you're not convinced?'

'I'm not sure. I'm going to phone Beth, see what she has to say.'

'All right, love, we'll speak to you soon. Love you.'

It was eerily quiet once she'd said goodbye and put the phone down. She wanted a hug from her mum. She sniffed and forced back tears. She wasn't going cry over Milo Blake and a fling she never had.

She was so glad her parents weren't on social media. She really couldn't bear the thought of them reading the comments on Twitter and seeing hashtags like #milodoesjenna and #milohotsex. Although no doubt Denise would be back round in the morning showing them Twitter memes and fuelling the rumours and gossip even more.

It was well past office hours and late to be phoning her agent, but the last message Beth had left explicitly said to phone her back at any time.

She scrolled through her mobile to Beth's number and plumbed the digits into the cordless phone.

'Hi Jenna.'

'Sorry it's late.'

'Oh, don't worry.'

'It's been a strange day.'

'Everyone's talking about you and Milo.' She could hear the excitement in Beth's voice.

'It's not true by the way, everything's been made up, despite what the photo suggests.'

'It doesn't make a difference either way, it's out there now, you're being talked about. You and Milo are trending on Twitter. I've had offers coming in for you all day long, almost from the second that magazine went live.'

'Offers?'

'For auditions, reality TV. You name it, they want you.'

Jenna leant back on the sofa. She'd dismissed everyone's excitement on set this morning about what hooking up with Milo could do for her career and yet now it was actually coming true.

Jenna's head immediately flooded with the possibilities and what ifs, but she made herself listen to Beth.

'I'll see what comes in over the course of the week and then we can make some decisions. It's incredibly exciting, Jenna. Whether you're into Milo or not, roll with it. He's a career maker.'

'Did you know he'd personally requested me to work on this film?'

'Uh huh.'

'Why didn't I know that?'

'Did I not tell you? I thought I had. Must have slipped my mind. Either way they really wanted you to be a part of the film. See what I mean by the influence he has; he's a good person to be seen with. Whatever you're doing or not doing, keep at it. Fuel those rumours.'

They said goodbye, the excitement in her agent's voice in stark contrast to the worry that consumed Jenna. She was too tired and emotionally drained to be wondering or even caring about the opportunities that were about to come her way. She checked her mobile again; still no message from Finn. It was too late to try and phone him again now. Maybe he was out with friends and maybe he'd been too busy working today to answer her call; perhaps he hadn't actually seen the article and wasn't ignoring her.

What she needed to do was talk to Milo, get his take on it, and find out what he was going to say about it. As nothing had actually happened between them he could deny it – people would listen to him. The only problem was how to actually go about seeing him without anyone else seeing them together.

Chapter Seventeen

Jenna woke with a start. Worry consumed her thoughts. She should have tried phoning Finn again last night however late. Why the hell hadn't she at least texted him, told him the photo and magazine article was completely made-up. Nothing more than gossip to sell some magazines. But then again if he hadn't even seen the article then keeping quiet about it was probably best. Unable to settle back to sleep she forced herself out of bed and jumped in the shower. Her call time was later this morning and Finn would be here before she left. They were starting work inside today so she'd get the chance to speak to him. She'd tell him all about the article, explain just how ridiculous and untrue it was and it would be fine.

Jenna got dressed in a maxi skirt and sleeveless top. It was overcast but humid, the heat still intense but the blissful hot and sunny summer days had seemingly stalled. The grey mugginess of the morning suited her mood.

She ate a piece of toast, downed a coffee and tidied the kitchen. Her bag was packed for the day. She had nothing left to do, except say hello to Finn when he arrived and then head off to the base at eight thirty.

She was wiping over the kitchen surface for the third time when she heard the van pull into the drive. The engine switched off and two doors slammed shut so Finn's dad was with him. Footsteps crunched along the gravel path and two shadowy figures passed the window before Gary appeared in the open doorway.

'Morning, Jenna, I wasn't sure if we'd get to see you today

or not.' He took off his sunglasses and tucked them in his T-shirt pocket.

'A later call time this morning, that's all.'

Gary stepped into the kitchen and Finn followed behind. He didn't look at her and she knew immediately that he'd seen the article.

'We're going to be working on the bathroom this week,' Gary said. 'Water's definitely going to be off today and tomorrow.'

'That's okay, I'll be out all day.'

'You might want to fill up some containers just in case.'

Finn dumped his tool box on the floor with a bang. 'Or you can always stay at your boyfriend's until the water's back on.'

He turned his back on her, squatted and rifled through his tools.

'Right, okay then.' Gary looked between his son and her. 'I'm going to get what we need from the van.' He stepped past Finn and out into the sunshine.

Jenna didn't know what to say to Finn. He was pissed off, his tone said as much and his dad had picked up on it. It was hard not to.

Finn stood upright, clutching something in his hand. 'Why lead me on when you're with him?' He slammed a crumpled copy of *Hot Now Magazine* on the kitchen table.

'I tried phoning you yesterday to warn you about the article because it's not true. I didn't think you'd really believe what's written in a gossip magazine.'

'It's not what's written, Jenna, it's the photos of you two all over each other. Why wouldn't I believe that? Seems blatantly evident to me. You've made a fool of me. That's all Jake's girlfriend was banging on about at the pub last night.'

'It's not what it looks like. Really it isn't.'

Finn picked up the magazine. '"Leggy Jenna Wilson in a romantic clinch with the hottest actor of the moment Milo Blake". You're half naked and all over each other. I don't care, it's up to you what you get up to, but don't go fooling around with me when you're with him. I'm done with being messed around.'

'Actually, you're right, it is up to me what I get up to and I'm sick of everyone assuming stuff about me that's not true. If you think I'm the type of person who'd be sleeping with one bloke and leading another one on at the same time, then it's because you don't know me very well at all.'

Jenna picked up the magazine and slammed it against Finn's chest. She stalked over to the sink, leant against it and stared outside, her heart thumping.

'Everything okay?' Gary made Jenna jump. Her cheeks flushed and she turned away. Even if he hadn't heard what they'd said, he'd have heard their raised voices. How unprofessional had she been; Finn was working on her parents' house. She was staying here for work and she was in this emotionally-charged mess with one of the builders and an even bigger mess with the lead actor. She'd spent the most amazing day with Finn on Sunday and had dinner with his parents afterwards, and now this. Unprofessional on all levels.

'Finn, why don't you make a start on the bathroom.' It was an order rather than a question.

Finn picked up his tool box and headed for the stairs, not looking at her as he went past.

Jenna's skin itched with heat and embarrassment, sensing Gary's eyes on her. She didn't want to turn round and face him. She wondered if he'd seen the article too, or if Finn had kept quiet about it. But either way, after seeing them so happy together on the weekend he must be wondering what had gone wrong.

She breathed deeply and turned round. 'I'm going to put the kettle on if you'd like a drink?'

'Tea for me please and I'm sure Finn'll have a coffee.' He went to pick up his tools and paused. 'You're sure everything's okay between you two?'

'There's no problem, really. Just a bit of a misunderstanding.'

Gary didn't look convinced. 'We'll have the water back on as soon as we can.'

~

Away from the toxicity of the hotel and the overpowering presence of Milo, it had been the best weekend. Lily and Amanda were great friends, chilled out and uncomplicated, and bumping into and spending time with people other than actors had been refreshing. And then Sunday on the beach with Finn; she'd loved spending time with him. She hadn't wanted the evening at the pub to end, and exploring that quiet little cove had been magical. She wanted more than the friendship they'd developed. She wanted more than just a kiss. And now this. What she'd got was the focus of unwarranted gossip and the one person she'd had feelings for in a very long time was well and truly pissed off.

It had felt wrong with Milo from the beginning. He'd been keen to spend time with her when he didn't even know her, almost like she ticked all his boxes – she was blonde, pretty and an actress; she'd do. He flirted like he was putting on a show, which, from what Jenna had gleaned over the past few days, was exactly what he was doing. With Finn... Her pulse raced and she flushed at the thought – it was anything but a show. They'd been hidden in the shadows of the rock on the beach, his firm strong body against hers as he kissed her passionately, not a pathetic brush on the cheek like it had been with Milo, all for the paparazzi. Whatever happened, she was going to find and confront Milo today.

With her mind firmly on Finn, and her heart not engaged with filming, Jenna got through the day. At least it was another relatively easy day filming in the tea shop in Porthleven. She wasn't around Milo or Heidi either, so that was a relief – the Heidi bit at least. She was determined to speak to Milo though. She didn't even have his mobile number to text him. That in itself spoke volumes; according to the world they were together, but in reality they were so un-together it was laughable. A sham. But after she wrapped for the day, having had no chance to speak to Milo, and no chance of seeing Finn either when she got back to an empty cottage, she headed straight back out. It was still light and she'd have enough time to drive to the hotel and back again before it got dark. She started the engine and pulled out of the drive.

It was probably a bad idea, she thought as she reversed into a space in the busy hotel car park. She had no clue if there were paparazzi hidden in the trees waiting for a money-making shot. What if the paparazzi knew where the cottage was? What if they'd followed her? It was possible. She switched off the engine and gripped the steering wheel. She stared at the hotel wondering what to do. Everyone had wrapped at least a couple of hours ago, including Milo. She knew he'd been driven back to the hotel. He was here and she could talk to him inside, somewhere private where no one would spot them.

She put her hand on the door handle. Except even a photo of her going into the hotel could be twisted a hundred different ways. Beth had told her the other evening to fuel the rumours, but did she really want to do that? Her thoughts returned to Finn and the hurt on his face when he'd slapped that magazine down on the kitchen table, the image of her in a bikini pressed against a topless Milo Blake like a huge wedge between them. She took her hand off the door handle, started the engine and drove back to Bramble Cottage.

Jenna decided to leave it until the next day at work. The base was a safer place to confront him. Security were on the entrance to the field and if anyone, whether cast or crew, felt the need to take a photo and sell it, well that was up to them and completely out of her hands. It was an early start and a busy filming day, so she was straight into hair and make-up before being bussed to location. At lunchtime when she saw Milo heading to his trailer she knew it was her chance. Food could wait, talking to Milo was the priority.

She stalked across the grass, which was dry and brown from the summer heat and thousands of feet trampling over it for the last few weeks. She reached the trailer, the sign on the door – MILO BLAKE – as bold and as assertive as he was.

She knocked and waited.

The trailer door swung open and Milo stood there in his 1940s soldier's uniform, his hair slicked back looking as delicious as he did in his normal clothes.

'Can I come in? We need to talk.'

Milo moved back and ushered her into his trailer, his hand grazing her back as he closed the door behind her.

'What's up?'

'You really need to ask?'

'The magazine article.' He shrugged. 'Get used to it – you're in the public eye. Comes with the territory.'

'But none of it's true, doesn't that bother you?'

'What's the problem with being linked to someone as gorgeous as you? We're both single.'

'But we're not having sex, we've not actually hooked up, and you've been flirting and leading me on ever since we met and all for what? A suggestive photo…'

'Are you saying you'd actually prefer us to be having sex so what they're writing about is true?' He moved closer, his dark eyes boring into her, the smell of his aftershave strong.

She closed her eyes, drew in a breath and put her hands on her hips, determined to stand her ground. She opened her eyes. 'Why do you feel the need to hide the truth?'

'About what?'

'That you're gay.'

He held her gaze. 'I'm not.'

'You're really going to do this? What's the point lying to me? I know, Milo.'

He licked his lips as if buying time. 'You know what?'

'Oh for God's sake, Milo.' She glanced at the closed trailer door and lowered her voice. 'You and Timothy were at it in the spare bedroom at the cottage.'

Milo folded his arms. 'Huh. You weren't asleep.'

'No, I wasn't. But it cleared up a lot of stuff for me, like the reason you flirted with me but never took it any further when you had the chance. So, you need to set the story straight and say those pictures were all taken out of context. We're not together, we're not having "hot sex", we haven't even kissed.'

'I can't do that.'

Jenna rubbed her fingers across her forehead. 'Why the

hell not?'

'Why are you so bothered about it? Most actresses would kill to be in your position, shagging Milo Blake. How many more followers do you have on Instagram since this story broke?'

'That's what you think I'm worried about? I don't care about that. My problem is that it's not true.'

'So what if it's not true. I bet your agent loves it. All the attention you're getting. Watch the offers roll in this week.'

'You're unbelievable.'

Milo shook his head. 'I'm doing you a favour, Jenna.'

'But you're blatantly lying. How can you be okay with that?'

'Seriously, why are you so upset?' Milo stepped back, studied her and chuckled. 'There's someone else, isn't there?'

'Will that change things? Will you tell the truth?'

'Who is he?'

'What does it matter who he is? I want this non-story straightened out.'

'It's that builder isn't it? He's hot as hell. I can see why you're with him.'

Jenna clenched her fists and breathed deeply. It was all a game to him, when actually he was messing with her life. She decided on a different tack.

'Why are you worried about people knowing you're gay? I mean, there are loads of gay actors. Why keep it a secret?'

Milo went over to the fridge and took out a bottle of water. 'You don't understand. I'm typecast, which actually is a really good thing because I get loads of work.' He unscrewed the lid and took a gulp of water. 'I'm the good looking guy next door, the leading man, the one the girl always falls for. I don't want to risk my personal life getting in the way of my work. Risk losing out on roles because a shitty casting director passes because of who I'm with. This is my life, my career.'

'I get that, but it's my life and my career too. My relationship with Finn.'

'Wow, Finn, that's a proper Cornwall surfer kinda of name.'

'Seriously, Milo, I need you to end this craziness.'

'Jenna, hun, apart from the Finn thing, I'm doing you and your career a huge favour. You'll thank me one day.'

Fuming, she left his trailer, ignoring the glances in her direction from some of the extras. Of course everyone would think they'd been having a quickie in his trailer, exactly as Milo wanted everyone to believe. He *wanted* to take the conversation away from anything he deemed negative. She wondered what Timothy thought about Milo being splashed across the media with her. She had no real idea about Timothy, he didn't have the same level of fame as Milo. Was he openly gay? Maybe that's why Milo was being extra careful that he wasn't gossiped about in that way. In his mind it was much more palatable to be seen with a blue-eyed blonde woman. He was spinning a web of lies and Jenna was caught helpless at the centre.

Chapter Eighteen

Work was her escape and the cottage her refuge. Despite Lily and Amanda repeatedly asking her all week to come back to the hotel with them after they wrapped, she kept refusing. They were concerned about her cutting herself off from everyone but she wanted to be on her own. The cottage felt far removed from all the gossip and people she wanted to avoid. Although she'd talked to Milo, she still hadn't got round to having *that* conversation with Heidi. Finn was definitely avoiding her. She'd only seen him once more during the week when she'd wrapped early and got back to the cottage before he'd left. He'd been working on the bathroom with his dad, which made it impossible for them to have a private conversation. He'd ignored her and she'd said little more to him than hello. It bothered her more than anything that she'd wrecked things between them by not being up front about the Milo situation to begin with.

At least the end of the week brought the promise of Carla coming down for the weekend. It was a hellishly long drive for just two days but Jenna appreciated it more than she could say. Building work stopped at the end of the day on Friday and they weren't going to be working on the cottage over the weekend, so she knew she wouldn't see Finn for a couple of days at least. She missed him like crazy and regret coursed through her at the way things had played out between her and Milo and her and Finn over the last week.

Carla arrived at lunchtime on the Saturday, pulling into the drive in her battered Ford Fiesta. She climbed out of the car, a familiar sight with her freshly-dyed pink hair, skin-tight trousers and layered tops that clashed with each other, yet somehow the colours and patterns worked.

Jenna flung her arms around Carla and clung on to her.

'Wowzers, someone needs a hug.'

'It is so good to see you.'

'You too.' Carla released Jenna and wandered round to the front of the cottage, her hand shading her eyes as she gazed up at it. 'Shit, Jenna. This place is insane. I'd never want to leave if I was here.'

'Yes you would, you love city life too much. You'd get bored.'

'Have you been?'

'What?'

'Bored?'

'Well no, but then I've been working.'

Jenna opened the door to the kitchen and Carla explored downstairs 'oohing' and 'aahing'. Jenna smiled as she grabbed hummus, olives and cheese from the fridge and put it on a tray with a fresh loaf of crusty bread.

'You hungry?' Jenna asked.

'Starving.' Carla leant on the work surface and watched Jenna slice the bread and spread butter on it. 'This place is lush.'

'Imagine what it'll be like when it's finished.'

'Are your mum and dad going to sell it?'

Jenna shook her head. 'The plan's to rent it as a holiday home.' She handed Carla a bottle of lemonade, picked up the tray and led the way outside and round to the garden at the back.

'Flip, it's huge, loads bigger than it looks when you first drive in.'

'It's great, isn't it? So many hidden bits too – my dream garden.'

'Does the wood belong to the cottage too?'

'Some of it. It's kinda hard to see where the garden ends – there's a fence but it needs repairing.'

Jenna put the tray on the middle of a picnic blanket

already laid out on the lawn. They sat down on either side and stretched out in the sunshine. Jenna was sure the run of sunny weather wouldn't continue, but while it did she was going to make the most of it. She was also going to make the most of having Carla here. However lovely Lily and Amanda were, she needed a friend who really knew and understood her, someone who didn't judge and who would also tell her the truth.

'So, spill, tell me everything, all the juicy details.'

'There are none.'

'Really, nothing at all?'

'Nothing. Well not with Milo at least.'

Carla dropped a piece of bread back on her plate and grabbed Jenna's arm. 'Woah, wait. What do you mean, not with Milo? There's someone else?'

'The builder. Well, one of them – the son, Finn.'

'Are you serious?'

'Yeah, we met up on the weekend, just happened to be out at the same place, got chatting, stayed out late, we went for a walk…'

'And?'

'And ended up kissing.'

'Sweet. You really like him, huh?'

Jenna nodded and felt a burning sensation in her throat like she was fighting back tears.

'We had an amazing day together on Sunday, but I messed things up. At least that bloody article did and me not being upfront with Finn. He saw the article and is understandably mad.'

'So he thinks it's true?'

'Yeah, everyone does.'

'He'll come round; wait and see. It'll blow over, all the craziness that's happening right now.'

Jenna toyed with an olive on her plate, no longer hungry. She stared past Carla to the trees which cast long shadows over the newly cut grass.

'Do you know, being here makes me feel far removed from all the shit that's happening in the real world. I feel cut off from everything – in a good way. My love life – my made up love life I should say – is being played out in gossip magazines.'

Carla picked up her mobile, clicked on something and scrolled through. She turned the screen round. 'You're trending on Twitter, Jenna. You're a fucking hashtag.'

'I never asked for this.'

'No one ever does; unless of course they want the attention and actively look for ways they can get themselves in the papers.'

'I don't crave attention. I don't want to be famous because someone thinks I've hooked up with a movie star.'

Carla pulled her sunglasses to the end of her nose and looked at her. 'I know I asked you this before, and obviously you have a thing for the builder, but you're honestly telling me you've done nothing with Milo Blake? I mean, he's hot as hell; even I would.'

'He didn't even kiss me at that pool party. He just made it look like we were about to kiss and put his hands on all the right places. He was the one being all touchy leading me to that quiet spot away from the others so it looked like there was no one with us.'

'But there were?'

'Yeah, loads of us.'

'Do you think he knew there were paps about?'

'I think he was the one who tipped them off.'

'Why would he do that?'

'To get those photos out.'

Carla frowned. 'He's famous enough without needing to do stuff like this. He's an A-lister not a Z-lister.'

'Don't you think it's odd that he was all over me when we were in public but nothing – and I mean nothing has happened between us in private. I was expecting him to invite me up to his room and I was in a total turmoil about whether I'd say yes or not, and then nothing. He just walked back round to everyone else in the pool. And then when he stayed overnight hooking up with me was the last thing on his mind.'

'Really? Nothing? You've honestly not slept with him?'

'No.'

'Cos social media's having a fucking field day with the two of you. Imagining how beautiful your children will be.'

Jenna shook her head. 'What if I told you Milo was gay.'

'Then I'd say either you're lying or he's an awesome actor.'

Jenna sat upright and hugged her knees to her chest.

Carla placed a hand on Jenna's leg. 'You're serious about him being gay? I'm usually pretty good picking up on if someone's gay or not. With him I got nada; I'd say he's straight as fuck.'

'I'm certain about it because the night I had that party at the cottage he slept with one of the actors. As in a male actor.'

'That's pretty bloody conclusive then.' She leant back, resting her hands on the blanket. 'Wow, so he's using you as a cover up for his sexuality. He has everyone fooled.'

'Except I know the truth and I don't want to play along – I could milk this as everyone seems to be suggesting and have my five minutes of fame, but I don't want to, it's not who I am.'

'You've got integrity, that's for sure. You know, it's so 'effing sad to live like that nowadays when he shouldn't have to hide it. Hell, everyone knows I'm bi.'

'Yes, but who you are, your look, your personality, your openness about being bi is what helps you get parts. Milo told me if everyone knew he was gay he's certain it'd stop him from getting the leading man, love interest roles. He told me he's got limited time at this kind of fame and he wants to get the most out of it as he can.'

'His whole life is one big performance. It must be fucking exhausting.'

After lunch they left the cottage and headed to Falmouth, away from anywhere Jenna thought either Finn or any of the cast would be, especially Milo. Apart from the first weekend, she hadn't really explored this part of the coast. There'd been little downtime to see much of the area outside the filming locations, so it was good to spend a few hours wandering about like a proper tourist, nosing around the independent shops, having a beer in a pub by the harbour, and buying fish and chips to take back to the cottage.

They ate them straight from the paper, sitting outside on the picnic table, birdsong the only sound apart from their munching. The cottage glowed in the evening light; the freshly painted walls were pristine now they were clear of the scaffolding. The windows had all been repaired, sanded and repainted, their glossy grey contrasting against the white walls. The newly laid slate roof looked smart. The outside at least was finished and appealing even if inside still needed a lot of work. The only trouble was, everything about the cottage now reminded Jenna of Finn: him on the roof relaying the slates; dipping his brush into thick glossy paint ready to transform the windows; shirtless on that insanely hot day working on the cottage's stonework.

Jenna sensed Carla watching her and looked across the table.

Carla pointed a chip at her. 'You need to switch off and stop thinking about stuff.'

'Easier said than done.'

'Always is. Getting drunk often helps.'

'To begin with, until the tearful bit happens.'

'Hey, I always think of you as a happy drunk.'

Jenna laughed. 'I'm so glad you're here.'

'You know, I was thinking, to take your mind off all this shit with Milo, how about we meet up with Heidi tonight? Have me as a mediator between the two of you?'

'I don't want to see her tonight; I don't want to spend what time I have with you focusing on Heidi and our messed-up friendship.' Jenna looked across the picnic table at Carla. 'Unless of course you'd like to see her, I mean you two are still friends…'

'We are, sort of. It's not like I've seen much of her over the past few months. She's been too bloody busy.' Carla raised a pierced eyebrow. 'And to be honest I think she's doing her best to avoid me and bringing up what happened between the two of you – she must know that she was totally the one in the wrong.'

'Who knows if she believes she wronged me or not.' Jenna stabbed her fork into the battered fish. 'I will talk to her, but not tonight.'

'That's fine, I just wanted to give you the opportunity, that's all. She'll be back in London soon enough; plenty of time for me to catch up with her. You never know, you two might actually be on speaking terms again by then.'

Jenna nodded but her gut was telling her otherwise. She couldn't imagine their friendship ever returning to how it was. Maybe she was burying her head in the sand turning down Carla's offer to support her when facing Heidi, but the last thing she wanted to do was add more stress into her life.

It was late on Sunday afternoon when Jenna waved Carla out of the drive on to the road and the long journey back to London. She wandered back to the cottage feeling lost. The place was quiet and lonely without Carla's company and laughter. Tomorrow Finn and his dad would be back working on the cottage, continuing to repair it bit by bit. She had an early call time and knew she'd leave before they arrived. Maybe that was for the best. She locked the front door and leant against it, thinking of the long evening stretching ahead with no company. She wondered if her Great Aunt Vi had ever felt lonely living here on her own for so many years. With effort, Jenna pushed herself away from the door and wandered over to the kitchen. She switched on the kettle. It was too early to go to bed but that's what she felt like doing. She had things to do though, a few lines to learn, and she needed to look through what she was filming in the coming week. She made herself a camomile tea and was heading into the living room with it when her agent phoned. She stared at Beth's name on the screen and let the call go to answerphone.

'Jenna, I've just had an email from one of the producers of *The Love Hotel*. They want you on next year's show. This is big, Jenna. You don't need to decide tonight or even in the next week, but soon. It's a massive deal we're talking about. I'll email you all the details when I'm in the office tomorrow. Just wanted to give you a heads up so you don't freak out too much when you see the offer. You're going to be huge, Jenna.' Huge.'

Chapter Nineteen

The same way Beth's words had rocked her to sleep the night before, they tumbled around her head as soon as she woke up. She felt wrung out and tense despite the promise of an opportunity that could change her life. She showered, dressed and ate breakfast in a daze and was out of the cottage and on her way to the base before Finn and Gary arrived.

Filming from the previous week had moved from inside the tea shop in Porthleven, to a second unit set up in Port Isaac to film the outside shots. The long drive to the north coast gave Jenna plenty of thinking time. White fishermen's cottages and the harbourside dressed with lobster pots and wooden boxes were the backdrop to the scene. This week Jenna had scenes with Milo, Timothy and Heidi. It was guaranteed to be an interesting week and today was the only day where she was unlikely to see any of them.

She spent the morning walking arm in arm with Lily along the harbour. They stopped to look out over the water and whispered together before continuing to the tea shop, at which point the scene cut. They'd filmed it in the opposite order, the inside scenes first in Porthleven, the outside ones in Port Isaac afterwards, which would be seamlessly put together in post-production. It was an easy and enjoyable day as filming went, with straightforward action to shoot from different angles and only one line. Between camera changes, they were able to sit on canvas chairs in the shade and look out over the picturesque harbour.

If she thought the gossip about her and Milo would cool

off, she was mistaken. The events of the past week were following her. She'd spotted paparazzi on the edge of the village as the minibus had driven them to the set, and although they couldn't get close – unless they hired a boat and took photos from out at sea – she knew they were there, stalking her like vultures. The thing that confused her was that Milo wasn't on location today, at least not here with her, and that left her worried that there was enough interest in her alone. The idea of a stranger staring at her through a long lens freaked her out.

The scene was being set up to shoot with the camera on Jenna's face this time, and while Lily was taken to the marquee to have a rip in the hem of her skirt mended, Jenna wandered over to the line of chairs set up against the bumpy white wall of a cottage.

'Hey Ade. Can I join you?'

'Of course.' He patted the seat next to him. 'The down time's not so bad in a place like this, is it?'

'It's pretty special.'

'Usually we're holed up in some crappy room with no windows. I like it on location.'

Jenna stretched her legs out and rested back in the chair. The tide was in and a couple of wooden boats painted half grey, half blue bobbed on the glittering water.

'You must have been on some amazing shoots, though?' Jenna asked.

'Yeah, I've had my fair share of interesting projects. I was down this way a few years ago filming one of the *Pirates of the Caribbean* films. I had a few days on *Game of Thrones* over in Ireland too. There're gems among the mundane. Is this the biggest film you've worked on?'

'It is for the length of time I'm on it.'

'Plus you got more than you bargained for, eh?' He winked.

'You've heard as well.'

'Course I've heard. Everyone's heard. Gossip doesn't stay quiet for long, particularly when it's being fuelled by someone.' He tapped the side of his nose.

'What do you mean?'

'I know what happened that night round the pool. Only a bloody romantic fixated on seeing something that wasn't there would think there was something actually going on between you and Milo. He's the biggest flirt on the planet and it's all for show.'

Jenna sat up properly in the chair and leaned closer to Ade. 'I can't tell you how good it is to hear you say that. Everyone else seems to question my sanity in saying nothing's happening between the two of us, like I should've been falling over myself to jump into bed with him.'

'Like that would ever happen...' Ade raised an eyebrow.

Jenna smiled and watched one of the sparks recover a cable and make sure it was out of shot. The knot of tension in her stomach felt like it had eased a bit, knowing that someone could see the situation from her point of view. Maybe Milo Blake and which side he batted for wasn't the best kept secret he thought it was.

She turned back to him. 'Was acting what you always wanted to do?'

Ade grunted. 'Thought it was, when I was a bright-eyed twenty-something, fresh out of drama school, all starry-eyed over the incredible life I was going to have, the money I was going to make, the women I was going to shag... We were sold a dream and the huge success of a lucky few. I mean some actors make it, like really make it and have Hollywood come calling like our boy Milo. Others like me have to graft. Sometimes it's not all about working hard that ensures you do well, as I'm sure you realise.' He nudged Jenna's shoulder with his. 'I'm old and bitter, you really shouldn't listen to me. I've been doing this shit for longer than I care to think about. But do you know the advice I wish my younger self had got when I was an eager young actor, turning up for every audition I could get, saying yes to every role I could however 'effing bad the script was. I wish someone had told me to only become an actor if it was the *only* thing I wanted to do with my life. The only thing.'

'Do you regret your career?'

'Regret is a strong word. Nah, I can't regret the things I've done – they're what's shaped me. But it's come at a price. Financially I've been comfortable but I ain't rich. I've had three wives; I've got five kids aged between twenty-two and four. I've never been able to stay in one place long enough to ever feel settled. That partly wrecked my home life and my marriages. That and I was always too tempted being away from home for long stretches at a time, if you know what I mean.' He tapped the side of his nose again. 'You're young; I'm a miserable old miser, disillusioned after years of this shit, bouncing from one job to the next. Also, apart from a window of about three or four years in my twenties, I was never a leading man. I made my name and paid the bills as a character actor, suited me just fine in the long run, but you're proper leading lady material.'

'But at what cost?'

'You're young. Why the hell not go for it while you're not tied down by a mortgage, family and responsibility. And I'm deducing by this Milo Blake gossip that you're single?'

Jenna nodded.

'Have fun then. Go for it. If there's no one special in your life to keep you in one place, then why not embrace all this acting life has to offer. All that "being with Milo" has to offer.'

'D'you know, off the back of the *Hot Now Magazine* article, I've been offered reality TV stuff. My agent emailed me the details about it this morning, but it's completely not what I want to do…'

'Pays well?'

'The pay's huge, it's just…'

'I'd take the money. You're only young once and these kinds of opportunities, well, you turn your back on them now, you're not going to be able to change your mind later on.'

'It feels like I'd be selling my soul.'

'And you want to be a serious actor, right?'

'Well, yes. I want to act. I don't want to play a version of myself that'll get twisted and abused on reality TV.'

'You've got your head screwed on, kid. I like that.

Looking at the bigger picture and all. But just think how many girls your age would jump at the chance you've been handed on an 'effing platter.'

Ade's take on her situation stayed with Jenna long after their conversation finished. Maybe she was overthinking it; maybe she should go against her gut and say yes, take the money and see what other opportunities came out of it. She was single, she didn't have responsibilities apart from the rent on her flat but even that could be given up with enough notice. She'd properly messed up any chance of a relationship with the only person she'd wanted to be with for a long time. And even before that, what chance did they realistically have with Finn in Cornwall and her in London. What did she have to lose? An acting career was what she'd wanted for so long and an opportunity was being dangled in front of her that could raise her profile and further her career in a huge way. Yet she felt unsettled, knowing that if she said yes, it would change her life forever but perhaps not in the way she wanted it to.

Adrian – Ade – Turner-Jones was in his fifties, a proper character actor, handsome in his own way but rugged with it. He got steady roles because he played a type, but what would Jenna do in ten or fifteen years' time if the leading lady roles dried up, when there was a queue of younger prettier blondes to take her place. She could set herself up for life now.

Of course her agent wanted her to say yes, she got a fifteen per cent cut of everything Jenna made. Most of her friends and fellow actors would say go for it. Her parents wouldn't like the idea but then they often struggled with some of the roles she played, let alone be comfortable with her parading about in a bikini on some tropical island for *The Love Hotel*. And there was Finn. Even if she could convince him that there really was nothing between her and Milo, why on earth would he want anything to do with her if she signed up for a show where the aim was to hook up with someone.

She phoned Carla the moment she got back to the cottage.

'It's fame for the sake of fame, Carla. Would you take it?'

'I'd never get offered it.'

'But if you did, if you were me. What would you do?'

'Honestly? I don't know. I think I'd be as torn as you are. There are positives and negatives.'

'Well, that's no help at all.'

'Sorry. I guess it all depends on the sort of career you want long term. Would prancing around in a bikini and snogging a fit bloke be a stepping stone to something amazing, or do you keep plugging away at the auditions and acting and see where it takes you. You're talented and beautiful; you've got tonnes going for you, with or without selling your soul.'

'What would Heidi do?'

'You know what she'd do.'

'Maybe I'm worrying too much. One of the actors told me today that you're only young once, take the opportunities while you have them, they'll soon dry up.'

'He's disillusioned by the business, huh?'

'Just a bit.'

'Well, he has a point. And I can see it now, "*The Love Hotel* starring Jenna Wilson". It's money, it's fame – well notoriety at least – it depends on what *you* want.'

'I don't want my words or actions twisted. I don't want to be manipulated. I'm an actor for a reason; I like hiding behind a character. It's my safety net not actually having to be me.'

'You could always create a persona. Play a version of you.'

'It's reality TV, not fiction.'

'It's all bloody fiction, Jenna. All of it.'

'Maybe you're right.'

'You don't have to decide about it yet, do you?'

'No, by next week; they're beginning casting then.'

'And they're giving you a place without an audition or anything. They just want you?'

'They just want me because they think I've screwed Milo Blake.'

It was only the third time since staying in the cottage that Jenna had felt lonely. The first time was when she'd spoken to her mum and she'd wanted a hug; the second when she'd waved goodbye to Carla. Yet again she felt a sadness ending the call with her friend, locking the cottage door and going upstairs. Sliding into an empty bed she realised what she was missing. There'd been so much potential with Finn. She hadn't felt so strongly about someone for as long as she could remember. That night at the pub, she could have invited him back. She should have, before everything got messed up. But then having sex with him would have complicated her feelings further. And considering how upset he'd been by the article about her and Milo, she couldn't even imagine how he would have reacted if they'd slept together and he thought she'd used him in the worst possible way.

She snuggled down beneath the sheet even though it was warm in the bedroom. Who was she kidding anyway? A relationship with Finn wouldn't work any more than an actual relationship with Milo. But at least Finn, unlike Milo, was uncomplicated. He wasn't a highly-strung actor; he had a sensible job, worked regular hours, lived with his family and had a close group of friends. He was a builder and Jenna an actor. She didn't know where her next pay cheque was coming from, didn't know where or who she'd be working with from one week to the next. The two of them were so different. She bet Aunt Vi never had this kind of trouble with men. She wondered what happened to the man who wrote her the letters and why her great aunt had ended up spending her life alone.

She closed her eyes but her brain wouldn't switch off. She had made her decision. Her career had to come first. She was only twenty-seven, while the opportunity was there she needed to run with it, take the money, enjoy the fame and reap the rewards afterwards wherever that led to. She'd phone Beth in the morning and tell her to say yes. If Heidi could play the fame game, she could too.

Chapter Twenty

Regret flooded through Jenna the next morning; beads of sweat covered her body and palpitations made her chest feel tight and constricted. She'd made her decision last night, yet she still felt stressed and unsure. Maybe it was natural when it was such a big decision, one that would affect her in a dramatic way. As everyone kept on saying; it would change her life. Maybe she wasn't ready for that?

She flung the covers off and stalked to the bathroom. Her head felt fuzzy like she'd been late-night drinking, when actually she'd gone to bed reasonably early and only had a glass of wine while she'd thought things through.

She washed away the sweat and worry, and emerged from the shower a little calmer. She wrapped a towel around herself and looked at the bathroom. Gary and Finn had done a good job in here, replacing the dated sink and toilet with contemporary white ones. They'd kept the beautiful roll top bath and made the most of the space with a modern walk-in shower to replace the old one. Everything reminded her of Finn. The palpitations intensified when she thought about him. There was no turning back now. No erasing what had happened; yet what she wanted more than anything was to make things right with him.

She had a nine o'clock call time, later than normal, which gave her enough time to have breakfast at home. She'd enjoyed the cooked breakfasts at the base during the first week or two of filming but a full plate of bacon, sausage, fried egg, mushrooms and beans got a bit much after a while. She poured muesli into a bowl and sat out on the steps to catch the morning sun.

She knew what else was bugging her. Today was her first filming day with Heidi. There would be no escaping her as the scene involved just the two of them. Jenna headed back inside, rinsed out her bowl and packed her bag for the day. Gary and Finn would be here soon. Part of her longed to see him; part of her wanted to be well clear of the place before he arrived.

Jenna's morning commute was familiar now, and rather than the dreaded bus then Tube journey into central London, she relished the ease of clear roads and beautiful countryside as she headed to work. No main roads choked with traffic, no monotonous grey of built up areas or the long hours spent travelling to auditions and filming locations. She started the engine, glanced in the rear-view mirror at the low-hanging tree branches swaying in the breeze above the gleaming new slate roof. She released the handbrake and started down the driveway, coming to a halt when Gary's van turning into the drive blocked her way.

Jenna put up her hand, catching Finn's eye as she did. She reversed the short distance to allow Gary to park the van next to her.

Jenna gripped the steering wheel, not knowing what to do. It would be rude to drive off without saying hello, but then she didn't know what to say to Finn in front of his dad.

She got out of the car but left the door open and leaned across it. Gary emerged from the driver's seat and smiled at her. 'Morning, Jenna, nice surprise to catch you.'

'Yeah, a later call time for once.'

The passenger door of the van opened and slammed shut. Finn stalked up the path to the cottage without saying hello or giving even a backwards glance. Jenna bit her lip.

'I'd better get going.'

'Yes, of course.' Gary closed his door. He made to go but turned back just before Jenna had the chance to get back in her car. 'I know it's none of my business, and I'm not exactly sure what's going on because Finn's not said much, but he's hurting. I'm not one for listening to gossip, unlike Sally… but if you get a chance to talk to him… We'll be here until six this evening, just in case you're back early enough.' Gary's cheeks flushed and Jenna realised how much Finn meant to him to bring the situation up with her.

The tightness in Jenna's chest was back. 'I will, talk to him, when I can. I'm just not so sure he wants to talk to me…'

She left it at that and ducked into the car. She slammed the car into first and drove the short distance down the drive and out on to the lane.

She arrived at the base well before her call time. She parked her car and made her way towards the holding area. She'd already had breakfast but she could do with a coffee while she waited for hair and make-up. She did have one thing she needed to do first, and perhaps after that she'd finally be able to relax. Her decision had been made she just needed to make it official.

She walked away from the trailers, took her phone out of her bag to check the time and phoned her agent. She'd be at work by now and there was no point in waiting any longer to speak to her.

'Hey Jenna, I wasn't expecting to hear from you so soon. I thought you were working today?'

'I am, just a little later.' She scuffed the hard dusty ground as she walked away from the base. 'It's just after your message and email, I had a good think about what I wanted to do, and what it would mean to be on *The Love Hotel*. What it could do for my career, and…' Jenna bit her lip and leaned against the fence.

'And?'

'Beth, I'll do it. Tell them yes.'

'Amazing, Jenna. I'm so happy for you. I'll contact them today.'

Jenna gazed across to the principal actors' trailers and wondered if Milo was there, tucked away in comfort, managing his love life via the paparazzi and gossip magazines.

The car park was to the right, make-up and costume in the centre and the catering truck and marquee for meals and down time to the left. Production offices edged the base. It was a mini city in the middle of a field, the once green grass now battered by thousands of trampling feet, leaving behind dust and straw. Jenna felt trampled too – emotionally at least. She watched the comings and goings of actors, production crew and extras, while attempting to focus on what Beth was saying.

'They'd like to meet you in person – not an audition, this is yours, no negotiation needed, they just want to get to know you better. The contract will be ready to sign as soon as you're able to come back and meet the producers.'

'Yes of course, I can sort something out.'

'Amazing, Jenna. I'm so pleased. This is an incredible opportunity and I can't think of a nicer person for it to happen to.'

They said goodbye. Jenna put her phone on silent and tucked it into her bag. She'd made her decision, had told Beth, and yet she still felt unsettled. She'd hoped committing to it would have eased the little voice in her head doubting that it was the right thing to do. It was a big decision to make and one that would change her life. People only regretted the things they didn't do, not the things they did. She needed to hold on to that thought.

It felt a hugely stressful day, not only because of her decision to say yes to *The Love Hotel*, but it was her first scene with Heidi. She didn't even have the comfort of Lily and Amanda as they were filming a different scene.

Jenna headed to costume first, which was already rammed with lots of extras about to be bussed to location. One of the costume ladies found Jenna's now-familiar 1940s skirt and blouse on a named hanger and ushered her to a quiet corner. Jenna pulled on beige stockings and the dark green skirt. The costume lady helped tuck the blouse in and tie the laces of the sensible brown heeled shoes. The costume immediately made her feel different, older, more responsible, like women would have felt while most of the young men were at or about to go to war. It made her think of Aunt Vi again and her wartime love. It was hard to imagine her white-haired, stern-faced great aunt ever happy and in love, wearing stockings and lipstick.

Jenna caught sight of Heidi on the other side of the trailer, a flash of her blonde hair between the sea of extras getting ready. Her heart sank. They'd be heading into hair and make-up together.

It was a relief to escape the noise, heat and the smell of body odour in the costume tent and breathe in fresh air as she walked the short distance to the principal make-up trailer.

'Morning, Jenna!' August called breezily as she swung the chair round for her.

Jenna sat down. 'Morning.'

'Any new gossip to share?' August winked and Jenna smiled at her through the mirror.

She couldn't be cross with August, the happiest, loveliest lady despite the long hours she worked day in day out. Her smile lit up her already welcoming face.

'I'm trying my hardest not to be the centre of gossip.'

'Aah, Jenna hun, you're no fun. We live off gossip in here, don't we, Vicky?'

The trailer door swung open and Heidi appeared, in a near identical costume to Jenna's.

'We certainly do.' Vicky turned to the open door. 'Here's our newest recruit. Morning, Heidi.'

'Morning, ladies. Hi, Jenna.' She lightly touched Jenna's shoulder as she walked past and sat in the free chair in front of Vicky.

'You two know each other then, do you?' August waggled a make-up brush between the two of them.

Heidi caught Jenna's eye in the mirror. 'Yeah, since drama school.'

'Have you worked on things together before?' Vicky squeezed foundation on her hand and dabbed a little on Heidi's cheek, blending it in with her fingers.

'A couple of things,' Heidi said.

'We're usually up for the same roles so it's not often we get to work together unless someone wants two blonde-haired, blue-eyed, twenty-something actresses. You know how it goes.' Jenna avoided looking at Heidi and instead focused on August sweeping blusher on her already rosy cheeks.

'Haven't you just finished working on the new Bond film, Heidi?'

Jenna's stomach did a little flip. She held her breath and waited for Heidi to answer.

Heidi coughed. 'Yeah, I wrapped a few weeks ago.'

'Oh go on, tell us all about it.'

'There's actually not a lot I can say.'

'It's all hush hush is it?'

'Pretty much. It's easier to not talk about it in case I let something slip by mistake.'

August finished dusting blusher over Jenna's cheeks and reached for an eyebrow pencil. 'You must be able to tell us if you're playing a goodie or a baddie. Or perhaps a love interest?'

'A sort of goodie. But love interest…' She pretended to draw a zip across her mouth.

August raised an eyebrow. 'Oh it's like that, is it?'

Jenna's fingers clenched the edge of her chair. She desperately wanted to be done and back outside. The last thing she wanted to listen to were the details of Heidi's time on the Bond set and to relive the jealousy and anger that even thinking about Heidi over the past few months had made her feel.

'What's Daniel Craig like?'

'As you'd expect, a dream, a total gentleman.'

'You lucky, lucky thing.' Vicky sighed and swept powder over Heidi's face.

'You must have worked on some amazing projects though?' Heidi asked, glancing between the two make-up ladies. 'And worked with your fair share of famous actors too?'

August carefully finished filling in Jenna's eyebrows. 'Yeah, yeah of course. We shouldn't complain really, should we?'

'Not really.' Vicky laughed. 'It's just you have a thing for Daniel Craig, don't you?'

'It's true, I do.' August grinned. 'But yes, I've worked on some amazing films – lots of period pieces which I love, so I get to do the rather gruesome side of make-up with blackened teeth and scarred faces, as well as the preened and powdered faces of the wealthy.'

'Ooh, tell us which films?'

'Too many to count, but I loved working on *Vanity Fair* with Reese Witherspoon – although that was a fair few years ago now. It was one of my first big films and I was in awe of the amazing talent. Other period films *King Arthur*, *Elizabeth*, *The Duchess*. More recently I worked on *Mary Queen of Scots* with the divine Saoirse Ronan and Margot Robbie.'

'So historical make-up is your speciality, is it?' Jenna said, relieved the conversation was moving away from Heidi and the Bond film.

'You could say that; I guess I've just fallen into it over the years. The more films I've done, the more experience I've had and the more I get hired – it's only natural I guess, but I love it.'

They were driven to location together, just the two of them. They sat in silence in the back of the car for the twenty minutes it took to reach the peaceful and picturesque setting of a whitewashed cottage on a hillside overlooking sloping fields down to a sheltered bay and the shimmering ocean.

The crew were already there, having set up earlier. Jenna knew this location had been used lots throughout filming, as it was Milo's character's parents' house. As well as the outside shots, the inside of the cottage was being used too, cramped but by all accounts, charming and full of character.

Jenna and Heidi's scene was taking place outside; the two women ironically love rivals for Milo's character. The scene required tension and dislike between the two women, and Jenna was confident she could pull that off with ease. She might even enjoy it.

~

'And action!'

Take five and the wind buffeted Jenna's face as she rounded the corner of the cottage. Tears stung her eyes and she stalked across the front garden to the gate. Her hand hovered over it as Heidi called after her, her words snatched away on the wind. Jenna swung the gate open and slammed it behind her, its banging joining the crunch of her heels on the path.

'And cut!'

Jenna turned round and headed back towards the cottage. The director was talking to Heidi, and the crew were getting ready to shoot the scene again.

The director turned to Jenna as she reached him. 'That was great – the perfect amount of moodiness. Heidi's face was a picture. Well done. We'll reset to film it from the other angle with the focus on your face, Jenna.'

And so the afternoon marched on with two scenes being filmed, one with dialogue and the two of them arguing, the other the aftermath as Jenna stormed off. They'd started filming later in the day and didn't wrap until early in the evening, just before the light began to fade. They'd been lucky with the weather again, patchy sunlight and high white clouds, a fresh breeze floating inland from the sea.

Somehow they'd managed to not actually talk to each other all day, apart from stuff related to what they were filming. They were civil and cooperative with each other then. They'd stopped for a late lunch and were driven back to the base, where they'd eaten separately, Jenna catching up with Lily, while Heidi disappeared off somewhere. The less time they spent with each other the better, at least while they were working.

When they wrapped, the tension between them in the car on the way back was palpable, to the point Jenna had no clue what to say to Heidi to even start a conversation.

Heidi broke the silence a couple of minutes away from the base. 'Are you planning on ever talking to me again?'

Jenna studied the back of the driver's head aware of him

being able to hear everything. 'I don't really have much to say.'

'You have plenty to say. We need to get this awkwardness between us out in the open and be done with it. Today's been unbearable tiptoeing around you.'

'Seriously? That's how you feel? That you have to tiptoe around me?' Jenna folded her arms. 'I've done nothing today to make you believe that. Maybe it's guilt making you feel that way.'

Heidi turned and stared out of the window. Hedges zipped by in a green blur. 'Come over to the hotel tonight and talk. Properly talk. We can't ignore each other forever.'

Jenna bit her lip. She'd felt stressed all day having to work together with an unbelievable amount of hatred coursing through her. 'I want to talk but I don't think coming over to the hotel's a good idea.'

'Milo won't be there if that's what you're worried about – he's got a night shoot. He'll have left the hotel by now and won't be back until the morning. Come on over whenever you like.'

The driver pulled into the base and stopped the car. 'There you go, ladies. Enjoy your evening.'

Chapter Twenty-One

All Jenna really wanted to do was head back to the peace of the cottage. Finn and Gary would have left by now and she'd have the place to herself. She could make a simple meal, sit outside in the garden and listen to the birds in the trees, the sigh of the wind, the rustle of creatures in the undergrowth. She could pull up some brambles before it got dark and take out her frustration on the weeds. But the tension in her chest told her otherwise. A talk with Heidi was long overdue and it wasn't healthy to feel so angry at someone who was once her best friend. It had been eating away at her for long enough. She needed to deal with it.

She stole a little time to herself though before she left; ten minutes sitting outside with a soothing camomile tea. She cupped her hands around the china mug and gazed across the garden, making a mental note of all the places she still needed to tackle. One of the best jobs she'd ever had was during the summer before starting drama school. A friend of her parents had put in a good word for her at a National Trust place and she got a job working in the garden for seven weeks. She'd learnt so much from the head gardener and loved the days spent digging, weeding and planting. For a week of that summer she'd also worked backstage at an amateur dramatics show. She'd been exhausted but happy; she also knew that she wanted to be on the stage rather than in the wings, but again it had been a last minute favour for a friend after one of the crew had pulled out. Thinking back on it now, sipping tea and looking over the wilderness she was trying to tame, it was the gardening she had the fondest memories of. It had been hard work physically, but less complicated with few people to deal with. Her week working for the amateur dramatics society had been full of drama both on and off stage. Big egos, big characters, lots of complicated relationships both romantic and otherwise. It would have made a good plot for a novel. She remembered being glad to escape on the show's last night. It reminded her of how she was feeling now about wrapping on the film. She drained her tea, swept her hair into a messy ponytail and took her cup inside.

This time when she reached the hotel and parked she didn't bottle it and head straight home. She turned the engine off and got out of the car. The hotel was bathed in the honey tones of the retreating sun. Heidi had said to meet her in the hotel bar, but Jenna took the longer more picturesque way around outside.

The terrace only had a couple of people sitting out but no one from the film, so Jenna headed inside. The bar overlooked the tropical gardens and had an incredible sea view from its floor-to-ceiling windows.

She'd only just stepped inside when someone called her name. She turned to see Lily waving to her from a table with Timothy and Ade.

'I didn't know you were joining us this evening?' Lily smiled and hugged her.

'I wasn't; I mean I might a bit later but Heidi wanted to talk.'

'Ah, okay.' Lily gave her a knowing look.

'She's over at the bar,' Ade said. 'Join us after if you have time.'

Jenna left them, her feet heavy as she walked to the long sleek bar. Heidi was perched on a stool, her long blonde hair cascading down her back. She was wearing a colourful print maxi dress with a denim jacket flung casually on top. Only a year or two ago they'd have both been sitting side by side like twins, looking the same, dressed the same, giggling together. Jenna hadn't changed out of the clothes she'd worn to work – not that it mattered as she'd been in costume all day, but she hadn't thought about it when she pulled on skinny jeans and an over-sized short-sleeved top that morning. She hadn't dressed to impress like Heidi had.

Jenna slid on to the stool next to her. Even with her back to them she was certain their cast mates were watching.

'Hey.'

'Hey.' Heidi turned to her. 'I wasn't sure you were going to turn up. You should be staying here, you know. Loads more fun than being on your own.'

'I like it at the cottage.'

'Of course you do; would you admit otherwise?'

'Why would I lie about it?'

Already the tension in her chest had intensified again.

The barman appeared in front of them, smiling and glancing between them both. She was used to the attention the two of them got when they were together. No doubt he knew that they were associated with the film too.

Heidi's hands clasped a large glass of rosé. The barman looked at Jenna. 'What can I get you?'

'Gin and tonic, please.'

Jenna watched him making it, unsure what to say to Heidi to get the conversation started and wishing she was sitting with Lily, Timothy and Ade instead.

The barman placed her drink on a napkin and she handed him a fiver.

'Let's go and sit outside.' Heidi jumped down from the stool, grabbed her drink and was off across the bar before Jenna could say anything.

Jenna picked up her drink and followed Heidi out into the fresh evening, joining her at a table on the edge of the terrace.

'So, you wanted to talk. Let's talk.'

'It was awkward as hell on set today,' Heidi said. 'I mean, the tension was great. Thank God we were acting a scene that required us to dislike each other, because if we were supposed to have been the best of friends there's no way we'd have been able to pull it off. No way.'

Jenna folded her arms. 'There's only one way we're going to be able to clear the air and I've been waiting for you to say it for the last God knows how many months. Now's your chance.'

Heidi sipped her wine, placed it on the table and stared out towards the sea. Apart from the murmur of chatter from the few other people outside, the only sound was the gentle rush of the waves on to the shore below. It should have been soothing but it accentuated Heidi's silence. Jenna clenched her fists beneath the table.

'Fine.' Heidi turned back to her. 'What I did wasn't right, but given the chance you'd have done exactly the same. It was a misunderstanding, that was all, and once I got there, even though they had your name down they let me audition because we looked so similar. In their mind, there was no difference.'

Jenna leant an elbow on the table and rubbed her forehead. She concentrated on breathing deeply and staying calm because all she wanted to do was scream at Heidi. This wasn't the place to cause a scene.

Jenna shook her head. 'I wouldn't have done what you did. I wouldn't have had the nerve and also I wouldn't have wanted to. We've always had each other's back, at least we used to. We used to be thrilled for each other when one of us got a role even if we'd both been up for the same part. Friendship, Heidi, that's what we had. Friends don't treat each other like that.'

Heidi leant forward and lowered her voice making Jenna realise that perhaps hers had been rising. 'It was an honest mistake. I only realised when I got to the audition and they were expecting you rather than me.'

'It was my agent who left the message. Don't you dare say you didn't realise, of course you did. You listened to the message, thought it was for you, knew it couldn't be for you because it was my agent but decided it was too good an opportunity to pass up. You knew I'd lost my mobile so the landline was the only way my agent could get hold of me. You used it to your advantage. You thought you'd turn up in my place and hope for the best. You deleted the message. You lied to my face. You stole a role that should have been mine.

It was deceitful, hurtful and so unbelievably selfish. Whatever happened to friends first, jobs second?'

'Truthfully?'

'Yes please, Heidi, it's about bloody time you were truthful.'

'My agent had been chasing that role for me, so I felt – rightly or wrongly – that it was *my* opportunity.'

'Okay fine, even if I were to believe you that it was a genuine mistake that you turned up at *my* audition, why the hell didn't you get in touch with my agent when you realised?'

Heidi folded her arms and sat back in her chair. Even in the softening light, Jenna could see that her eyes were brimming with tears.

'Because I knew you'd get the bloody part, Jenna. You always do. And I wanted it so badly.'

'No I don't always get the part.'

'You're beautiful and talented…'

'So are you…'

Heidi raised her hand. 'Let me finish. I've always had to try harder next to you. Yes, we're similar in so many ways, but you're stunning, Jenna, beautiful not just pretty. Your bone structure is to die for. You're the perfect height, the perfect build. The only thing I've got going for me apart from the similarity to you with blonde hair and blue eyes, is big boobs and bum. I can do sexy but not understated and stunning. *Everyone* notices you walking into the room, just like Milo Blake does.'

'What has any of this got to do with Milo?'

'It's just the opportunities you get, that's all.'

Jenna frowned. 'What do you mean?'

Heidi waved her hand. 'Nothing. The simple answer is, I did what I did because I was so jealous you got the call and I didn't. I took advantage of the situation that your agent couldn't reach you; I took advantage of the fact she didn't specifically say the message was for you, although of course I bloody knew it was. I wanted my chance, I wanted my big break to happen. I didn't honestly expect to get the goddam role and for that I'm sorry.'

Jenna swigged her gin. 'You're sorry you got the role, but you're not sorry for deceiving me? That's unbelievable, Heidi. How am I ever supposed to trust you again? How can I forgive you when you won't even apologise for being a bitch and stealing the role from right under me? Did you ever stop to think that it could've been my big break too? My opportunity? We'll never know now.'

'You've just got your big break.' She made speech marks with her fingers. 'By "shagging" Milo Blake and having the whole bloody world know about it.'

'You think what's happened over the past couple of weeks is my big break? Complete lies are being spun about me and Milo, and what you consider to be a big break is actually reality TV and stuff I've never craved. It's notoriety and fame for fame's sake, and not because I'm good at my job and have furthered my career because I'm talented.' Jenna downed her drink and stood up. 'I really can't hear any more of this. I thought an apology from you could be the starting point of us trying to repair our friendship, but you're so full of yourself and bitter that you can't see how wrong you were.'

'You're really not into him? Milo?'

'No, I'm really not, and he has nothing to do with our issues, you realise that, right?'

Jenna walked away, feeling even more fired up and annoyed with Heidi. It was a half-hearted apology and one that Jenna didn't want to accept, not if Heidi couldn't see the truth. She'd always thought they'd been on an even footing when it came to everything – their looks, their talent, the opportunities that came their way. It was a shock to know that Heidi didn't see it like that.

Jenna walked back to the bar without thinking. The sensible thing would have been to go back to the cottage; instead she found herself getting another gin and tonic and joining Lily, Ade and Timothy at their table. She had a rare weekday off and nothing planned for tomorrow, so she could enjoy herself tonight, safe in the knowledge that Milo Blake wasn't around to mess things up for her again.

~

Unlike the day before when she woke up feeling like she had a hangover, Jenna actually did wake with a hangover the morning after her evening at the hotel. That first gin and tonic with Heidi had turned into a fair few more, and her anger at Heidi dissipated with an evening of laughter with Lily, Ade and Timothy. Heidi hadn't joined them. Although a little while after she left her outside, Jenna had seen her sidle through the bar. Jenna knew she should care, after all, they'd been best friends for years, yet at the same time a little voice kept telling her that friends didn't treat each other the way Heidi had treated her. Friends supported each other and were honest. So, she'd ignored her and had a good evening with her new friends before calling a taxi to take her back to the cottage.

She had no idea what she was going to do with her day off. Finn had no clue that she'd be home, so maybe it was best if she spent the day somewhere else, away from the cottage and his anger, but with her car still in the hotel car park it felt like too much of an effort. She'd had a run-in with Heidi yesterday, she couldn't face another one with Finn, someone she actually cared about. Unlike Heidi, he'd done nothing wrong, apart from making assumptions.

But she couldn't avoid him forever.

And the garden was calling. With long hours filming and busy weekends, she'd hardly had a chance to get outside and continue working on it. She'd made such progress in the beginning that she didn't want the momentum to stop. She only had until the end of the summer to make a real difference, to transform the outside the way Finn and his dad were working wonders on the inside.

She was outside at the front of the cottage trying to untangle brambles entwined around a rose when she heard the van pull into the drive. Her heart raced as the engine turned off and a door slammed.

Just the one door.

Finn came round the corner of the cottage, carrying his tool box. He was deliciously familiar, his hair windswept, wearing tan builder's shorts, a fitted cream T-shirt and work boots, yet his smile was missing.

'Morning,' he said and headed straight inside.

Jenna threw down her secateurs. She took off her gardening gloves. She couldn't stay out here and ignore him. There was no excuse, particularly as his dad wasn't with him.

It took a moment for her eyes to adjust to the dimness inside. Finn's tool box was on the table, and he had his back to her as he filled the kettle with water.

He'd obviously heard her come in. 'I wasn't expecting you to be here.'

'I have a day off.'

'Do you want a coffee?'

'I can make it.'

Finn flicked the kettle switch and faced her. 'I'm working in the living room today – knocking out the old fireplace. It'll be loud and messy; hope you don't mind.'

'No, it's fine, don't let me get in the way.'

They were being too polite, like they didn't know each other past a professional working relationship. Maybe she should just let him get on. Was it really a good idea to have *that* conversation first thing in the morning when he was dying for a coffee and she was yearning to rip out weeds in the garden?

He answered her question by picking up his tool box and heading towards the living room. 'I'll get on then.'

She sighed and took two mugs out of the cupboard and made them both a coffee. She poked her head round the living room door. 'Coffee's on the kitchen table.'

The weeds and brambles took the brunt of her frustration and it wasn't long before she managed to untangle the rose and she had a mountain of brambles piled next to her. She retrieved two large bags from the tumbledown shed and snipped the brambles into smaller pieces, compacting it down into the bags before going back to detangle the next rose.

Thump, thump, thump.

Jenna looked up, put her hands on her hips and stretched, her back sore from bending over for too long. The thumping was coming from the living room and Jenna imagined Finn bashing away at the ugly 1960s fireplace. Alongside the cottage's beamed ceiling and sash windows, the concrete monstrosity was completely out of place. Jenna had wanted to take a lump hammer to it when she'd first visited the cottage with her parents. Apart from needing a break, she was desperate to see what would be revealed once the concrete was ripped away. Plus it was an excuse to talk to Finn. She dropped her gloves and secateurs on the grass and headed inside.

Finn's T-shirt was covered in dust. He had a mask over his mouth but the rest of his face gleamed with sweat and his hair was grey with dirt. He grasped a lump hammer in his hands and rhythmically hit it against the fire surround. His arm muscles took the strain every time he smashed the hammer down. Fine dust and bits of chipped concrete flew from the fireplace, scattering over the floor and on to the sofa and armchair covered with old sheets. It was a messy and back-breaking job, but she did wonder if he was venting more anger on the fire surround than was necessary.

He caught sight of her, swung the lump hammer into the surround and then stopped. He dropped it to the floor with a thud and wiped the back of his hand across his face.

Jenna moved further into the dust-covered room. 'Are you likely to find anything behind it?'

Finn pulled the mask down from his mouth. 'It'll definitely reveal the old brickwork, not sure what the surround will be like though. But it'll open it up and once it's repaired it'll look a hundred times better. Are you going to put a wood burner in or have an open fire?'

'Not sure; if the place is going to be rented out I imagine my parents will go for a wood burner.'

With the sun pouring through the windows highlighting the dust dancing in the light, it was hard to imagine a wood burner pumping out heat in the middle of winter. Although it had returned to normal British summer temperatures after the July heatwave, Jenna was still hot from working on the garden in the hazy sunshine. She also felt heat rising to her cheeks at the thought of the conversation she knew they had to have.

Finn picked up the hammer again.

'Can we talk?' Jenna asked.

'I don't think there's anything to say.'

'That's because you've ignored my texts and phone calls.'

'With good reason.'

Jenna rubbed her fingers across her forehead. With his fist tense around the lump hammer and clenched cheeks, anger simmered off him. How could she make him believe that she was telling the truth? She folded her arms. That was exactly what she needed to tell him, the truth. So what if Milo was desperate to hide who he really was and she was taking a risk by telling Finn. With no other option it was all she could do.

'The funny thing about the situation – and it's not actually funny, I know that, is Milo is more likely to want to shag you than he would me.' She met his eyes.

Finn dropped the lump hammer on the floor and folded his arms.

'What the hell are you talking about?'

'Do I really have to spell it out?' Jenna raised her eyebrows, but Finn stood his ground, his frown not shifting. 'He's gay. Somehow it's managed to be the best kept secret in the film world. I think a few people know but pretend they don't. He has a hell of a lot of influence and is determined to keep who he is a secret. I don't think anyone would actually risk spilling the beans. He used me as a cover story, that's all it was. All it is.'

Finn began to slow clap. Dust puffed into the air each time his work gloves connected. 'I got the feeling you'd be a good actress, but you're fucking awesome.'

He pulled the mask back over his mouth, lifted the hammer and swung it at the fireplace.

Crash.

Concrete tumbled to the floor in a dust cloud.

Jenna wanted to scream. She was telling the truth and yet he *still* didn't believe her. What the hell did she have to do to prove her innocence? She breathed deeply. He was too angry to talk to her right now. Maybe taking it out on the fireplace was the best thing he could do. Perhaps he'd be more amenable later. Wishful thinking, Jenna thought as she retreated back outside to continue taking her own frustration out on the brambles.

Chapter Twenty-Two

Hot Now Magazine had a new photo on the cover. The pristine white walls of the hotel and one of its balconies was instantly recognisable. The people on it were familiar too: Milo and Heidi. Kissing. The headline read MILO BLAKE'S LOVE TRIANGLE. Jenna's heart sank as she thumbed through the magazine and found the four-page spread detailing the ins and outs of Milo's supposed love life. The photos jumped out; another grainy one of Milo and Heidi snogging, this time in his hotel room with the doors and curtains conveniently left open; another of her and Heidi animated and angry out on the hotel's terrace; plus, one of Jenna getting in a taxi late at night looking worse for wear.

She read the article with an increasing tightness in her chest. The love triangle was meant to be between her, Milo and Heidi. They'd made it look like Milo had cheated on her with Heidi, and rather than the actual truth of Jenna confronting Heidi about their friendship and the role she stole from her, the magazine instead insinuated that Jenna had been confronting Heidi about *her* relationship with Milo.

Somehow Heidi had been drawn into Milo's game and Jenna was still caught in his web of lies. She flung the magazine down. So, because she'd refused to play along, he'd twisted it to make himself look lusted after by not just one but two pretty blonde actresses. Had Heidi asked her to meet her at the hotel because she knew there'd be a photographer there? Was that a set-up too? It felt as if she was being manipulated on all sides, first by Milo and now by someone she'd once called a friend.

There was absolutely no way Finn would listen to her now. He hadn't believed her when she told him the truth about Milo being gay, and now there was more 'evidence' that Milo was involved with both her and Heidi. She might as well give up on the idea of ever mending her relationship with Finn. It was never going to last anyway. Without the Milo thing, it would have been a summer romance and then they'd have to kiss goodbye when she headed back to her life in London and he continued with his in Cornwall. The fact that they only got to spend two blissful days together rather than the whole summer irked her more than anything, but she couldn't turn back time or erase all the crap that had been written about her.

She was wrapped for the day and instead of going back to the cottage she drove to the coast and parked in a small National Trust car park. She closed the car door, disturbing birds in the undergrowth, sending them flapping into the air.

She walked to clear her head, to get away from the incessant questions and speculation. The beach was off the beaten track, like the one Finn had taken her to, with a steep path cutting into the hillside. It was early evening and people were beginning to pack up from their day on the beach and head back to wherever they were staying. The view as she made her way down was epic: white sand kissed by turquoise sea and rock stacks towering out of the water. Although there were still lots of people about it was peaceful and that was the main thing. Her day had been filled with noise: the hairdryer to style her hair; the constant chatter of the make-up ladies; the music in the scene they'd shot, followed by applause after applause after applause, take after take after take. How difficult was it to get a scene right that simply involved clapping and a couple of 'looks'? Very, it seemed by the length of time it took today. Lunch had been filled with people talking, cutlery clashing, the scrap of plates, laughter. She craved peace and quiet to clear her head and to allow herself to think straight.

The sand was soft underfoot, making it slow-going

walking across to a quiet spot backed by one of the dark grey and rust-red hued rocks. It was an antidote to the noise in her head. Birds soared and the only other movement was the white foamy peaks of gentle waves bubbling on the sand.

Although she wanted to be alone, she needed to talk to Carla, the only person who knew the truth about the situation with both Milo and Heidi. She took out her mobile and rang her. It went to voicemail. She didn't leave a message. She sat down and stared across the beach to where the dry sand had darkened from the waves. Someone had drawn a heart, but Jenna couldn't make out the names in the middle of it. She imagined it said Finn and Jenna, then imagined dragging her foot through it until it resembled nothing more than a pile of damp sand.

It took three tries to reach Carla.

'Sorry, you're not working are you?'

'Nah, not today. Kickboxing class. Finished now though, so you've got a couple of minutes before I hit the showers. Let me guess, Heidi?'

'I'm so bloody predictable, aren't I? I'm down in Cornwall working on the most incredible job and the last couple of weeks all I've done is moan about it.'

'Actually, you've not moaned once about the job. It's Milo fucking Blake who's the problem. And I totally get why you're stressed with Heidi being there, particularly when you weren't expecting her to be.'

'You're too good to me, Carla.'

'I'm your friend, silly. So what's happened?'

'You've not seen the latest copy of *Hot Now*?'

'Oh shit, no.'

'Apparently there's now a love triangle between me, Heidi and Milo. Photos and everything. My conversation with Heidi played out beautifully for a pap to capture, and a gossip mag to turn it into something it isn't.'

'Bloody hell, Jen. Is Heidi playing along with it? Actually, I know the answer to that.'

'*He's* directing the narrative, Carla. He's bloody clever about it, getting actresses like me cast at a point in their career where it's an incredible opportunity. Flirt with them, lead them on, suggest the pretence of hooking up would do wonders for their career. And if you don't play along, well then, he just makes something else up.'

'And as we already know, she'll do anything to get bigger and better parts.'

Jenna ran her fingers through the cool grains of sand. 'While Milo gets to maintain his position as a Hollywood heart throb with women falling all over him.'

'How miserable to live with that kind of pretence, particularly when he's famous enough to be scrutinised constantly.'

'But people buy into it, don't they? They're not looking further than him snogging Heidi in his hotel room, and "oh my goodness, what a terrible mistake, we left the curtains open…"'

'Or suggestively putting his hand on your bum and whispering in your ear when he knew the paps were there. He's a snake.'

'He's protecting himself by screwing around with other people's lives, thinking he's doing them a favour.'

'He probably is doing Heidi a favour. She'll be loving the attention. You wait, her agent will be getting calls just like your agent did.'

Despite her made-up life being played out online and in gossip magazines, Jenna's real life continued as normal. She was back to work the next day. It was mid-August and much like her mood, the weather had turned from the blissful heat and sunshine of the earlier part of the shoot, to the usual unpredictability of a British summer. Some days it poured with rain and shooting was taken inside; the next day it could be hot and humid, causing havoc with continuity.

Jenna couldn't leave the situation with her, Milo, and Heidi be, not any longer, not after the latest gossip and not after the anger Finn had directed at her. They had scenes together but there was never a chance to talk to Milo – at least not privately. She knew she was being scrutinised. Everyone on set was talking about it; she knew paparazzi were camped outside the hotel, which made her wonder if they knew where she was staying. Was there a long lens spying on her through the trees at the end of the garden?

Instead of making the most of the last couple of weeks' filming, she was longing for it to end, counting down the days until she could escape what had essentially turned into a fish bowl – everyone watching her, everyone having an opinion about her life. And when she really thought about it, what Milo was actually doing could be seen as sexual harassment. With all the attention around #metoo she didn't quite understand how he could get away with it, not in this day and age.

She finished her morning's filming and went back to base on her own for once. She got a coffee and sat in her car, leaving the door open to let in what little breeze there was on the humid and overcast day. She thought back over the events of the past few weeks and her reaction to Milo. She was angry with him now, believing he was harassing her, and yet in the beginning hadn't she encouraged it? She fancied him the same as everyone had – Lily, Amanda, all those extras who'd been lusting after him. She'd felt special when he paid her more attention than anyone else. Nothing untoward had happened then. He was a tactile person; he put his arm around everyone: the costume ladies, the assistant director, the caterers. He chatted with everyone too. Jenna had warmed to him because he was friendly with everyone, whatever their job. He didn't act like a diva, like he was more important than anyone else because he was the star of the film.

And then, at the hotel and at the party back at the cottage, hadn't *she* wanted him to kiss her? Wouldn't she have welcomed it? She'd enjoyed flirting with him. He was good looking and seemed a decent bloke, regardless of his fame. She remembered feeling confused when he didn't kiss her that night on the landing, but by then she'd seen him kissing Timothy. Her feelings towards Milo became muddled from that point onwards, but was he completely to blame?

She drummed her fingers on the steering wheel and gazed

across the base. The place had been drenched by a huge downpour and now the dampness was evaporating in the muggy afternoon sun. More people had arrived at the base since she'd been sitting in her car, and it was now busy with actors grabbing a drink or heading to the tent for a costume change. Then she caught sight of Milo, striding across the flattened grass, a coffee cup in his hand as he headed to his trailer.

Jenna downed her cold coffee and got out of her car. She took the long way round, up along the top of the car park in an attempt to avoid anyone. Now was her chance to talk to him again, in private. She stormed up to his trailer and knocked before she could change her mind and bottle it. She wasn't even sure what she wanted to say to him but she knew she needed to say something.

The trailer door swung open. Milo stood with his coffee cup in his hand, the top few buttons of his shirt undone so it flapped open, giving a glimpse of his toned chest.

'Hey, I wasn't expecting you, seeing as though you've been avoiding me.'

Jenna folded her arms. 'I, uh… Yeah, well, with good reason.'

'Don't just stand out there, Jenna. Get your arse in here.'

She was about to glance behind her, but then figured what the hell. Did it really matter if anyone saw her go in? She closed the trailer door behind her with a bang.

'You look pissed.'

'You think?'

'The Heidi thing, right?'

'You even have to ask?'

He wandered over to the seating area of the trailer, sat down and patted the space next to him. 'Let's talk then.'

She sat down opposite.

'Whose idea was it to go for the love triangle angle? Yours or Heidi's?'

'To be honest, it's been a happy accident.' He sipped his coffee and placed the cup on the table between them. 'You aren't interested in being a part of "Milo and Jenna", but

Heidi seems happy enough. The story kinda played out by itself.'

'Yeah right. You honestly expect me to believe you didn't have any part in orchestrating those photos?'

'Jenna, hun, I thought you'd be happy to finally not be with me.' He rested his arms on the back of the seat and watched her intently with his mesmerising hazel eyes.

'I'm not out of it though, am I? I'm still in the papers; my face is still being splashed everywhere, just part of a different lie this time. And not only that, you're leading Heidi on. You flirted with me; but you've taken it further with her.'

'Why do you care? You two don't even like each other.'

Jenna looked at him sharply. 'Has she told you?'

He shook his head. 'I have no fucking clue what happened between you two, but it's pretty bloody obvious you don't like her, Jenna. You're civil enough when you're working together, but you both go out of your way to avoid spending time with each other. I've tried talking to Heidi about you but she keeps saying there's nothing to talk about.' He picked up a lighter from the table and twisted it between his fingers. 'From your face I'd say you think otherwise.'

'You ever had someone hurt you so badly that you can't stand the sight of them?'

'Wow, that bad, huh?'

'I can't trust her, not after what she did.'

'Was it over a bloke?'

Jenna shook her head. 'No. If only. That might have been less of a betrayal.'

'If she hurt you that much, why the hell do you care if she gets hurt now? Why would you care if I'm using her? Surely from your point of view it's a little bit of payback?'

'It's true, I don't really care about her.'

'Then what's the issue?'

'You do realise she's using you just as much? Whether she has real feelings for you or not, she's all about her career, and trust me, she's ruthless about it. Maybe I'm naive, not playing the game, but think about it. She had her sights on you from the moment she got here – straight in there flirting with you even though, like everyone else, she thought you were with me.'

'I'm well aware of what she's doing, Jenna. I've encouraged it; it works to my advantage. To be honest, I expected you to lap up the attention, but you're different. Not ruthless like Heidi is. Works out fine for me though, so don't go feeling too sorry for me. Seriously though, you two have quite the competition going, don't you?'

'Except I don't want to be in competition with her, I never have done. She's my friend.' Jenna looked sideways at Milo. 'She was my friend.'

'What do you want me to do, Jenna?'

'Leave me out of it. All this shit you've got going on. Tell the press you've dumped me – or even better, tell them there was never anything going on between us and it's always been Heidi. I mean, that's if you're happy to continue lying to them. You could just say it's only ever been about Timothy.'

Jenna didn't wait for an answer. She got up and battled with the trailer door until it swung open. She clambered down the steps, letting the door bang closed behind her. She stormed off across the base, relieved that she'd already been wrapped and all she needed to do was get out of her costume. She had a welcome distraction with a night out with Lily and Amanda later, although she knew their choice of pub was made in the hope that they'd bump into Finn. Jenna wasn't convinced that bumping into Finn when he'd been drinking would be a wise idea. Either way, an evening spent with cheerful company rather than wallowing in self-pity on her own was preferable.

After spending the rest of the afternoon in the garden, Jenna took her time getting ready. She scrubbed away the dirt and sweat with a leisurely shower, painted her toenails, straightened her hair and did her make-up. She tugged on skin-tight jeans and a short-sleeved sequinned top. She looked at herself in the bathroom mirror and wondered who she was trying to impress. Nobody, she realised, she was only trying to make herself feel better. She tucked her sleek blonde hair behind her ears. Her silver earrings flecked with blue were flattering against her lightly tanned skin. She'd always thought her deep blue eyes framed by naturally long eyelashes were one of her best features, but she had high cheekbones and full rosebud lips too. It was all skin deep, all meaningless in the end. She was a look, a commodity, a pretty face that could gain attention because of how she looked and who she associated with. She'd done enough work as an actor and a model to know that an awful lot of the time looks came before talent, but this last couple of weeks had been even more of an eye opener.

How vain was she staring at herself in the mirror? She left the bathroom and booked a taxi to pick her up at eight. She needed a drink tonight. While she waited, she made a chicken salad and picked at it on the cottage step. She watched blue tits flit between trees and fat wood pigeons waddle across the lawn.

It was a much cooler evening than the last time they'd been to the pub. By the time the taxi picked her up it was overcast and threatening to rain, so Jenna headed inside and found Lily and Amanda tucked away at a table in the corner. It was a week night and not as busy as the balmy evening when Finn and his friends had turned up. How had everything gone so wrong in such a short time?

She hugged her friends and sat down, a gin and tonic clasped in her hands. 'Let's not talk about work, or men or anything related to what's happened over the past couple of weeks.'

'Oh God, Jenna,' Lily said, laughing. 'What on earth's there left to talk about?'

'I don't know, holidays?'

'Being down here is like being on a permanent holiday.' Amanda raised an eyebrow and sipped her wine.

'A working holiday, maybe,' Jenna said.

Lily folded her arms on the table. 'Okay, how about this. Let's do some quick one-word answer getting-to-know-you questions. Jenna, Amanda, then me.' She grinned at them both. 'Favourite ever holiday?'

'Rock-pooling in Cornwall when I was a kid.'

'Croatia with my boyfriend last year.'

'New Zealand road trip after I graduated from uni.'

'I'd love to go to New Zealand,' Jenna said. 'Knocks my childhood holiday out of the park.'

'Okay, next one.' Lily clapped her hands. 'Film role you would love to have had. Jenna first.'

'Katniss Everdeen in *The Hunger Games*.'

'I could totally see you playing her,' Amanda said. 'Would have to dye your hair though. Katniss is totally dark-haired. Kick-ass role though.'

'How about you, Amanda?'

'Oh, there are so many amazing roles to choose from... Princess Leia, Hermione in *Harry Potter*, or Rey in *Star Wars*.'

'Lily?'

'I'd definitely go for a period film like *Elizabeth* – the Cate Blanchett version – anything where I can get my hair and make-up done and have incredible costumes.'

'You wouldn't get fed up of having to wear a corset?' Jenna asked.

'Probably, but I just love the theatrics of it.'

'I can see you as Elizabeth with your stunning red hair.'

Lily smiled and tucked a stray red curl behind her ear. 'You ask one, Amanda.'

'Okay,' she said slowly, drumming her fingers on the table and looking at Lily. 'Love of your life?'

'Easy. My boyfriend, hands down. You?'

'Matt Tulsa, a boy I met on holiday when I was thirteen. I fell completely head over heels in love with him.'

'Not your boyfriend?'

Amanda laughed. 'He comes a close second.' She looked across the table at Jenna. 'How about you?'

While listening to the others, Jenna had been trying to think who was the love of her life so far, and had come up with no one.

'I'm not actually sure. Perhaps I've not met him yet.'

'You've been in love though, right?' Lily asked. 'Had butterflies in your stomach when you see someone, want to spend every minute with them, your thoughts constantly consumed with them.'

'That could be seen as just lust, though, couldn't it?' Amanda said. 'Love is that feeling when you just know. It's hard to explain; I guess it might be different for everyone.'

Jenna bit her lip, realisation flooding through her that the only person who'd ever affected her in that way was Finn.

'Greatest acting ambition?' Lily moved the questions swiftly on, meaning Jenna had no time to dwell on the fact that Finn meant more to her than just a fling.

'By the way, Timothy and Ade should be here soon,' Lily said, once they'd exhausted their one-answer questions. 'We invited them, hope you don't mind?'

'Well technically they invited themselves.' Amanda sipped her wine. 'We saw them back at the hotel and were itching to do something this evening.'

'Is Milo coming?'

Lily shook her head. 'Don't think so.'

'Ah, yes of course.' Jenna sat back in her seat. 'Silly me, he'll be with Heidi.'

'Do you mind?' Amanda asked.

'You have to ask?' Jenna immediately felt the earlier tension return. 'I'm not with Milo, I don't want to be with him and I couldn't care less what Heidi gets up to.'

'Okay. Sorry for asking.' Lily folded her arms.

'It's just what it looks like, that's all, Jen. Lily wasn't meaning anything by it. We're just checking that you're okay.'

'Sorry, yes.' She gave Lily a weak smile. 'I didn't mean to snap – I'm just fed up with the whole situation. I attempted to talk to Milo this afternoon, but he's enjoying the attention too much to be bothered about how I'm feeling.'

'You know what you need to do…' Amanda placed a cool hand on Jenna's arm. 'Get laid, but like for real.'

'Amanda!' Jenna playfully slapped her arm.

She held her hands up. 'Sorry, it's just with all this gossip of affairs and "hot sex" with Milo, and you not actually getting any, I figured you might be a tad sexually frustrated.'

'Well, I lost my chance, didn't I, to do anything about that.'

'You've not spoken to Finn?' Lily asked.

'If you count arguing with him, then yes.'

'That bad, huh?' Amanda gave her a sympathetic look.

'He doesn't want to listen; and he doesn't believe me. He's been shown up in front of his friends. I think he's been hurt by a woman in the past and just saw red. The whole thing's a mess.'

'He'll calm down eventually, I'm sure. He'll see the truth and then it'll be fine.' Lily slid her arm across Jenna's shoulders.

'And by then we'll be done filming and leaving Cornwall for good. Realistically it was only ever going to be a one summer thing, so maybe I should just forget about him and move...'

'Hey ladies.' Timothy appeared by their table with a pint in his hand.

'You made it.' Lily smiled at him. 'Where's Ade?'

Timothy motioned across the bar. 'He's got a larger table over there, if you want to join him. I just need a minute with Jenna.'

Lily glanced at Amanda, then Jenna. 'Yeah, of course.' She patted Jenna's shoulder as she and Amanda picked up their drinks and headed across the bar.

Timothy sat down next to her. He clasped his hands around his pint and stared across the pub.

'Lily and Amanda said this was a decent place. They also said you bumped into that builder of yours here the other week.'

Jenna leant back against the cushioned seat. 'He's certainly not mine any longer. Milo put paid to that. And if you're here to threaten me into silence, then don't worry, I'm not going to say a thing. I don't bloody care what you and Milo get up to in private. What I do care about is being dragged into the situation and being lied about.'

Timothy placed his hand over hers. 'Jenna. I came over here to thank you. You have every right to go to the papers

179

and spill the beans and put the story straight, but you haven't. Who knows if they'd believe you or not, but as you well know, once gossip gets out there – whether true or made-up – it takes on a life of its own.'

'Do you mind? Milo behaving like this? Hiding your relationship, flirting with every girl he can lay his hands on?'

'If I want to be with him, that's just the way it is. On his terms.'

'It's sad, you know.'

'I know. A lot of things are sad. It's sad he feels the need to hide he's gay for fear of ruining his career.' Timothy picked up his pint and knocked it gently against Jenna's glass. 'Are me and you okay?'

'Yeah.'

'I never wanted you to get hurt, and honestly, Milo had the best intentions for you. Yes, you were unwittingly helping him, but he genuinely thought it would raise your profile and open up all sorts of opportunities. He hadn't factored in that you might be into someone.'

'It's not your fault, Timothy.' She touched his shoulder. 'And yeah, it's brought me opportunities but it's messed up my relationship with the first person I've really cared about in a long time. Without the truth – and trust me, he doesn't believe me – I can't see how I'm ever going to get him back. But like I just said to them.' Jenna indicated to where Lily and Amanda were talking to Ade on the other side of the pub. 'Maybe it's for the best; if I was with him I'd only end up with my heart broken by the end of the summer.'

'I'm really sorry, Jenna. Truly I am. The one thing I'm happy about though is that you're not shallow – I mean, Milo had you pigeon-holed as a blonde, blue-eyed, beautiful actress with a modelling background and figured you'd jump at the chance he was offering you. But you don't play by the rules, do you?'

'So, because I'm blonde and pretty he figured I'd sell my soul?'

'Heidi has.'

Jenna folded her arms. 'Yeah, well, I'm not Heidi. She

sold her soul a long time ago.'

'I heard there was bad blood between the two of you.'

'Nothing stays a secret, does it?' Jenna downed the rest of her gin. 'If you're truly sorry, then tell Milo to back down about me – leave me out of everything. If Heidi's willing to be gossip for him, then let her. You don't need me.'

Chapter Twenty-Three

It felt like the longest week since she'd got to Cornwall. Jenna hated wishing time away but with most of Friday off, she decided to go home and visit her parents. She'd not seen them since filming began and she was craving normality and home comforts.

It was odd driving away from the winding narrow roads, leaving behind picturesque fishermen's cottages and the glinting blue of the sea for motorways edged by fields, which eventually turned into the built-up city she was used to. Home. Except, as she let herself into her flat and closed the door on the traffic and exhaust fumes, she realised she'd never felt less at home. Most of her clothes were down at the cottage in Cornwall, and as she was renting a furnished place, she actually had few belongings of her own: a handful photos, a toaster and a kettle didn't really make a home. Her parents had insisted she stay with them for the weekend, and apart from checking her flat and collecting her post, she wasn't going to hang about.

After spending weeks in the cottage in Cornwall, she knew she never really thought of her flat as home. It was a place to crash after a long day, but that was about it – unlike Bramble Cottage, a place she'd truly fallen in love with. She closed the door to her flat and locked it. The communal hallway smelt damp and stale and the carpet was grubby from numerous feet and tyre marks. Two bikes leant against the tired-looking cream wall. She gathered the post that had been left out for her on the shelf above the radiator. Not that it was ever actually on. In winter, the hallway was cold and unwelcoming, and she was always glad to get into her small but warm flat.

Jenna got back into her car and drummed her fingers on the steering wheel, delaying getting going in the rush hour traffic. She felt foolish, at the age of twenty-seven, being worried about seeing her parents, but they weren't used to witnessing their daughter's supposed love life played out in the media. She wasn't used to it either. She wasn't used to paparazzi shouting her name and trying to get a reaction as she left set. Everything about the last couple of weeks was far removed from her normal life. Her taste of fame was not as exciting as she thought it would be.

She pulled up outside her parents' house and switched off the engine. She hesitated, acknowledging that the sick feeling in her stomach was the thought of her parents being disappointed in her. She got out, her legs still stiff from hours spent driving and grabbed her overnight bag from the boot. Her mum had the door open and was standing on the step before Jenna made it halfway up the garden path.

'Hiya, love.' Her mum wrapped her in a hug. Jenna sank into her arms realising how much she'd needed to see her parents. Kath pulled away and looked her up and down. 'Are you okay? You look tired.'

'It's a long drive.'

'A cuppa is what you need.' She ushered her into the hallway and closed the front door behind them.

Jenna left her bag on the floor and followed her mum into the kitchen. She sat at the table while her mum fussed about, switching on the kettle, pulling two mugs from the cupboard and dropping in teabags.

'Where's Dad?'

'Not back from work yet.'

Jenna looked at her watch. 'I've kinda lost track of time today.'

'Were you filming this morning?' Kath slid the biscuit tin across the table.

'Only for an hour.'

'Well, at least you can have a rest for a day or two now, can't you.'

Jenna nodded and hunted about in the tin for a chocolate digestive.

'Have they been feeding you well on set?'

'We always get fed well, so yes. I've been eating if that's what you're worried about.'

Kath placed two cups of tea on the table and sat down. 'I'm not worried about that. Well, I am worried; I'm worried because I know how stress and anxiety have affected you in the past. And the last time I spoke to you, well, you sounded *so* stressed.'

It was the elephant in the room, her mum skirting around the topic Jenna knew she was dying to talk about.

Jenna dunked a digestive in her tea. 'I assume you've seen the latest gossip?'

Kath nodded and cupped her hands round her tea. Her knuckles turned white. 'About you, Milo and Heidi. How did she get dragged into all of this?'

'She dragged herself in – actually no, there was no dragging needed. She wants the attention.'

'So she's really with Milo?'

'As much as anyone can be with Milo.'

'What does that mean?'

'Nothing. I'm not with Milo, never have been, never will be. I don't care what Milo and Heidi get up to, I just want to be left out of everything.'

Jenna watched her mum sip her tea; she knew she was trying to work out what to say.

'What about your agent. What has she said about the situation?'

'Oh, she loves it. She's had offers pouring in.'

'Really? Well, that's good, isn't it?'

'Sort of.'

'What have you been offered?'

'Well, that's the problem, it's mostly been reality TV.'

'Okay…'

'The main one being *The Love Hotel.*'

'Oh.' Her mum's eyes widened. 'That's quite an opportunity, isn't it?'

'It pays loads. Super high profile.'

'You don't sound sure.'

'I don't really feel sure about anything. What do you think? What would Dad think about it?'

'Your dad will say go for it – you know what he's like, always one for jumping in headfirst and thinking about it afterwards.'

'And you?'

'I don't know what to think really. You don't sound happy about it, but then the amount of attention you've received because of this Milo Blake thing… The truth is, I'm worried about you, love. You were so happy when you first went down to Cornwall, and now, I don't know. You seem to have the weight of the world on your shoulders. I don't think I'm in the best position to advise what you should or shouldn't do. What do your friends say? People you know in the business? They're the best ones to judge.'

'Everyone can see both sides – the good and bad. It could be the best thing ever or it could destroy everything I've worked hard for.'

Kath tipped her head back and closed her eyes. 'What is it they say? You only regret the things you don't do, not the things you do.' She looked directly at Jenna.

'So you're saying I should do it?'

Kath placed a warm hand on her arm. 'I'm not sure what I'm saying. I guess I can't say I like the idea of you parading about on TV…'

'It's not parading…'

Kath shot her a look. 'They're half naked most of the time; I've seen the show, it's all about sex and flouncing about in a bikini. But what I think shouldn't stop you from doing it, if that's what you really want. You're young and beautiful, Jenna. What young woman wouldn't go for that kind of opportunity? I mean, if I was thirty years younger, as gorgeous as you and single, well…' She raised an eyebrow.

Jenna stood up and went over to the sink. She leant on

the side and looked out across the garden. The olive tree she'd bought for her parents' thirtieth wedding anniversary last year was doing well, its silvery green leaves looking beautiful beneath the late afternoon sun.

She turned back to her mum. 'I already said yes to it.'

'Oh, you did. Well, that's fine then, isn't it, love? Your decision's made.'

Jenna bit her lip. Was that disappointment in her mum's voice? Or maybe it was worry. Her parents would support her whatever she did, wouldn't they?

Kath scraped her chair back. 'Well, your dad will be back soon. We thought we'd get a takeaway this evening. You can invite Carla over if you like.'

Jenna nodded, downed her tea and took her bag up to her old bedroom, which was now another spare room. It didn't take long to unpack. She messaged Carla about coming over and immediately got a reply, simply saying, 'hell yeah!'

Jenna was glad of Carla's reassuring presence as they sat together at the dining table, half-empty trays of curry between them. Carla had been a staple in their lives since Jenna was eighteen and had started drama school, but it felt like they'd known each other longer than that.

Kath broke off a piece of poppadum and turned to Carla. 'What do you think of all this stuff going on with Milo then?'

'Honestly, I'm conflicted. I keep thinking what I'd do if I was in her position. I mean, Milo wouldn't touch me with a bargepole. I'm not his type.' She winked at Jenna. 'The wrong kind of blonde, too many tattoos and piercings for his liking. But if I looked like Jenna I'd probably lap up the attention and accept the opportunities with open arms – but that's because I'm not used to it.'

The tips of her faded pink hair were dyed purple, a change since the last time Jenna had seen her. Jenna hated the way she thought of her 'girl next door' looks as a curse rather than a blessing. She'd had so many people being jealous of her over the years, when at times she'd have traded it all in to look like Carla, beautiful in her own way: individual and full of character. She was cursed by being the perceived idea of beauty. She had nothing to complain about and yet she felt trapped by her looks into being something she wasn't.

Carla glanced between Kath and Tony. 'Milo's a sleazeball playing Jenna and Heidi against each other.'

'But why's he doing it?' Kath frowned. 'He's famous enough as it is. Why does he need the extra attention?'

Carla scooped up a forkful of pilau rice. 'Because he can.'

Jenna played around with the food left on her plate. It was difficult to explain the reasoning behind Milo's actions without spilling the truth. Maybe she should? Why the hell was she protecting him? She gripped her fork tighter and skewered a piece of onion bhaji. She knew why, because as easily as he could raise her profile and help her get offers and auditions, he could destroy her too. She could lose everything she'd worked so hard for. There was no way Milo would allow her to reveal the truth without hurting her for it. She could trust her parents to stay quiet, the same way she could trust Carla, but what if they told Denise next door – she'd be happy to sell the gossip to the highest bidder the moment her mum said anything. No, she had to skirt round the truth, not just to protect Milo, but to protect herself too.

Jenna piled the empty plates together and her mum took them over to the kitchen sink.

'Anyone want coffee?' she called back.

'I'll have one, love.' Tony stood up, patted Jenna's shoulder, and went and sat in his armchair by the TV.

'Decaf for me please, Kath.'

'Jenna, you want anything?'

'Camomile tea, please.'

'You have a permanent frown on your face, Jenna.' Carla leaned closer and put her hands on Jenna's. 'It doesn't suit you. You're my happy easy-going friend; I'm the one who should be all angst-ridden.'

Tony turned on the TV and flicked through the channels. The kettle started to boil and Kath pottered about getting cups out of cupboards.

Jenna gritted her teeth. 'I'm expected to act a certain way because I look a certain way. You've just said it – I can't possibly be gloomy and emotional because I'm a bubbly blonde.'

'I'm sorry, Jenna, I didn't mean it like that…'

Jenna shook her head. 'No, it's fine. I know you didn't. But I'm typecast in real life as well as for roles. I'm expected to behave and react a certain way because I'm a bloody blonde actress. Milo expected me to lap up the attention and got a shock when I didn't.' Jenna gazed past Carla at her mum pouring boiling water into mugs. 'All this shit with Milo has taken over my life; it's all I can think about. It's driving me mad.' Carla's hands squeezed tighter over hers. Jenna looked at her friend. 'If I'm feeling this uncomfortable about a story that's bullshit, do I really want to be famous? I mean famous for fame's sake?'

'Well, I guess you need to ask yourself why you wanted to be an actor. Was it for the love of the craft or the idea of celebrity, being someone?'

'Can't you "be someone" without having to be famous?'

'Of course you can, but unfortunately we now live in a society where being famous because you're pretty or an actress, a model, or because you take your clothes off or go on reality TV, is given more importance than being a nurse or a paramedic, a scientist, a humanitarian. In fact, it's given more importance than just about anything.'

'That's not right, is it?'

'Of course it's not, but it's the world we live in. Reality TV, fake news, Trump as President and Brexit. I mean, it's all gone to shit. But play the game right, Jen, and you'll make millions, but you might have to sell your soul in the process.'

Chapter Twenty-Four

The drive back to Cornwall felt even longer. On her way to Surrey, she'd been looking forward to seeing her parents and staying with them, and now she was heading back to an empty cottage and the prospect of work the next day. The holiday traffic didn't help, and she ended up crawling along the motorway with lorries, caravans and camper vans heading in both directions. She'd been mad to travel this distance in such a short space of time, but she'd been homesick. She'd hoped her visit would have made things clearer, and although she felt like it had been a break – however brief – somehow she was even more confused.

Jenna knew her parents would support her whatever she decided to do. Her mum had been right; it was Jenna's life and she needed to make a decision based on what she wanted, and not be influenced by her parents. They weren't going to stop her, but it didn't mean they were going to like it.

The thoughts that continued to swirl around her head eased a little as she reached Cornwall. As the roads narrowed and the surroundings became greener, she felt calmer. But she didn't go straight to Bramble Cottage, instead she headed to the coast and the beach Finn had taken her to. She parked in the same car park and checked the time; she had a couple of hours before it started getting dark. She grabbed her shoulder bag and a bottle of water and set off, finding the path through the long grasses that led away from the busy beach in front. Her feet pounded the sandy path and she was glad she'd thrown a jumper on over her T-shirt. Her legs were bare in denim shorts and the grass tickled as she walked. The further she went, the quieter it became, the sound of people and cars disappearing as she rounded the headland. The view was as stunning as the first time she'd seen it with Finn. The rugged coastline from high on the cliff was bathed in a golden light.

She waited at the top of the steps to the beach to let a family go past, parents and three kids with an assortment of rucksacks and bags, with colourful nets poking out of the top of the dad's bag. They smiled and said hello as they went by, probably off to get changed before going out to a pub for Sunday dinner. Maybe they were lucky enough to be staying in one of the hillside holiday houses with their far-reaching sea views.

As Jenna started down the steep stepped path, her stomach rumbled. It had been a long time ago since she'd eaten a sad-looking sandwich at a service station on the M5. She'd do anything for a roast dinner right now. Like the roast she'd had at Finn's parents' back when life had been so damn good. She wished Finn was with her now, his broad shoulders and windswept blonde hair leading the way. He'd stopped at the awkward steep bits and held his hand out to help her down. She made it down now in one piece, jumping the last bit and landing on soft pale sand. She knew she was torturing herself by coming here when the memories of Finn were still fresh. She kept walking anyway, planting footprints into the damp sand.

The cove was empty, still and quiet, no voices, only the gentle waves bubbling on to the sand. Jenna relished the peace after the last couple of weeks of being surrounded by people intent on knowing every detail about her life, her past, her relationships. Her taste of fame was not what she'd been dreaming about since drama school. It wasn't Oscar-worthy, scene-stealing fame, but fame for seemingly hooking up with someone who actually was famous. She ploughed across the sand, giving herself time to think. She could choose the reality TV route and the potential of what it might lead to – a bigger profile and better roles. There were possibilities that was for sure, but would it be worth it? What if it backfired and messed up her acting career? What if she ended up selling out for money and fame rather than knuckling down and working hard to gain roles because of her talent? Or her looks?

She sat down and wrapped her arms around her bare knees. The sea was so clear and blue, a turquoise shimmer in the late afternoon sunshine. The location should have lifted her spirits. Part of her wanted to wallow in self-pity, but the other half felt like she should embrace the opportunity. Would she really be selling her soul? Other people would jump at the chance. Without a doubt, Heidi would.

Maybe she should be more like her, more ruthless in her ambition for fame and fortune, whatever the cost. Acting was what she'd always wanted to do and success on a big scale went hand in hand with fame. But was it the only thing she wanted to do with her life? She thought back to her conversation with Ade – there was a time limit to the kind of success she could have as a young actor.

It was late, and quite cool despite the sun shining in a nearly cloudless blue sky. A breeze swept in off the sea, wrapping itself around her. Goosebumps formed on her legs. Everything about this place reminded her of Finn. They'd hiked together over grassy clifftops, taking in the view of glimmering sea and craggy cliffs, pockets of sandy beaches and seaside cottages. They'd walked along the beach hand in hand, leaving footprints. They'd dangled their feet in rock pools and watched shadowy fish swim past their toes and spied crabs in crevices, while seaweed swayed beneath the clear saltwater. They'd kissed in the shadows of an outcrop of rocks, their hands exploring each other. They'd laid down together and gazed up at the bluest sky which had only a wisp of white cloud that looked like it had been brushed on by mistake. They'd kept their fingers entwined, holding on to each other not wanting the day to end or anyone to spoil their peace. She'd lost all that to fame. No, actually to notoriety. She wasn't famous; Milo was. She'd become infamous because as far as anyone who didn't know her was concerned, she'd slept with Milo to further her career. A lie had the same effect as truth, and now it was doing wonders for Heidi, except Milo had taken it one step further with her. Jenna knew it would all end in tears, for Heidi at least, if not for Milo.

There was a reason she felt this disconcerted and unsure about everything. There'd been moments over the past few years where she'd questioned what she was doing particularly when she'd landed certain roles – the hooker who was murdered in a back street; the clubber grinding against a semi-naked man; the babysitter who seduced the dad. She got those roles because she looked the way she did. That had been playing on her mind all weekend. From a young age friends had told her she had what it took to be a model, but apart from dabbling in modelling to pay her way through drama school, acting was what she'd wanted to do – at least what she thought she wanted to do. Those roles allowed her to at least play a character, not a version of herself.

Jenna stood up and wiped away the sand stuck to her shorts. She knew what she needed to do. The stress she'd felt over the last couple of weeks had manifested itself this weekend in worry about herself, about what her family would think about the choices she was making. Her parents' friends who'd known her since she was little would be able to watch her on TV 'parading about in a bikini'. Her friends would all have their own opinion – those who supported her, and those who would sneer and gossip about her 'selling out', swapping serious acting roles for reality TV. But actually it didn't matter what anyone else thought as it was her choice to make. What had finally occurred to her, while sitting on an empty beach staring out at the wide endless sea, was how *she* really felt about that choice.

The tension in her chest built up again on the drive back, but by the time she turned into Bramble Cottage's drive her pounding heart had slowed. It was almost dark, the sun was low on the horizon, the trees edging the garden silhouetted against the softening scarlet, amber and gold light. She grabbed her overnight bag from the boot and walked to the front of the cottage, her trainers crunching on the gravel the only sound apart from the soft cooing of wood pigeons. It was funny, considering how desperate she'd been to leave just over forty-eight hours earlier, she was so glad to come back. It felt like home.

The moment she got inside, closed the front door and turned on the kitchen light, tiredness and hunger washed over her. It had been a long day, driving all that way, followed by the detour to the beach. She couldn't be bothered to cook anything, and her earlier dream of a Sunday roast would remain just that; she wasn't going to go out again. She ate a bowl of cereal and watched *Live at the Apollo* but even that failed to make her laugh. She forced herself to not look at Facebook, Twitter or Instagram. She contemplated texting Finn but had no clue what to actually say, so she switched off her mobile.

However much Jenna wanted to make her decision permanent, it was far too late to phone her agent, particularly to give her bad news on a Sunday evening. Instead she went to bed and slept fitfully, with the thought that it was her last week of filming *and* she was about to turn down potentially the biggest opportunity of her life.

Jenna made the phone call on her hands free while driving to base the next morning. Beth wasn't even in work yet, and they ended up having to hold the conversation while on her commute into central London.

'I know I'm supposed to sign the contract for *The Love Hotel* when I'm back in London next week, but I can't. I've thought long and hard about this, but I can't be on the show. I don't want the scrutiny, I don't want to be talked about and pulled apart in the media in the way I have over the last couple of weeks. I'm so sorry, Beth. It's just not for me, however much an opportunity it may be career-wise. I'm not going to commit to something when it feels so wrong.'

The disappointment in her agent's voice was obvious. Ultimately Jenna knew it was her decision to make, and yet she couldn't shake off the feeling that she was letting down herself, her agent, her friends, her ambition, even Milo bloody Blake for giving her the opportunity to begin with, however twisted that seemed. Yes, it was her life, her career, yet it also meant Beth losing out on fifteen per cent of a huge pay cheque. It was her agent's career too. Maybe she was foolish. So many well-meaning friends had told her to jump at the chance and take the money. Who knew what opportunities that sort of high profile exposure would lead to? She'd been trying to live by the mantra of saying yes to everything even if it terrified her, but this opportunity had left her with a feeling of vulnerability. Being plastered over the front of *Hot Now Magazine* she'd experienced that kind of exposure and didn't like it one bit.

Jenna clenched her fists, drew in a deep breath and expelled it slowly. She didn't like letting people down, particularly Beth who'd worked so hard to get her to where she was in her career, but she couldn't ignore her gut feeling. Whether she ended up regretting her decision in weeks or even years to come, she knew it was the right one to make. At least it was for now.

Chapter Twenty-Five

'I can't believe it's our last week.' Lily sat down with a thump opposite Jenna and Amanda, making her plate of Moroccan chicken and couscous jump a little on the tray. 'I'm going to miss everything about it, the place, the filming, the cast and crew, but most of all you guys.'

'We'll all be back in London next week; we can still see each other. Friends forever, right?' Jenna put her hand in the middle of the table and laughing, Amanda and Lily put theirs on top.

'Too right, you're not going to get rid of me that easily.' Lily winked.

'You are both staying until the end of the week though?' Amanda bit into an apple. 'I'm gutted I'm wrapping before you both,' she said through a mouthful of fruit.

'Well I'm wrapping tomorrow so it's only one extra day. When do you finish again, Jen?'

'Friday.'

Three more days of filming and then that would be it, her summer on a movie in Cornwall would be over and she'd be heading back to the smog and noise of London.

'Can I join you?'

Apart from the familiarity of her voice, it was the waft of Marc Jacobs Daisy Dream perfume that let Jenna know it was Heidi standing behind her. She caught a knowing glance between Lily and Amanda.

'If you like.' Jenna motioned to the empty chair next to her.

Heidi put her plate on the table and sat next to Jenna. She opened the ring pull on her can of Diet Coke.

Their easy conversation had stopped, and Jenna could tell from Lily and Amanda's expressions that they were at a loss at what to say. To make it even more awkward all they now needed was Milo to join them.

'I wrap this afternoon,' Heidi said, digging a fork into her chicken salad. 'I've got a costume fitting and an audition in London on Thursday. Thought this might be the last chance we get to talk.'

'Okay then, so talk.' Jenna didn't feel like making polite conversation with Heidi; but if she wanted to say something then she wasn't going to stop her.

'I miss talking to you, Jenna. I miss knowing what's going on in your life…'

'Everyone knows what's going on in my life. It's been splashed all over the internet.'

'I mean what's really going on with you.'

Jenna caught Lily's eye from across the table. 'There's nothing going on besides working on this film and being at the cottage. That's it, that's my life – until I go home on the weekend. Then it's back to the endless cycle of auditions, castings, meetings, filming, promo. Rinse, repeat. You know the drill.' She moved the couscous around her plate, her appetite gone.

Lily started talking to Amanda, giving Heidi the chance to lean closer to Jenna. 'I know you've not forgiven me for the Bond thing, but are you okay about me and Milo? I really don't want our friendship to be strained any more than it…'

'Are you serious?' Jenna turned to face her. She lowered her voice, even with the amount of background chatter and Lily and Amanda no longer listening in, she was aware of so many people surrounding them. 'You set me up – the other evening at the hotel, you knew there'd be a photographer there, knew they'd be taking photos of us.'

'I didn't know that was going to happen, honestly I didn't.' She placed her hand on Jenna's arm. She was still wearing the oversized silver ring Jenna had given her for her twenty-first birthday.

'Really? You had nothing to do with it?'

Heidi's eyes dropped from Jenna's. 'It wasn't my idea. Milo had been talking about you and he kinda suggested that we should meet up, get all our past shit out in the open. It was something I'd been meaning to do anyway. I don't want us to be like this, act like strangers and never talk.'

'Well, you've been going about making amends in totally the wrong way, Heidi. All I see is you putting your career first, every single time. It's the reason you're cosying up to Milo, despite thinking he was with me.'

Heidi shook her head. 'You've got that wrong. Don't forget, I know you, Jen. I knew you weren't into Milo. Yeah he's good looking but he's not your type.'

'And what's he been saying to you? That I'm not interested in him or simply that he likes you more?'

'He's the biggest flirt on the planet, Jenna. He flirted with you, he's flirting with me. He flirts with everyone. You're not actually with him and I'm single, so there's no problem, is there?'

'So, if you're heading home tomorrow, is whatever you're supposed to have with Milo over?'

'Nope, I'm coming back on Friday, going to stay until the end of the shoot and then head back to London.'

'And so what's the actual deal with you and Milo? Are you sleeping with him?' Jenna held her gaze, wondering if she was going to lie to her about that as well.

'Does it really matter if I am or not?'

Jenna bit her lip. She had no clue if Heidi knew if Milo was gay. And how far would he take things to make the press believe his cover story? After all he really had kissed Heidi. Jenna sighed, it wasn't her problem. Heidi was a big girl; she could deal with Milo Blake on her own.

'I hear you've said no to *The Love Hotel.*'

Jenna swung back to Heidi. 'How the hell do you know?'

'Tabitha told me.' She glanced sideways at Jenna and stuck her fork in a piece of chicken. 'Our agents talk, Jen. They work in the same flipping office. Are you sure you don't want to do it?'

'I'm certain; the relief I felt once I told Beth was immense.'

'We could have been on it together. How much fun would that be?'

'You're doing it?' Jenna shook her head. 'I should have known.'

'Not for definite, no. Tabitha's setting up a meeting with the producers. She's convinced they'll be gutted that you've pulled out…'

'And let me guess, she's going to sell you as the alternative; Milo's new fling; a sexy blonde actress.' Jenna threw her fork down on her half-finished plate of food. 'Oh Heidi, I really hope you know what you're doing.'

Jenna thought she knew Heidi. They'd clicked from the minute they'd met at drama school, and instead of being rivals they'd become firm friends. But when she really thought back on their friendship, there had been signs of a rivalry from early on. Just little things in the way Heidi would draw attention to herself – if they were both wearing skirts, Heidi's would be shorter; if they found themselves among a group of blokes on a night out, Heidi would be louder and flirt more. Jenna had always put it down to personality – despite them both being drama students, Heidi was more outgoing, the attention seeker. And over the years, despite Carla being the opposite of both her and Heidi, Jenna realised now they'd built a stronger bond. She was dependable and straightforward. Maybe it was easier because being so different there never was any risk of rivalry. She also knew that Carla fancied Heidi. It was the big boobs and big personality, and even if she fancied Jenna, she hid it well, knowing that their friendship came first and she didn't want to ruin that.

Jenna had no clue how she and Heidi were ever going to repair their friendship, or if they ever would. Without a doubt their relationship had changed and the closeness they once had was gone forever. She was relieved when Heidi was wrapped that afternoon and on her way back to London. She was one less thing to contend with. The remaining days ticked by, the countdown to the end, and there were tears when each of the cast wrapped. The end of the summer brought the end of an unforgettable few weeks' filming.

It was also her last chance with Finn. Since he'd gutted the fireplace, the dirty, dust-filled room had been stripped bare and cleaned, the walls had been plastered and an undercoat had been put on. With early call times all week she'd been out before Finn and Gary arrived in the morning and got back after they'd left, the only evidence they'd been at the cottage the smell of wet paint.

On Thursday she was unexpectedly wrapped early and with her heart beating in anticipation of catching Finn before he left, she drove straight back to the cottage. The van was still in the drive. Jenna parked next to it and walked up the path. She wondered if Finn would be on his own, but wasn't sure if she'd prefer Gary to be here or not. She faltered outside the open front door, took a deep breath, strode in and collided with Gary.

'Sorry, Jenna, didn't mean to walk right into you.' He motioned towards the living room. 'Finn's in there; I'm just getting something from the van.' He gave her a knowing smile, brushed past her and disappeared out of the front door.

Jenna took another deep breath. Now she had to talk to Finn.

She walked over to the living room and hovered in the doorway. There was a massive improvement from the week before. The room was bright and clean and old sheets covered what little furniture there was. Finn had his back to her, painting the wall to the left of the opened-up fireplace.

'Hey there,' she said quietly. 'I wrapped early. Was hoping to catch you before you finished.'

Finn slapped the remainder of paint on the wall and turned to her.

The frown on his face made her falter.

'I, um… I was er, really hoping we could talk. Maybe go out for a drink…'

'Jenna, what's the point? Aren't you leaving soon?'

'Saturday.'

'Well, then, what more's there to say? You messed me around just like every other girl. You're leaving in a couple of days. End of.' He dipped the brush into the Farrow and Ball paint her parents had chosen called Sudbury Yellow, and turned his back on her again.

'And you're being a dick, you realise that right?' she muttered as she left the room.

She wanted to scream in frustration at his inability to allow her to talk. But he was right when he'd said what was the point. It was back to real life next week. It was the briefest of summer flings that had ended in tears before it had really started, and all she was left with was the memory of watching him work on the cottage and two blissful days together.

'And that's a wrap for Jenna!'

Cast and crew clapped as the director shook Jenna's hand. She could only imagine the wrench of leaving a long-running series; she'd been working on the film for eight weeks, a short time in the scheme of things, yet it felt a monumental time in her life. Part of her was relieved it was over, the other part was anxious about the future. She had a casting for another film the week she got back, and then the following week she was jetting off to Ibiza to film an advert for a travel company – both off the back of the made-up feature about her and Milo. But then of course, once the gossip about them died down, it would be back to the endless cycle of auditions, luck and looking right for the part. She'd turned down the biggest opportunity she'd ever had – financially at least – so next year, instead of a huge job waiting for her, her diary was pretty empty.

It wasn't the final day of filming, just the last day of filming for her, and as she walked from the minibus back to the costume tent, everything was continuing as normal with a handful of crew grabbing a late lunch and extras in costume getting on another minibus to take them to location. Apart from Milo and a couple of the other principal actors, most people had finished, and so there was a wrap party at the hotel later.

Jenna arrived at the hotel fashionably late. A taxi dropped her off and she'd already booked one to take her home later – she needed to drink tonight, let her hair down and celebrate the end of a crazy few weeks. She wasn't sure if the party was taking place inside or out, so she made her way to the bar first. It was pretty empty apart from a middle-aged couple not associated with the film, and Timothy ordering a drink. He spotted her and waved her over.

'What you having, Jenna?'

'Oh, a gin and tonic for me, please.' She joined him up at the bar.

'You're not driving tonight then?'

'No way; I feel like I deserve to celebrate.'

'You and me both.' He passed her the gin, handed the barman a note, picked up his beer and knocked it against Jenna's glass. 'To the end of filming.'

'I can't believe it's over – well for us at least.'

'Tell me about it.' He slid off the bar stool. 'Everyone else is outside.'

They walked out together, back into the beautiful August evening. The light was beginning to fade, the sky clear and starlit, the air warm. Among the cast and crew, Jenna spotted Lily and Amanda on the other side of the terrace. She was about to make her way over when Timothy put his hand on her arm.

'I've had a chat with Milo.' He led her to an empty table on the edge of the terrace, pulled out two chairs and they sat down.

'He won't go back on what's already been said, I'm so sorry, Jenna. If it's any consolation I've made him promise that he doesn't mention you in the press again, at least not "romantically". He's got Heidi for all that now.' Timothy looked away, a wobble in his voice as if the words were difficult to say.

Jenna took his hand in hers. She really felt for him, having to keep his feelings secret, and his relationship with Milo reduced to them creeping around in the middle of the night to see each other. Carla had been right; it must be exhausting to keep up the pretence. And for how long? What if they wanted to take their relationship to the next level? Move in together or even get married? It would never happen, not while Milo clung on to his lies to keep himself firmly in the limelight.

Jenna squeezed his hand. 'You okay?'

He nodded. 'It is what it is.'

A slight breeze swept in off the sea. The water glimmered red and gold from the fading sun. The terrace was edged by solar lights, and warm light spilt from the hotel.

'How's things with your builder?' Timothy asked.

'He's not my builder.'

'You know what I mean.'

'They're non-existent. He won't talk to me; he won't listen. He's been shown up in front of his friends and family because of everything in the media.' She stopped and frowned. 'You know this already. Why ask if Milo's not going to put the record straight?'

'I just really hoped you'd made up with him, that's all.'

'Fat chance of that, but it doesn't matter now. I'll be heading home tomorrow.'

'He lives round here, does he?'

'Yeah, in Mullion with his parents, so not far from here. He wants to move out but it's expensive. He's kinda got a good thing working with his dad, and they live in this amazing new-build in a quiet little cul-de-sac on the edge of the village. I'm not sure I'd want to move to some crappy little flat miles from the sea either.' She looked at Timothy and shook her head. 'Why the hell am I even talking about him? It's over. It was over before anything really started.'

'He's still with his parents, huh?'

'Circumstances. His folks are lovely though.'

'You've met them?'

'Had Sunday dinner at their house. Pretty certain that's why he's so pissed at me – one day he's introducing me to his parents, the next day I was splashed across *Hot Now Magazine* in a bikini with Milo. He's had his heart broken before and I know he thinks I've made a fool of him.' Jenna pulled her hand from Timothy's. 'I'm fed up talking about it, the whole situation makes my blood boil and I want to enjoy tonight.'

'I'm sorry, truly I am.'

Jenna grabbed her drink and stood up. 'Timothy, it's really not your fault. Don't beat yourself up about it; Milo sure as hell isn't.'

Jenna clocked him sidling on to the terrace with Heidi. So she'd kept her promise of returning after a casting in London, back for more photo opportunities with Milo. It must be heartbreaking for Timothy to watch the person he loved cosying up with a woman he didn't actually fancy. Milo had his arm around Heidi's waist and a beer clutched in his other hand as they chatted to the first assistant director and one of the producers. Timothy was watching them. A frown darkened his handsome face. Jenna wanted to slap Milo on Timothy's behalf. Not that it would do any good. Timothy was fully aware of what Milo was doing, and if he wasn't comfortable with it, he was old enough to deal with it himself. She just couldn't help feel sorry for the guy, a far more sensitive and thoughtful person than Milo deserved.

She squeezed Timothy's shoulder. 'I'm going to see Lily and Amanda.' She motioned to the lawn. 'Want to join us?'

'I will, in a bit… I just need to do something…' He stood abruptly and walked across the terrace, away from Milo and Heidi, and disappeared through the open doors of the hotel's bar.

Chapter Twenty-Six

It felt strange, wandering around the cottage for the last time after calling it home for two months. She wondered if Aunt Vi would have approved of the changes made to her home. Jenna ran her fingers along the oak mantel that Finn had uncovered when he knocked the fireplace out. The thought crossed her mind that she could end up growing old on her own just as her great aunt had. She wiped away a tear. She was being silly and emotional; it wasn't like she'd never meet anyone else or never come here again. It belonged to her parents and she could have a holiday down here whenever the place was free. And it would be ready to rent out soon. The outside was finished, the upstairs too with its beautiful new bathroom, spacious landing, freshly plastered and painted bedrooms, and polished wooden floors. Downstairs the fireplace in the living room had been restored to its former glory, ready for a wood burner to be bought and fitted. Jenna had a flashback to the argument in the dust-covered room, the lump hammer clutched in Finn's fist while he'd been hacking away at the old 1960s tiled fire surround. Jenna wiped away another tear and closed the living room door with a bang.

There was only the kitchen left to do and that was scheduled for next week when she was back in London. The old kitchen was being ripped out and replaced, but the lovely old butler sink and the flagstone floor were remaining, the old married with the new.

Her head thumped with a wine and gin hangover from the night before. She'd already had two strong black coffees and the thought of driving all the way home didn't fill her with joy.

Jenna placed a bottle of wine and chocolates on the kitchen table, along with two envelopes; one for Gary, the other for Finn. Gary's was to thank him for all the work they'd done on the cottage, and Finn's, well Finn's had taken most of the morning to write. In the end she opted for something short and truthful. She ran her fingers across Finn's name. She was being bloody soppy over someone she'd barely got to know, someone she'd only spent a couple of days with in a summer filled with new friends and film stars.

She leant the envelopes against the bottle and went outside. She wished it was raining; it would make it easier to leave if it was miserable. Instead, it was a charmed day, warm yet fresh with blue sky and sunshine. Tears welled again as she wandered around the garden and took in the neat lawn edged by a defined border; the jumble of undergrowth and brambles tamed to reveal the beauty of what lay beneath; lavender, hebes and gladioli bringing splashes of colour to beneath the trees which cast long shadows over the sunny lawn. There was still lots of work to do; she hadn't had the chance to tackle the wooded area of the garden, but the transformation was immense.

Her suitcase and bag were packed, but as she stood in the middle of the lawn with her hands on her hips, eyes closed, head tilted back relishing the warmth of the sun on her face, she was reluctant to leave. She wasn't sure that she wanted to go back to the monotony of castings, auditions, long filming days and working on a different job from one week to the next. She'd loved the stability of the summer, knowing where she'd be each day and what she'd be doing. Despite the drama that had ensued over the last few weeks, she'd got to know the cast and had made new friends. But it was over. It was back to her tiny flat with no garden and a road choked with traffic, all the things this summer had promised an escape from.

Birds twittered in the trees and she watched them swoop across the garden. She'd hung a bird feeder on a branch of a tree close to the cottage, so she could watch the birds from the kitchen window.

Jenna shoved her hands in the pockets of her denim skirt and walked round to the front. She'd feed the birds, then go. She found the birdseed tub in the cupboard below the sink and took it outside. She started to fill one of the feeders when a vehicle pulled into the drive. She frowned. It was Saturday. She wasn't expecting anyone, unless Lily had decided to call in on her way home but that was unlikely, and Amanda's boyfriend wasn't driving down until later. A car door slammed, just one. A tingle shot across Jenna's shoulders. Footsteps crunched over gravel. She dumped the birdseed tub on the grass and raced around to the front of the cottage. There was no one there.

'Hello?'

Finn's voice from inside the cottage made her heart falter. 'Out here!'

He appeared in the doorway, his blonde hair ruffled, and a familiar cream Ripcurl T-shirt hugged his chest. 'I thought I wouldn't get here before you left,' he said, breathlessly.

'Oh?' Jenna shielded her eyes from the sun with her hand. 'You're about to leave?'

'Uh huh.' Jenna met his blue eyes. He seemed to be less angry than the last time she'd seen him, his face more open, happier, like he'd be willing to talk. 'I was just feeding the birds.'

They looked at each other, their silence only interrupted by birdsong and a breeze rustling branches.

Jenna put her hands in her pockets. 'Why are you here?'

'An actor from your film came over last night. Timothy.'

'He did what?'

'He was feeling massively guilty about you.'

Jenna remembered back to the night before and how conflicted he'd been. He'd said he needed to do something. Is that what he'd meant? She'd been too wrapped up in celebrating with Lily and Amanda to notice if Timothy had been there or not. 'How did he even know where you lived?'

'He found out from the pub landlord – it's a small enough place, everyone knows everyone.'

Jenna wasn't used to that. Where she lived, she only knew the person who lived in the flat opposite to say hello to, and she had no clue who lived above her.

'Why did he want to see you?' She hoped she knew the answer but she held her breath anyway.

'To explain everything – the whole situation with you and Milo. Or not as it turned out.' He watched her intently and her heart thudded faster at his words. 'He said the whole thing had been a set-up, from Milo handpicking you for the role, all the flirting, and a photographer being paid to take suggestive photos.'

Jenna bit her lip in an attempt to contain her emotions. 'Did he tell you why Milo did it?'

'He was totally upfront to the point he had bloody photos on his phone of him and Milo together.'

'Woah, he showed you them?'

'Not like that.' Finn laughed. 'A selfie of them kissing. Pretty bloody persuasive though. I'm so sorry I didn't believe you. It just seemed so definite – I couldn't unsee those photos of you two and that's obviously why Milo did it, because people believe what they see, don't they? Even something that's not real. I get it now that there was no photo of you actually kissing. I saw you in a bikini with Milo Blake half naked, his hand on your bum, looking like you were about to kiss and I saw red. You were everywhere – friends kept messaging me with stuff from Twitter and photos from Instagram… I bought the story the same way everyone else did…'

Jenna stepped closer and took his hands. 'I'm sorry about everything too, Finn. But you've got to understand you hurt me just as much by not believing I was telling the truth.'

He nodded. 'I'm so sorry. It's just I've been hurt before… And the thing with Milo…'

'I know. It's what he does, plays the fame game and he's epically good at it. He just picked the wrong person to spin a lie around – to begin with at least; he's having a ball with Heidi.'

'Does she know he's gay?'

Jenna shrugged. 'I have no idea, but either way I doubt she'd care. She wants the fame as much as he does.'

'And you don't?'

Jenna ran her thumbs along Finn's. 'No, not like this, not at the cost of friendship or a relationship.' She met his eyes again. His smile lit up his face, making the tension in her chest disperse. She shook her head. 'I can't believe Timothy went round to yours to put the story straight. He's a decent bloke; I knew he felt guilty for everything Milo had done.'

'I kinda felt sorry for him. I mean, his boyfriend refuses to be honest about their relationship and feels the need to pretend he's with women.'

'And yet Timothy stays with him. He must trust you not to say anything. I wonder if Milo knows Timothy spoke to you?'

'I'm not going to say a word. You've got more risk of a story getting out because of my mum. She had a bloody fit.' Finn laughed. 'I had no clue who Timothy was until he introduced himself but Mum recognised him straight away from that Jane Austen series she's been watching. She was totally giddy that someone famous was in the house.'

Jenna smiled at the thought of Finn's mum telling all her friends about a famous actor popping over for a cuppa. And then sadness washed over her at the memory of the evening she'd spent with Finn and his parents and how it had all been so brief and was now over.

'Hey, don't look so sad.' Finn lifted her chin. 'Are we good? I don't want you leaving with us still being on bad terms.'

'We're good. I'm just sorry that what we had got ruined over gossip.'

'What I don't get is why you didn't tell me right at the beginning that you weren't with him in that way? You know, the morning I saw him in the cottage?'

'I tried to but you were adamant that he was my boyfriend. He was walking round the cottage naked – I totally understand how you could jump to conclusions. I figured me trying to deny things further would make me seem guiltier.

Except I had nothing to be guilty about. It's not like we were actually together.'

'But did you want us to be?' His hands tensed in hers. 'Do you want us to be?'

His words hung heavy in the brightness of the morning.

'That weekend we had together, you know, before that bloody magazine article, was the best couple of days of this summer.' She wiped away a tear from her cheek. 'I live hundreds of miles away from you, Finn, my whole life, most of the work I do is in London... I don't know how we could work...'

He put a finger to her lips. 'But if it wasn't for that. If there weren't any obstacles...'

'Then I'd be with you in a heartbeat.'

His grin said it all.

'Do you have to go today?'

'I've got an audition in London on Monday.'

'But that's Monday. You could go tomorrow instead...'

His blue eyes didn't move from hers. One more day. One more night. One night with Finn. Jenna swallowed; heat flushing the top of her chest. Wouldn't that make it even harder to leave tomorrow? She knew she was overthinking, like she'd been overthinking everything for the last couple of weeks, getting herself into a mess emotionally. But it was also only ten in the morning. They had the rest of the day together, so why rush back.

She stood on tiptoes and closed the distance between them with a kiss. He kissed her back, wrapping his arms around her until she was cocooned in his embrace. The sun warmed them both. Those butterflies Lily had talked about in the pub the other evening were back, along with the desire to stay wrapped in his arms forever.

Jenna took his hand and led him inside, past the kitchen table with the bottle, chocolates, and the card for him that was no longer needed. She'd been staying in the cottage long enough to know where all the creaks were as she led him upstairs. Her heart beat faster as they reached the landing, now a peaceful uncluttered space. The walls were a calming fern-green and there was a comfy armchair by the window that looked out over the garden and the wood.

Her room was finished too with a deep sunshine-yellow on the walls. The old wrought iron bed had a new mattress and a colourful bedspread which injected warmth into the room unlike the first time she'd walked in here, when the place looked sad and grey. It was as much Finn's room as it was hers; he'd repaired the cracks in the walls, repapered and painted, sanded the floors and stained them. There were still finishing touches to do, things to buy like a rug and new curtains to replace the faded flowery ones, but that would happen in good time.

The bedsprings groaned as they tumbled on to the bed together. Jenna kicked off her shoes and pulled Finn's T-shirt over his head, and he kissed her while helping her to wriggle out of her skirt.

'I've been dreaming about this moment all summer,' Finn said. His hands explored her body, his lips kissing her neck and the top of her chest. He unhooked her bra with one hand and grinned. She ran her fingers slowly across his chest, tracing the outline of his tattoos, down to the defined muscles of his stomach until her hand reached the button of his shorts. Jenna had dreamt of this moment too, the perfect end to her summer.

Chapter Twenty-Seven

Leicester Square was bathed in light, from the restaurants and bars, the cinemas and street lights, and it made no difference that it was an overcast autumnal evening. A sea of people clutched their mobiles as they stood waiting behind barriers lining the square outside the Odeon. Milo Blake's handsome face beamed down over the square from the poster above the entrance, a 1940s fighter plane in the sky above him, the backdrop a Cornish setting.

Jenna was blinded by flashes from the photographers as she slowly made her way down the red carpet. People shouted her name in an attempt to get her to look their way. The nervous fluttering in her stomach intensified with each photo taken, and each autograph she signed. Up ahead she spied Milo charming the crowd, happy to take selfies with adoring fans. Heidi was not far behind him, lapping up the attention, a star in her own right after the year she'd had. Timothy was signing autographs further down the red carpet. It was a bizarre set-up they had, but one that was seemingly profitable for them all.

Jenna squeezed Finn's arm tighter and he squeezed her back. If she felt this nervous in front of all these people and the bank of photographers, she could only imagine how nervous he was. He didn't show it though and looked as much a film star as anyone. She was certain the pictures the girls in the crowd were taking were more about him than they were for her. Even so, as Jenna stopped to sign a couple of autographs and pose for selfies, she still couldn't get over the fact that people knew who she was. Finn didn't stray far from her, yet he held his own, laughing and joking with the crowd. He looked so different in a suit instead of his usual casual surf-wear. And she'd spent a small fortune on a long and sparkly designer dress that hugged her slender curves. She knew she looked good and she knew her and Finn looked good together.

Milo was posing for photos next to the cinema entrance. He'd brought his mum as his date, a clever move which no doubt would win him more fans, and also leave him free to be with Timothy later on. Jenna wasn't sure if she was happy or sad for Timothy, but he had a choice and at least Milo wasn't lying to him about anything; just to himself.

Of course after filming had wrapped and the weeks had gone by with Jenna back in London and Milo filming in the US, the gossip about them had died down. Her brief notoriety had been usurped by Heidi, and her 'fling' with Milo carried on for months afterwards, cementing Heidi as a firm fixture in the gossip magazines. Far from feeling jealous of the attention Heidi got, Jenna felt only relief. Although she was enjoying the glitz and glamour of the premiere, she didn't want that kind of scrutiny to be a part of her everyday life.

Finn stood back and grinned at Jenna as she had a photo taken with two young girls in the crowd. She signed autographs for them and took hold of Finn's hand again. They reached the wall of photographers and journalists and the noise intensified. People shouted her name, bombarding her with questions from all sides. She'd worked as a model and she knew her best angle, so she posed, one leg crossed in front of the other beneath her red carpet-skimming dress. She held her clutch bag in one hand and put the other on her hip, and with her chin tilted slightly down, she focused on the cameras flashing in front of her. Finn stood back, allowing her a moment in the limelight.

'Are you upset your relationship with Milo Blake is over?' a journalist called out.

'Not at all. I'm really happy.' She looked at Finn and he joined her. The journalist smiled and gave her a knowing look.

There was no point in correcting the media. As far as they were concerned, she had a brief fling with Milo while they made the film until he moved on to Heidi and she found new love with a Cornish builder. She was certain everyone thought Heidi got the better deal, but Jenna knew the truth. Heidi may have gained notoriety from having a 'famous boyfriend' but it was for show only, a kiss here and there for the paps and no real affection beyond that. What a life to lead. The supposed 'hot sex' she'd been having with Milo was far from fiction with Finn.

'Jenna! Jenna!' Whistles and shouts from the press grew as they reached the cinema entrance.

Jenna turned, and with her arm firmly hooked in Finn's she smiled and waved. She leant closer to him. 'Let's get inside.'

She didn't want to get used to this kind of attention. The truth was, the more fame she gained, the more she shrunk away from it, which in the end had helped her to get her priorities right over the past twelve months.

The cinema was packed. Nearly two thousand faces gazed up as Jenna made her way on to the stage with the rest of the cast, the producers and the director. Her heart beat faster as the director introduced the film, and she zoned out as he sung Milo's praises. She heard Cornwall mentioned and the incredible welcome the production had received when it took over Mullion and the surrounding area for a whole summer.

Jenna only realised that Heidi was standing next to her when she took Jenna's hand in hers and whispered, 'This is insane, isn't it?'

Jenna nodded, but couldn't quite believe in the sincerity of her words, not when less than a month earlier she'd walked the red carpet for the Bond premiere, the biggest movie of the year. It eclipsed this one by a long shot.

Milo took the microphone from the director and stepped to the front of the stage. Someone wolf-whistled from the back and laughter echoed around the cinema. He was dressed impeccably in a smart fitted-suit, and his dark hair, tanned skin and handsome face commanded attention. Jenna squinted in the dim light of the auditorium to make out Finn sitting next to Ade. She could see Lily and Amanda too and suddenly felt a fraud up on the stage, even more so when Milo mentioned her. She had no idea what he said, she just smiled politely and was glad when the audience erupted in to applause and they could return to their seats.

The theatre lights dimmed and the filming board classification for *The Cornish Affair* came on to the screen. There was an air of anticipation in the movie theatre as voices hushed. Jenna squeezed Finn's hand tighter. Amanda was on the other side of Jenna, her hand gripping the armrest between them. It was a big moment. Jenna had seen herself on screen before but to be featured in a film as big as this one was something special.

Along with almost everyone else, Jenna watched the film for the first time. Scenes and locations were so very familiar, and yet in post-production the sense of history and the way it had been edited together made it fresh and new. It was like watching a film she barely knew the storyline of. It surprised and elated her in equal measure, and despite cringing when she first appeared on screen, she slowly relaxed and actually enjoyed it for what it was, an entertaining period drama and love story.

The post-premiere party was held in an old chocolate factory-turned-swanky bar. Apart from the principal cast and crew, there were a lot of other celebrities whose agents had managed to snag them an invite. A few A-listers and lots of reality TV faces. Jenna had no clue who many of them were, apart from *The Love Hotel* contingent who'd been on at the same time as Heidi. Heidi of course seemed to know everyone.

Finn took two glasses of champagne from a passing waitress and handed one to Jenna.

'I feel out of my depth.' He looked around the bar packed with people glammed up for the evening. It was filled with lots of sparkle, little black dresses, tuxes and over-the-top air kissing.

'You and me both.'

'Yeah, but I'm not used to any of this and I've just watched you killing it on the big screen. Doesn't really compare.' His eyes widened. 'Heads up, Milo's coming our way.'

Apart from on the red carpet and on stage before watching the film, Jenna hadn't seen Milo for months. He'd been on the press tour in the US and around Europe, while she'd only done some press about the film in the UK. He was the big star, the one booked for *The Graham Norton Show* and interviewed on BBC Radio 1. His fame was stratospheric compared to hers.

He reached them, his hand immediately finding her shoulder. 'Hey, how you both doing? Finn, good to see you again.' They shook hands and Jenna couldn't help but think of the ridiculous situation they'd found themselves in the summer before last.

'You too,' Finn said.

Jenna wasn't convinced that there was any truth in that reply; there was no love lost between Finn and Milo.

'Do you mind if I talk to Jenna for a moment.'

Finn looked at Jenna and she nodded.

'I'll be over there.' He kissed her cheek and walked off.

'I'm glad you're with him, Jenna. He seems a nice guy.' He sidled closer, the waft of his aftershave strong as his hand rested on her hip. 'And fit as anything.'

'Yes he is. Timothy's fit too if you took time to notice.'

Milo glanced behind them.

'Don't worry,' Jenna said. 'I won't say a thing. I never will, I promise you that.'

'Well thank you, I appreciate it because after how it all kicked off, well, I wouldn't blame you if you had spilt the beans.'

'You realise I'm doing it for Timothy, not you.'

'I gathered that.'

'He's a bloody decent bloke. You should do right by him.'

'I know, I know.' He waved at a passing actor. 'I will do,

one day.'

Jenna folded her arms. 'One day. What are you waiting for? Someone to force you to speak out? I don't understand why you don't do it on your own terms?'

He rubbed the stubble on his chin. 'It's not that simple, Jenna.'

'It really is. You either love someone or you don't.'

Milo took her arm and steered her away from the group of people next to them. 'What I wanted to come over and say to you is, I'm sorry. Deeply sorry about the stress and upset I caused you when we were filming. I was selfish. I made assumptions about you and didn't mean to mess around with your life quite as much as I did. I think you're unusual – in a good way. You don't seem to want fame for fame's sake.'

'It's not that I don't want to be famous, it's just I want to be known for acting, not anything else.'

'That's what I mean by unusual. Most twenty-something's whether they're actors or not crave fame and would lap up the attention. I mean, look at Heidi. But not you. I like that about you, Jenna Wilson.' He touched her bare arm. 'And I really am glad you've kissed and made up with Finn. He's quite a catch.'

His stubble tickled her skin as he kissed her cheek. He turned to go.

'Milo.' Jenna caught his hand. 'You're too good an actor to ever lose out on parts because of your sexuality. You're incredible in the film, you know that right? Just wait until the reviews are published tomorrow. And if casting directors have an issue with you being gay, well then that's their problem and they'll be the ones to lose out. All the fame, all the gossip that constantly surrounds you, it totally gets in the way of how awesome you are when you're on that big screen.' She squeezed his hand and looked intently into his hazel eyes. 'You shouldn't have to lie about who you are, and certainly not when you're so damn talented.'

Jenna walked away, adrenalin pumping through her. Yes, he'd messed her around that summer, but she had initially liked him. His bad judgement may have clouded that for a time but now they were out the other side and the gossip had died down, she couldn't help but warm to him again. But without Timothy's honesty, she and Finn may have lost their chance of getting together forever.

She smiled at familiar and unfamiliar faces as she made her way to join Finn, Ade, Carla, Lily and Amanda and their partners at a large circular table.

Jenna slid on to the seat next to Finn.

'What did he want?' Finn asked.

'Believe it or not, to apologise.'

'Are you sure? Not the opportunity for a photographer to take a picture with his arm around you?'

'You noticed huh?'

'Yep. And even through all these people, I'm sure a photographer somehow managed to get that shot.'

'I gave him a piece of my mind too...'

'Is Heidi with Milo again?' Lily shouted across the table above the thump thump thump of the music.

Jenna shrugged. 'Who knows? I don't think either Milo or Heidi know what they want from each other.'

'Well.' Amanda motioned towards the crowded bar. 'Heidi's just cornered him so...'

Jenna wondered where Timothy was and what the hell Milo and Heidi were playing at. It was frustrating to see Milo constantly hiding behind a lie. Maybe she shouldn't have been so blunt with him, but she'd told the truth. One day someone less forgiving than her or Finn, someone wanting to make lots of money off a huge story would out him and then he'd lose all control over the situation.

'They've got it all planned out,' Carla said, leaning closer to Jenna so no one else could hear. 'Now Heidi's finished on *The Love Hotel* and that relationship fizzled out, she said Milo thought it might be good for them to "hook up" at the premiere – you know, for one night only. Then once all the fuss with this film has blown over they're going to split up, which of course will gain them more column inches. Heidi will move on with her life having gained roles and shedloads of money off the back of being Milo's lover, while Milo can just be single for a while, enjoy flirting and all that crap that he's so damn good at.'

'And perhaps spend some time with Timothy?'

'I have no idea how they're going to manage to do that without raising suspicion unless they work together again.'

'Well, Milo handpicked me, I'm sure he can do the same with Timothy.'

'Yeah, like that wouldn't be obvious at all.' Carla raised a pierced eyebrow.

'Have you seen much of Heidi?'

'A bit, before she went on *The Love Hotel*. And then of course we all saw a bit too much of her while she was on that. Flipping hell, Jen, did you dodge a bullet by not going on it.'

Jenna knew she had. It was nothing short of torture watching the emotional turmoil Heidi went through on the show. The intense focus on her life didn't sit comfortably with Jenna. The way she bared her soul and everything else all for the viewers' entertainment, assured Jenna that she'd made the right choice.

Watching Heidi's ups and downs in love and out of love, and the way she was talked about and discussed on social media had made Jenna feel sorry for her. It was like watching a car crash; she was unable to tear her eyes away despite hating what she saw. However much Heidi had hurt her, Jenna still wanted to give her a hug when she broke down on TV for the world to see after getting turned down by the guy she'd fallen for. How much was scripted and played up for the cameras Jenna really had no idea. She saw a version of Heidi, a mix of real and fiction. She played up her sexiness, and at times left little to the imagination. It made for uncomfortable viewing. So Jenna knew exactly what Carla meant by her having dodged a bullet. Jenna had made a wise choice, which had led to a quieter life. Out of the two of them, Heidi was the centre of attention tonight; Heidi was the one who knew most people here; Heidi would be the one in the gossip magazines tomorrow and trending online.

'I feel sorry for her,' Jenna said. 'Is she happy? Do you know?'

'I have no idea. She comes across like she is when you

speak to her, but she's not the same person we became friends with at drama school. I don't know, maybe it's to be expected, she's playing the game and she's playing it well. She's making a load of money, she's getting roles, she's become a household name, but at what cost…'

At what cost indeed. Jenna sat back against the cushioned seat. Heidi was a household name but that was all down to having a 'fling' with Milo and then sleeping with at least one of the blokes on *The Love Hotel*. Even with the release of the latest Bond, she was getting the attention because she played a sexy – albeit smart – woman who caught Bond's eye and featured in one of the most exciting set-pieces in the whole film.

A tapping noise on a microphone caught Jenna's attention. One of the producers was standing on the stage at the other side of the bar.

'Sorry to interrupt but Milo would like to say a few words.'

The music faded and chatter petered out. Milo leapt on to the raised platform, took the microphone from the producer, and cleared his throat.

'I, um. So I just want to say something. It seems like the right time to say it…' He stared down at the floor for a moment lost in thought. Even from across the room Jenna could tell from his flushed face that he was nervous, something she'd never seen before. 'Throughout my career I've had well-meaning advice from my agent, producers, directors, fellow actors, casting directors, magazine editors, you name it, everyone has advised me about everything, particularly when it comes to money and my career. But actually, I've never really listened to those few people in my life who talk sense, who aren't all about fame and money.' Milo looked directly at Jenna and she sank lower in her seat. 'They're about integrity and friendship, supporting one another; they're about love and being true to yourself…'

He swigged his champagne and loosened his bow tie. He looked across the crowded room, every single person looking at him, watching and waiting. Jenna's heart thumped.

'Timothy, could you come up here please.'

The thudding in Jenna's ears dissipated; she'd heard him crystal clear that time. Timothy weaved his way through the crowd, frowning as he jumped up on to the stage next to Milo. Milo smiled at him and took his hand. 'We've got something to tell you that we should have told everyone about a long time ago.'

Chapter Twenty-Eight

'Last night was one of the greatest of my life.' Carla leant against the work surface in her kitchen, yawned and stretched her arms above her head.

Jenna switched on the coffee machine and turned to her. 'Tell me about it. Did you see Heidi's face when Milo said that him and Timothy were in love?'

'Her face was like thunder – impossible to miss.'

'I actually feel sorry for her. I mean she's going to get lynched by the media for being a part of Milo's lies to further her career.'

Carla took three mugs from a cupboard and turned back to Jenna. 'I'll be here for her, don't worry. It might be a good thing, snapping her out of the mad world she's been living in the past couple of years. She can't carry on like she is without burning out.' She splashed milk into two of the mugs. 'Will Finn want coffee?'

Jenna had left him in bed in Carla's spare room. They'd managed a few hours' sleep after the excitement of the night before. The hangover and her fur-lined mouth were an unwelcome result. She desperately needed coffee and she knew Finn would too.

'I'll wake him. We should go out for brunch.'

The cafe was just around the corner from Carla's, a chilled-out place with wooden tables and mismatched chairs. Compared to the night before in her slinky dress, with her make-up and hair done by professionals, she felt relaxed and comfortable in skinny jeans and boots, her hair wound up into a messy bun.

Their plates of breakfast arrived, Finn's filled with bacon, eggs, sausage, mushrooms and hash browns, Jenna with a poached egg and salmon, and Carla with smashed avocado and halloumi. They tucked in greedily, feeling more alive with food and more coffee.

'I did not see that coming,' Finn said through a mouthful of bacon. 'What the hell did you say to Milo?'

It was all they'd talked about since the moment Milo told a roomful of people that he was gay. Less than an hour later he was trending on Twitter and the world seemingly went mad over the 'shocking news'.

'I told him the truth – that some day someone would find out about him and Timothy and sell the story. I suggested he's better than the persona he's hiding behind, basically making himself out to be a womanising bastard. Or words to that effect. I'm sure he didn't come out just because of me. He had to have been thinking about it for a while.'

'Probably his whole damn adult life.' Carla picked up her flat white. 'I think it's a smart move. I mean, he wanted the column inches, which is why he was talking to Heidi about them "getting back together". Well, he's certainly got the attention he craves – the media are having a field day. And, most importantly, he's got so much support for being honest.' She sipped her coffee and looked across the table at them. 'Anyway, enough about Milo. When are you two lovebirds getting the keys to your flat?'

Finn smiled. 'A week Monday.'

'Great, so you can stick around here for a few more days. You're welcome to stay at mine unless your parents want you back for a bit.'

'Actually I'm really sorry, we can't,' Jenna said. 'We're going down to Cornwall.'

'And I've got a job lined up in Bristol the week after next which is going to take me through to Christmas,' Finn said. 'So it's our last opportunity to have a break for a while.'

'Ah bugger, I thought you'd be hanging around for longer.'

'Plus I've got a garden to weed.'

Carla laughed.

'You think she's joking?' Finn put his arm around Jenna's shoulder.

'In fact I've got two gardens – Bramble Cottage when we're in Cornwall and then the garden flat in Bristol.'

'Ah, Jenna Wilson, you're the most unshowbizzy, showbizzy person, you know that right? You look like a film star without even trying but you love everything that's not about being in the limelight. I think it's amazing that you know your own mind and are following your heart.'

Jenna reached across the table and took Carla's hand. 'I'm going to miss you.'

'Don't be so soppy. You spent weeks away down in Cornwall last year, what's the difference?'

'The difference is this move is permanent.'

'And yet you've already told me you'll be back in London in two weeks for a casting. We'll get to see each other loads. Now let's talk about something else before I start crying.'

The two sides of Jenna's life felt like ying and yang. In the space of a weekend, she'd gone from walking the red carpet of a major film that she'd starred in, to driving down to Cornwall in Finn's van for a quiet few days pottering around the garden, going to the beach, surfing, and eating fish and chips by the sea.

The move to Bristol had happened naturally in the end. After her summer working on *The Cornish Affair* had come to an end, along with her last day and night in Cornwall with Finn, holed up together in the cottage, she was torn when she left on the Sunday. The start of a relationship with Finn seemed to finish the moment she got in her car and drove out of the gate leaving him and Bramble Cottage in the rear-view mirror. She'd cried all the way back to London.

The pull of Finn was bigger than the pull of Cornwall, and although she missed the peace of the cottage and its garden, the sea air and the countryside, she embraced the opportunities that came her way back home. With auditions lining up she began to be choosey about the roles she went for and when the opportunity to work on a mini-series in Bristol came her way, she jumped at it. It was closer to Cornwall and that meant being closer to Finn.

It was only for a week, but Jenna realised there was the possibility of living somewhere other than London and still being able to work as an actor. Not only did she realise it was a vibrant and creative city, but it was also a filming hub. An idea began to form. Cornwall had stolen her heart as much as Finn had, but Finn was eager to escape his quiet country life, even if it was a wrench to move away from the coast. He was desperate to move out of his parents' house and an offshoot of Harrison & Son in a city location seemed the ideal solution, and so their new life together had taken shape.

It felt like coming home, pulling into Bramble Cottage's weed-free drive. Although Finn's parents lived close by, Jenna and Finn wanted to stay in the cottage while it wasn't being rented out, to have a proper mini-break in the place where their romance had started.

Jenna got out of the van and slammed the door shut; the noise sent wood pigeons flapping into the tops of the trees. She looked up at the cottage as she walked along the path.

'You and your dad did such a good job.'

'Goes without saying, doesn't it?'

Jenna reached the front door, now painted a mint green, in keeping with the surroundings. She unlocked it and pushed it open.

The kitchen had been transformed from a set of tired 1970s units to a sleek country kitchen. Extra touches finished the place off beautifully: a new blind on the window over the sink, a vase of dried wild flowers on the table, and a new light shade where a bare bulb had been for so long.

Finn dumped his bag on the kitchen table and looked around. 'Do you know, being back down here has made me realise how completely mad this weekend has been.'

'It's not always going to be like this. You know my life is rarely as glamorous as it has been these last couple of days.'

'Thank God.' He pulled Jenna to him. 'It's been fun

though.'

'And now we have five days down here to enjoy the cottage like holidaymakers. Lazy mornings, days on the beach...'

'Sounds blissful.'

'Even the weather is perfect.' Jenna went over to the fridge and pulled open the freezer compartment. They were still there from earlier in the year when she helped her parents do some work on the garden. Jenna turned back to Finn and waggled an ice cream at him.

'For old time's sake.' She handed him one, took his hand and pulled him outside and around to the back of the cottage.

It was late September; the sun was shining but Jenna was glad of her chunky cardigan thrown over her sleeveless top. A cool breeze whistled through the trees, rustling leaves and branches, but back out on the daisy-speckled lawn she could still feel the sun.

Jenna sat down on the grass and stretched her legs out. Finn joined her and ripped open his ice cream. He leant back on his hand. 'Aah, the good old days. I loved working on this place.'

Jenna gazed at the cottage with its neat slate roof, the walls repaired and painted, the sash windows all renewed. The cottage had been transformed from the tired shell of a place she'd first seen.

They sat in silence eating ice cream and listening to the birds chirping in the trees.

'Do you remember how hot it was that day?' Jenna wiped the ice cream from her lips and turned her gaze to the pale blue sky with wisps of white cloud. 'Doesn't even seem possible now.'

Finn shuffled closer and wrapped his strong arms around her. She thought back to that first brief and unexpected kiss, the way the jolt of excitement had gone through her, along with the desire for him to kiss her again. To know their fates had been so aligned made this moment perfect.

'I'm so glad I met you.' She nestled her head in the crook of his shoulder. 'The scary thing is we so easily couldn't have.

If Milo hadn't hand-picked me for the film, if I hadn't persuaded my parents that I should stay here while the place was being done up; if my dad hadn't clicked with your dad when he popped round to give him a quote – so many factors came in to play for us to meet and fall in love.'

Finn squeezed her tighter and kissed her again. 'It was one hell of a summer.'

ACKNOWLEDGEMENTS

The inspiration behind *A Starlit Summer* came from the time in my twenties and early thirties when I worked as a Supporting Artist in film and TV. I was on Mad Dog Casting's books and got to work a few times on the long-running TV series *Casualty* (which at the time was filmed in my home city of Bristol), as well as the BBC costume drama *The Young Visitors*, and the comedy *Trollied*. I was also lucky enough to work on three films. I spent a day in a field with dirt smeared on my face as part of a crowd of equally peasant-like fellow extras for *King Arthur*; I was a member of an eighteenth century theatre audience jeering at Keira Knightley and Ralph Fiennes in *The Duchess*; and in *Vanity Fair*, I played one of the wealthy ladies who snubs Reese Witherspoon's Becky Sharp.

I always knew that I wanted to set a book on a film set, and the idea of a young actress escaping London for a summer in Cornwall working on a movie seemed like the perfect match. And so that's how the idea of *A Starlit Summer* came about.

The Cornish setting is both real and fictional. Bramble Cottage is a fictional place in an unspecified location within driving distance of Mullion and Falmouth on the Lizard Peninsular, which of course are real places, as is Porthleven and Port Isaac. I've taken liberties with the beach Jenna and Finn visit by not naming it and by giving the beach near it a fictional name, although it's not dissimilar to many of the beaches found along the Cornish coast.

A huge thank you as always goes to Judith van Dijkhuizen who beta read an early version of the book. Always honest and thoughtful with her comments, she never fails to help me make a novel better because of her suggestions. My wonderful editor, Helen Baggott, polished the final manuscript ready for publication.

Jessica Bell worked on the covers for the whole of my Romantic Escape series at the same time and I could not be happier with the results. The cover for *A Starlit Summer* evokes the setting and the idea of an escape to the countryside, which I love.

I wrote the first draft of *A Starlit Summer* in 2019, well before the world was turned on its head with Covid-19. I think it's important for fiction to allow readers a virtual escape from the real world, so there's no mention of coronavirus and there won't be in the subsequent novels in the series either. They're romantic escapes and I want them to remain uplifting, heartfelt and hopeful with a good dash of romance. Pure escapism.

Thank you to all my readers who have read my books, supported me and left such lovely reviews, it means the world. Lastly, a huge thank you to my husband Nik, my son Leo, and my parents for their never ending support.

ABOUT THE AUTHOR

Kate Frost is the author of contemporary women's fiction and children's fiction. Her women's fiction, which includes *The Butterfly Storm*, *Beneath the Apple Blossom* and *The Baobab Beach Retreat*, often tackles serious subjects such as infertility, broken families and infidelity, often with a romantic element running through them. The long-awaited sequel to *The Butterfly Storm*, Kate's most popular book, is called *The Birdsong Promise* and was released in autumn 2018.

Kate Frost's children's books couldn't be more different – *Time Shifters* is a time travel adventure series for 9 – 12 year-olds. *Time Shifters: Into the Past* was published in autumn 2016 and the second book in the trilogy, *Time Shifters: A Long Way From Home* followed in 2018. The final book, *Time Shifters: Out of Time* completes the adventure.

Bristol, in the south west of England is home, which Kate shares with her husband, young son and their Cavalier King Charles Spaniel. Bristol is a vibrant and creative city offering plenty of opportunities for writers. Kate is director of Storytale Festival, an exciting new children's book festival she co-founded in 2019 with the aim of inspiring children and teens through creative and interactive events.

If you'd like to keep up to date with Kate Frost's book news please join her Readers' Club. To sign up simply go to www.kate-frost.co.uk/minetokeep and enter your email address. Subscribers not only receive a free ebook on sign up, but occasional news about Kate's writing, new books and special offers.

If you enjoyed *A Starlit Summer* please consider leaving a review on Amazon and/or Goodreads, or recommending it to friends. It will be much appreciated! Reader reviews are essential for authors to gain visibility and entice new readers.

You can find out more about Kate Frost and her writing at www.kate-frost.co.uk, or find her on Facebook, Twitter and Instagram @katefrostauthor.

KATE FROST

OTHER BOOKS BY KATE FROST

A Starlit Summer is the second book in a standalone series of Romantic Escape novels that can be read in any order. They're uplifting, heartwarming stories of love, romance, hope, friendship, new beginnings and second chances, featuring different characters in different locations.

The Baobab Beach Retreat
An ex-husband, two potential lovers, one reckless decision. Will Connie ever be happy in love?

The Greek Heart
A broken heart, an island escape, a boy from the past. Will Lottie's search lead to love?

The Amsterdam Affair
A new start, a chance encounter, a Christmas to remember. Will Iris's new year be happy ever after?

The Love Island Bookshop
A dream job, two opposing men, one destructive act. Will Freya's opportunity of a lifetime end in tears?

ALSO BY KATE FROST

The Butterfly Storm
The Birdsong Promise
The Honeysuckle Dream

Beneath the Apple Blossom

Time Shifters
(a time travel adventure trilogy for 9-12 year olds)

To be the first to hear about future releases, you can join my Readers' Club at www.kate-frost.co.uk/minetokeep.

KATE FROST

Printed in Great Britain
by Amazon